Fathers and Sons

Ivan Turgenev

Translated By
Richard Hare

EasyRead Large

ReadHowYouWant Classics Library

Copyright © 2010 Accessible Publishing Systems PTY, Ltd.
ACN 085 119 953

The text in this edition has been formatted and typeset to make reading easier and more enjoyable for ALL kinds of readers. In addition the text has been formatted to the specifications indicated on the title page. The formatting of this edition is the copyright of Accessible Publishing Systems Pty Ltd.

Set in 16 pt. Verdana

ReadHowYouWant partners with publishers to provide books for ALL Kinds of Readers. For more information about Becoming A RHYW Registered Reader and to find more titles in your preferred format, visit:
www.readhowyouwant.com

TABLE OF CONTENTS

Chapter 1	1
Chapter 2	6
Chapter 3	9
Chapter 4	18
Chapter 5	25
Chapter 6	34
Chapter 7	39
Chapter 8	48
Chapter 9	59
Chapter 10	64
Chapter 11	82
Chapter 12	88
Chapter 13	96
Chapter 14	105
Chapter 15	112
Chapter 16	119
Chapter 17	134
Chapter 18	150
Chapter 19	158
Chapter 20	169
Chapter 21	184
Chapter 22	209
Chapter 23	218
Chapter 24	228
Chapter 25	253
Chapter 26	269
Chapter 27	282
Chapter 28	305

Dedicated to the memory of
Vissarion Grigor'evich Belinsky

Chapter 1

"Well, Pyotr, still not in sight?" was the question asked on 20th May, 1859, by a gentleman of about forty, wearing a dusty overcoat and checked trousers, who came out hatless into the low porch of the posting station at X. He was speaking to his servant, a chubby young fellow with whitish down growing on his chin and with dim little eyes.

The servant, in whom everything – the turquoise ring in his ear, the hair plastered down with grease and the polite flexibility of his movements – indicated a man of the new improved generation, glanced condescendingly along the road and answered, "No, sir, definitely not in sight."

"Not in sight?" repeated his master.

"No, sir," replied the servant again.

His master sighed and sat down on a little bench. We will introduce him to the reader while he sits, with his feet tucked in, looking thoughtfully around.

His name was Nikolai Petrovich Kirsanov. He owned, about twelve miles from the posting station, a fine property of two hundred serfs or, as he called it – since he had arranged the division of his land with the peasants – a "farm" of nearly five thousand acres. His father, a general in the army, who had served in 1812, a crude, almost illiterate, but good-natured type of Russian, had stuck to a routine job all his life, first commanding a brigade and later a division, and lived permanently in the provinces, where by virtue of his rank he was able to play a certain part. Nikolai Petrovich was born in south Russia, as was his elder brother Pavel, of whom we shall hear more; till the age of fourteen he was educated at home, surrounded by cheap tutors, free-and-easy but fawning adjutants, and all the usual regimental and staff people. His mother, a member of the Kolyazin family, was called Agatha as a girl, but as a general's wife her name was Agafoklea Kuzminishna Kirsanov; she was a domineering military lady, wore gorgeous caps and rustling silk dresses; in church she was the first to go up to the cross, she talked a lot in a loud voice, let her children kiss her hand every morning and gave them her blessing at night – in fact, she enjoyed her life and got as much out of it as she could. As a general's son, Nikolai Petrovich – though so far from brave that he had even been called a "funk" – was intended, like his brother Pavel, to enter the army; but he broke his leg on the very day he obtained a commission and after spending two months in bed he never got rid of a slight limp for the rest of his life. His father gave him up as a bad job and let him go in for the civil service. He took him to Petersburg as soon as he was eighteen and placed him in the university there. His brother happened at the same time to become an officer in a guards regiment. The young men started to share a flat together, and were kept under the remote supervision of a cousin on their mother's side, Ilya Kolyazin, an important official. Their father returned to his division and to his wife and only occasionally wrote to his sons on large sheets of grey paper, scrawled over in an ornate clerkly handwriting; the bottom of these sheets was adorned with a scroll enclosing the words,

"Pyotr Kirsanov, Major-General."

In 1835 Nikolai Petrovich graduated from the university, and in the same year General Kirsanov was put on the retired list after an unsuccessful review, and came with his wife to live in Petersburg. He was about to take a house in the Tavrichesky Gardens, and had joined the English club, when he suddenly died of an apoplectic fit. Agafoklea Kuzminishna soon followed him to the grave; she could not adapt herself to a dull life in the capital and was consumed by the boredom of retirement from regimental existence. Meanwhile Nikolai Petrovich, during his parents' lifetime and much to their distress, had managed to fall in love with the daughter of his landlord, a petty official called Prepolovensky. She was an attractive and, as they call it, well-educated girl; she used to read the serious articles in the science column of the newspapers. He married her as soon as the period of mourning for his parents was over, and leaving the civil service, where his father had secured him a post through patronage, he started to live very happily with his Masha, first in a country villa near the Forestry Institute, afterwards in Petersburg in a pretty little flat with a clean staircase and a draughty drawing room, and finally in the country where he settled down and where in due course his son, Arkady, was born. Husband and wife lived well and peacefully; they were hardly ever separated, they read together, they sang and played duets together on the piano, she grew flowers and looked after the poultry yard, he busied himself with the estate and sometimes hunted, while Arkady went on growing in the same happy and peaceful way. Ten years passed like a dream. Then in 1847 Kirsanov's wife died. He hardly survived this blow and his hair turned grey in a few weeks; he was preparing to travel abroad, if possible to distract his thoughts ... but then came the year 1848. He returned unwillingly to the country and after a rather long period of inactivity he began to take an interest in improving his estate. In 1855 he brought his son to the university and spent three winters in Petersburg with him, hardly going out anywhere and trying to make acquaintance with Arkady's young comrades. The last winter he was unable to go, and here we see him in May, 1859, already entirely grey-haired, plump and rather bent, waiting for his son, who had just taken his university degree, as once he had taken it himself.

The servant, from a feeling of propriety, and perhaps also because he was anxious to escape from his master's eye, had gone over to the gate and was smoking a pipe. Nikolai Petrovich bowed his head and began to stare at the crumbling steps; a big mottled hen walked sedately towards him, treading firmly with its thick yellow legs; a dirty cat cast a disapproving look at him, as she twisted herself coyly round the railing. The sun was scorching; a smell of hot rye bread was wafted from the dim entrance of the posting station. Nikolai Petrovich started musing. "My son ... a graduate ... Arkasha..." kept on turning round in his mind; he tried to think of something else, but the same thoughts returned. He remembered his dead wife. "She did not live to see it," he murmured sadly. A plump blue pigeon flew on to the road and hurriedly started to drink water from a puddle near the well. Nikolai Petrovich began to watch it, but his ear had already caught the sound of approaching wheels...

"It sounds as if they're coming, sir," announced the servant, emerging from the gateway.

Nikolai Petrovich jumped up and fixed his eyes on the road. A carriage appeared with three posting horses abreast; inside it he caught a glimpse of the band of a student's cap and the familiar outline of a dear face...

"Arkasha! Arkasha!" cried Kirsanov, and he ran out into the road, waving his arms ... A few moments later his lips were pressed to the beardless dusty sun-burnt cheek of the young graduate.

Chapter 2

"Let me shake myself first, Daddy," said Arkady, in a voice rather tired from traveling but boyish and resonant, as he responded gaily to his father's greetings; "I'm covering you with dust."

"Never mind, never mind," repeated Nikolai Petrovich, smiling tenderly, and struck the collar of his son's cloak and his own greatcoat with his hand. "Let me have a look at you; just show yourself," he added, moving back from him, and then hurried away towards the station yard, calling out, "This way, this way, bring the horses along at once."

Nikolai Petrovich seemed much more excited than his son; he was really rather confused and shy. Arkady stopped him.

"Daddy," he said, "let me introduce you to my great friend, Bazarov, about whom I wrote to you so often. He has kindly agreed to come to stay with us."

Nikolai Petrovich turned round quickly and going up to a tall man in a long, loose rough coat with tassels, who had just climbed out of the carriage, he warmly pressed the ungloved red hand which the latter did not at once hold out to him.

"I am delighted," he began, "and grateful for your kind intention to visit us; I hope – please tell me your name and patronymic."

"Evgeny Vassilyev," answered Bazarov in a lazy but manly voice, and turning back the collar of his rough overcoat he showed his whole face. It was long and thin with a broad forehead, a nose flat at the base and sharper at the end, large greenish eyes and sand-colored, drooping side whiskers; it was enlivened by a calm smile and looked self-confident and intelligent.

"I hope, my dear Evgeny Vassilich, that you won't be bored staying with us," continued Nikolai Petrovich.

Bazarov's thin lips moved slightly, but he made no answer and merely took off his cap. His fair hair, long and thick, did not hide the prominent bumps on his broad skull.

"Well, Arkady," Nikolai Petrovich began again, turning to his son, "would you rather have the horses brought round at once or would you like to rest?"

"We'll rest at home, Daddy; tell them to harness the horses."

"At once, at once," his father exclaimed. "Hey, Pyotr, do you hear? Get a move on, my boy." Pyotr, who as a perfectly modern servant had not kissed his master's hand but only bowed to him from a distance, vanished again through the gates.

"I came here with the carriage, but there are three horses for your tarantass also," said Nikolai Petrovich fussily, while Arkady drank some water from an iron bucket brought to him by the woman in charge of the station, and Bazarov began smoking a pipe and went up to the driver, who was unharnessing the horses. "There are only two seats in the carriage, and I don't know how your friend..."

"He will go in the tarantass," interrupted Arkady in an undertone. "Don't stand on ceremony with him, please. He's a splendid fellow, so simple – you will see."

Nikolai Petrovich's coachman brought the horses round.

"Well, make haste, bushy beard!" said Bazarov, addressing the driver.

"Do you hear, Mitya," chipped in another driver, standing with his hands behind him thrust into the slits of his sheepskin coat, "what the gentleman just called you? That's just what you are – a bushy beard."

Mitya only jerked his hat and pulled the reins off the steaming horses.

"Hurry up, lads, lend a hand!" cried Nikolai Petrovich. "There'll be something to drink our health with!"

In a few minutes the horses were harnessed; father and son took their places in the carriage: Pyotr climbed on to the box; Bazarov jumped into the tarantass, leaned his head back against the leather cushion – and both vehicles rolled away.

Chapter 3

"So here you are, a graduate at last – and home again," said Nikolai Petrovich, touching Arkady now on the shoulder, now on the knee. "At last!"

"And how is uncle? Is he well?" asked Arkady, who in spite of the genuine, almost childish joy which filled him, wanted as soon as possible to turn the conversation from an emotional to a more commonplace level.

"Quite well. He wanted to come with me to meet you, but for some reason he changed his mind."

"And did you have a long wait for me?" asked Arkady.

"Oh, about five hours."

"You dear old daddy!"

Arkady turned round briskly to his father and gave him a resounding kiss on the cheek. Nikolai Petrovich laughed quietly.

"I've got a splendid horse for you," he began. "You will see for yourself. And your room has been freshly papered."

"And is there a room ready for Bazarov?"

"We will find one all right."

"Please, Daddy, be kind to him. I can't tell you how much I value his friendship."

"You met him only recently?"

"Quite recently."

"That's how I didn't see him last winter. What is he studying?"

"His chief subject is – natural science. But he knows everything. Next year he wants to take his doctor's degree."

"Ah! he's in the medical faculty," remarked Nikolai Petrovich, and fell silent. "Pyotr," he went on, stretching out his hand, "aren't those our peasants driving along?"

Pyotr looked aside to where his master was pointing. A few carts, drawn by unbridled horses, were rolling rapidly along a narrow side-track. In each cart were seated one or two peasants in unbuttoned sheepskin coats.

"Just so, sir," replied Pyotr.

"Where are they going – to the town?"

"To the town, I suppose – to the pub," Pyotr added contemptuously, and half turned towards the coachman as if including him in the reproach. But the latter did not turn a hair; he was a man of the old type and did not share the latest views of the younger generation.

"The peasants have given me a lot of trouble this year," went on Nikolai Petrovich, turning to his son. "They won't pay their rent. What is one to do?"

"And are you satisfied with your hired laborers?"

"Yes," said Nikolai Petrovich between his teeth. "But they're being set against me, that's the worst of it, and they don't really work properly; they spoil the tools. However, they've managed to plough the land. We shall manage somehow – there will be enough flour to go round. Are you starting to be interested in agriculture?"

"What a pity you have no shade," remarked Arkady, without answering the last question.

"I have had a big awning put up on the north side over the veranda," said Nikolai Petrovich; "now we can even have dinner in the open air."

"Won't it be rather too like a summer villa? ... But that's a minor matter. What air there is here! How wonderful it smells. Really it seems to me no air in the world is so sweetly scented as here! And the sky too..." Arkady suddenly stopped, cast a quick look behind him and did not finish his sentence.

"Naturally," observed Nikolai Petrovich, "you were born here, so everything is bound to strike you with a special..."

"Really, Daddy, it makes absolutely no difference where a person is born."

"Still..."

"No, it makes no difference at all."

Nikolai Petrovich glanced sideways at his son, and the carriage went on half a mile farther before their conversation was renewed.

"I forget if I wrote to you," began Nikolai Petrovich, "that your old nurse Yegorovna has died."

"Really? Poor old woman! And is Prokovich still alive?"

"Yes, and not changed a bit. He grumbles as much as ever. Indeed, you won't find many changes at Maryino."

"Have you still the same bailiff?"

"Well, I have made a change there. I decided it was better not to keep around me any freed serfs who had been house servants; at least not to entrust them with any responsible jobs." Arkady glanced towards Pyotr. *"Il est libre en effet,"* said Nikolai Petrovich in an undertone, "but as you see, he's only a valet. My new bailiff is a townsman – he seems fairly efficient. I pay him 250 rubles a year. But," added Nikolai Petrovich, rubbing his forehead and eyebrows with his hand (which was always with him a sign of embarrassment), "I told you just now you would find no changes at Maryino, ... That's not quite true ... I think it my duty to tell you in advance, though...."

He hesitated for a moment and then went on in French.

"A severe moralist would consider my frankness improper, but in the first place I can't conceal it, and then, as you know, I have always had my own particular principles about relations between father and son. Of course you have a right to blame me. At my age ... To cut a long story short, that – that girl about whom you've probably heard...."

"Fenichka?" inquired Arkady casually.

Nikolai Petrovich blushed.

"Don't mention her name so loudly, please ... Well, yes ... she lives with me now. I have installed her in the house ... there were two small rooms available. Of course, all that can be altered."

"But why, Daddy; what for?"

"Your friend will be staying with us ... it will be awkward."

"Please don't worry about Bazarov. He's above all that."

"Well, but you too," added Nikolai Petrovich. "Unfortunately the little side-wing is in such a bad state."

"For goodness' sake, Daddy," interposed Arkady. "You needn't apologize. Are you ashamed?"

"Of course, I ought to be ashamed," answered Nikolai Petrovich, turning redder and redder.

"Enough of that, Daddy, please don't..." Arkady smiled affectionately. "What a thing to apologize for," he thought to himself, and his heart was filled with a feeling of indulgent tenderness for his kind, soft-hearted father, mixed with a sense of secret superiority. "Please stop that," he repeated once more, instinctively enjoying the awareness of his own more emancipated outlook.

Nikolai Petrovich looked at his son through the fingers of the hand with which he was again rubbing his forehead, and a pang seized his heart ... but he immediately reproached himself for it.

"Here are our own meadows at last," he remarked after a long silence.

"And that is our forest over there, isn't it?" asked Arkady.

"Yes. But I have sold it. This year they will cut it down for timber."

"Why did you sell it?"

"We need the money; besides, that land will be taken over by the peasants."

"Who don't pay their rent?"

"That's their affair; anyhow they will pay it some day."

"It's a pity about the forest," said Arkady, and began to look around him.

The country through which they were driving could not possibly be called picturesque. Field after field stretched right up to the horizon, now gently sloping upwards, then slanting down again; in some places woods were visible and winding ravines, planted with low scrubby bushes, vividly reminiscent of the way in which they were represented on the old maps of Catherine's times. They passed by little streams with hollow banks and ponds with narrow dams, small villages with low huts under dark and often crumbling roofs, and crooked barns with walls woven out of dry twigs and with gaping doorways opening on to neglected threshing floors; and churches, some brick-built with the stucco covering peeling off in patches, others built of wood, near crosses fallen crooked in the overgrown graveyards. Gradually Arkady's heart began to sink. As if to complete the picture, the peasants whom they met were all in rags and mounted on the most wretched-looking little horses; the willows, with their broken branches and trunks stripped of bark, stood like tattered beggars along the roadside; lean and shaggy cows, pinched with hunger, were greedily tearing up grass along the ditches. They looked as if they had just been snatched out of the clutches of some terrifying murderous monster; and the pitiful sight of these emaciated animals in the setting of that gorgeous spring day conjured up, like a white ghost, the vision of interminable joyless winter with its storms, frosts and snows ... "No," thought Arkady, "this country is far from rich, and the people seem neither contented nor industrious; we just can't let things go on like this; reforms are indispensable ... but how are we to execute them, how should we begin?"

Such were Arkady's thoughts ... but even while he was thinking, the spring regained its sway. All around lay a sea of golden green – everything, trees, bushes and grass, vibrated and stirred in gentle waves under the breath of the warm breeze; from every side the larks were pouring out their loud continuous trills; the plovers were calling as they glided over the low-lying meadows or noiselessly ran over the tufts of grass; the crows strutted about in the low spring corn, looking picturesquely black against its tender green; they disappeared in the already whitening rye, only from time to time their heads peeped out from among its misty waves. Arkady gazed and gazed and his thoughts grew slowly fainter and died away ... He flung off his overcoat and turned round with such a bright boyish look that his father hugged him once again.

"We're not far away now," remarked Nikolai Petrovich. "As soon as we get to the top of this hill the house will be in sight. We shall have a fine life together, Arkasha; you will help me to farm the land, if only it doesn't bore you. We must draw close to each other now and get to know each other better, mustn't we?"

"Of course," murmured Arkady. "But what a wonderful day it is!"

"To welcome you home, my dear one. Yes, this is spring in all its glory. Though I agree with Pushkin – do you remember, in *Evgeny Onegin,*

"'To me how sad your coming is,
Spring, spring, sweet time of love!
What–'"

"Arkady," shouted Bazarov's voice from the tarantass, "give me a match. I've got nothing to light my pipe with."

Nikolai Petrovich fell silent, while Arkady, who had been listening to him with some surprise but not without sympathy, hurriedly pulled a silver matchbox out of his pocket and told Pyotr to take it over to Bazarov.

"Do you want a cigar?" shouted Bazarov again.

"Thanks," answered Arkady.

Pyotr came back to the carriage and handed him, together with the matchbox, a thick black cigar, which Arkady started to smoke at once, spreading around him such a strong and acrid smell of cheap tobacco that Nikolai Petrovich, who had never been a smoker, was forced to turn away his head, which he did unobtrusively, to avoid hurting his son's feelings.

A quarter of an hour later both carriages drew up in front of the porch of a new wooden house, painted grey, with a red iron roof. This was Maryino, also known as New Hamlet, or as the peasants had nicknamed it, Landless Farm.

Chapter 4

No crowd of house servants ran out to meet their master; there appeared only a little twelve-year-old girl, and behind her a young lad, very like Pyotr, came out of the house; he was dressed in a grey livery with white armorial buttons and was the servant of Pavel Petrovich Kirsanov. He silently opened the carriage door and unbuttoned the apron of the tarantass. Nikolai Petrovich with his son and Bazarov walked through a dark and almost empty hall, through the door of which they caught a glimpse of a young woman's face, and into a drawing room furnished in the most modern style.

"Well, here we are at home," said Nikolai Petrovich, removing his cap and shaking back his hair. "Now the main thing is to have supper and then to rest."

"It wouldn't be a bad thing to have a meal, certainly," said Bazarov, stretching himself, and he sank on to a sofa.

"Yes, yes, let us have supper at once," exclaimed Nikolai Petrovich, and for no apparent reason stamped his foot. "Ah, here comes Prokovich, just at the right moment."

A man of sixty entered, white-haired, thin and swarthy, dressed in a brown coat with brass buttons and a pink neckerchief. He grinned, went up to kiss

Arkady's hand, and after bowing to the guest, retreated to the door and put his hands behind his back.

"Here he is, Prokovich," began Nikolai Petrovich; "at last he has come back to us ... Well? How do you find him?"

"As well as could be," said the old man, and grinned again. Then he quickly knitted his bushy eyebrows. "Do you want supper served?" he asked solemnly.

"Yes, yes, please. But don't you want to go to your room first, Evgeny Vassilich?"

"No, thanks. There's no need. Only tell them to carry my little trunk in there and this garment, too," he added, taking off his loose overcoat.

"Certainly. Prokovich, take the gentleman's coat." (Prokovich, with a puzzled look, picked up Bazarov's "garment" with both hands, and holding it high above his head went out on tiptoe.) "And you, Arkady, are you going to your room for a moment?"

"Yes, I must wash," answered Arkady, and was just moving towards the door when at that moment there entered the drawing room a man of medium height, dressed in a dark English suit, a fashionable low cravat and patent leather shoes, Pavel Petrovich Kirsanov. He looked about forty-five; his closely cropped grey hair shone with a dark luster like unpolished silver; his ivory-colored face, without wrinkles, had exceptionally regular and clear features, as though carved by a sharp and delicate chisel, and showed traces of outstanding beauty; particularly fine were his shining, dark almond-shaped eyes. The whole figure of Arkady's uncle, graceful and aristocratic, had preserved the flexibility of youth and that air of striving upwards, away from the earth, which usually disappears when people are over thirty.

Pavel Petrovich drew from his trouser pocket his beautiful hand with its long pink nails, a hand which looked even more beautiful against the snowy white cuff buttoned with a single large opal, and stretched it out to his nephew. After a preliminary European hand shake, he kissed him three times in the Russian style; in fact he touched his cheek three times with his perfumed mustache, and said, "Welcome!"

Nikolai Petrovich introduced him to Bazarov; Pavel Petrovich responded with a slight inclination of his supple body and a slight smile, but he did not give him his hand and even put it back in his pocket.

"I began to think that you weren't coming today," he began in a pleasant voice, with an amiable swing and shrug of the shoulders; his smile showed his splendid white teeth. "Did anything go wrong on the road?"

"Nothing went wrong," answered Arkady. "Only we dawdled a bit. So now we're as hungry as wolves. Make Prokovich hurry up, Daddy; I'll be back in a moment."

"Wait, I'm coming with you," exclaimed Bazarov, suddenly pulling himself off the sofa. Both the young men went out.

"Who is he?" asked Pavel Petrovich.

"A friend of Arkasha's; according to him a very clever young man."

"Is he going to stay with us?"

"Yes."

"That unkempt creature!"

"Well, yes."

Pavel Petrovich drummed on the table with his finger tips. "I fancy Arkady *s'est dégourdi*," he observed. "I'm glad he has come back."

At supper there was little conversation. Bazarov uttered hardly a word, but ate a lot. Nikolai Petrovich told various anecdotes about what he called his farming career, talked about the forthcoming government measures, about committees, deputations, the need to introduce new machinery, etc. Pavel Petrovich paced slowly up and down the dining room (he never ate supper), occasionally sipping from a glass of red wine and less often uttering some remark or rather exclamation, such as "Ah! aha! hm!" Arkady spoke about the latest news from Petersburg, but he was conscious of being a bit awkward, with that awkwardness which usually overcomes a youth when he has just stopped being a child and has come back to a place where they are accustomed to regard and treat him as a child. He made his sentences quite unnecessarily long, avoided the word "Daddy," and even sometimes replaced it by the word "Father," mumbled between his teeth; with exaggerated carelessness he poured into his glass far more wine than he really wanted and drank it all. Prokovich did not take his eyes off him and kept on chewing his lips. After supper they all separated at once.

"Your uncle's a queer fellow," Bazarov said to Arkady, as he sat in his dressing gown by the bed, smoking a short pipe. "All that smart dandyism in the country. Just think of it! And his nails, his nails – they ought to be sent to an exhibition!"

"Why, of course you don't know," replied Arkady; "he was a great figure in his day. I'll tell you his story sometime. He was extremely handsome, and used to turn all the women's heads."

"Oh, that's it! So he keeps it up for the sake of old times. What a pity there's no one for him to fascinate here! I kept on looking at his astonishing collar, just like marble – and his chin, so meticulously shaved. Come, come, Arkady, isn't it ridiculous?"

"Perhaps it is, but he's a good man really."

"An archaic survival! But your father is a splendid fellow. He wastes his time reading poetry and knows precious little about farming, but he's kindhearted."

"My father has a heart of gold."

"Did you notice how shy he was?"

Arkady shook his head, as if he were not shy himself.

"It's something astonishing," went on Bazarov, "these old romantic idealists! They go on developing their nervous systems till they get highly strung and irritable, then they lose their balance completely. Well, good night. In my room there's an English washstand, but the door won't fasten. Anyhow, that ought to be encouraged – English washstands – they stand for progress!"

Bazarov went out, and a sense of peaceful happiness stole over Arkady. It was sweet to fall asleep in one's own home, in the familiar bed, under the quilt which had been worked by loving hands, perhaps the hands of his old nurse, those gentle, good and tireless hands. Arkady remembered Yegorovna, and sighed and wished, "God rest her soul" ... for himself he said no prayer.

Both he and Bazarov soon fell asleep, but others in the house remained awake much longer. Nikolai Petrovich was agitated by his son's return. He lay in bed but did not put out the candles, and propping his head in his hands he went on thinking. His brother was sitting till long after midnight in his study, in a wide arm-chair in front of the fireplace, in which some embers glowed faintly. Pavel Petrovich had not undressed, but some red Chinese slippers had replaced his patent leather shoes. He held in his hand the last number of *Galignani,* but he was not reading it; he gazed fixedly into the fireplace, where a bluish flame flickered, dying down and flaring up again at intervals ... God knows where his thoughts were wandering, but they were not wandering only in the past; his face had a stern and concentrated expression, unlike that of a man who is solely absorbed in his memories. And in a little back room, on a large chest, sat a young woman in a blue jacket with a white kerchief thrown over her dark hair; this was Fenichka; she was now listening, now dozing, now looking across towards the open door, through which a child's bed was visible and the regular breathing of a sleeping infant could be heard.

Chapter 5

The next morning Bazarov woke up earlier than anyone else and went out of the house. "Ugh!" he thought, "this isn't much of a place!" When Nikolai Petrovich had divided his estate with his peasants, he had to set aside for his new manor house four acres of entirely flat and barren land. He had built a house, offices and farm buildings, laid out a garden, dug a pond and sunk two wells; but the young trees had not flourished, very little water had collected in the pond, and the well water had a brackish taste. Only one arbor of lilac and acacia had grown up properly; the family sometimes drank tea or dined there. In a few minutes Bazarov had explored all the little paths in the garden; he went into the cattle yard and the stables, discovered two farm boys with whom he made friends at once, and went off with them to a small swamp about a mile from the house in order to search for frogs.

"What do you want frogs for, sir?" asked one of the boys.

"I'll tell you what for," answered Bazarov, who had a special capacity for winning the confidence of lower-class people, though he never cringed to them and indeed treated them casually; "I shall cut the frog open to see what goes on inside him, and then, as you and I are much the same as frogs except that we walk on legs, I shall learn what is going on inside us as well."

"And why do you want to know that?"

"In order not to make a mistake if you're taken ill and I have to cure you."

"Are you a doctor, then?"

"Yes."

"Vaska, did you hear that? The gentleman says that you and I are just like frogs; that's queer."

"I'm frightened of frogs," remarked Vaska, a boy of seven with flaxen hair and bare feet, dressed in a grey smock with a high collar.

"What are you frightened of? Do they bite?"

"There, paddle along into the water, you philosophers," said Bazarov.

Meanwhile Nikolai Petrovich had also awakened and had gone to see Arkady, whom he found dressed. Father and son went out on to the terrace under the shelter of the awning; the samovar was already boiling on the table near the balustrade among great bunches of lilac. A little girl appeared, the same one who had first met them on their arrival the evening before. In a shrill voice she said, "Fedosya Nikolayevna is not very well and she can't come; she told me to ask you, will you pour out tea yourself or should she send Dunyasha?"

"I'll pour myself, of course," interposed Nikolai Petrovich hurriedly. "Arkady, how do you like your tea, with cream or with lemon?"

"With cream," answered Arkady, then after a brief pause he muttered questioningly, "Daddy?"

Nikolai Petrovich looked at his son with embarrassment. "Well?" he said.

Arkady lowered his eyes.

"Excuse me, Daddy, if my question seems to you indiscreet," he began; "but you yourself by your frank talk yesterday encouraged me to be frank ... you won't be angry?"

"Go on."

"You make me bold enough to ask you, isn't the reason why Fen ... isn't it only because I'm here that she won't come to pour out tea?"

Nikolai Petrovich turned slightly aside.

"Perhaps," he at length answered, "she supposes ... she feels ashamed."

Arkady glanced quickly at his father. "She has no reason to feel ashamed. In the first place, you know my point of view," (Arkady much enjoyed pronouncing these words) "and secondly, how could I want to interfere in the smallest way with your life and habits? Besides, I'm sure you couldn't make a bad choice; if you allow her to live under the same roof with you, she must be worthy of it; in any case, it's not for a son to judge his father – particularly for me, and with such a father, who has always let me do everything I wanted."

Arkady's voice trembled to start with; he felt he was being magnanimous and realized at the same time that he was delivering something like a lecture to his father; but the sound of his own voice has a powerful effect on any man, and Arkady pronounced the last words firmly and even emphatically.

"Thank you, Arkasha," said Nikolai Petrovich thickly, and his fingers again passed over his eyebrows. "What you suppose is in fact quite true. Of course if this girl hadn't deserved ... it's not just a frivolous fancy. It's awkward for me to talk to you about this, but you understand that it's difficult for her to come here in your presence, especially on the first day of your arrival."

"In that case I'll go to her myself!" exclaimed Arkady, with a fresh onrush of generous excitement, and he jumped up from his seat. "I will explain to her that she has no need to feel ashamed in front of me."

Nikolai Petrovich got up also.

"Arkady," he began, "please ... how is it possible ... there ... I haven't told you yet..."

But Arkady was no longer listening to him; he had run off the terrace. Nikolai Petrovich gazed after him and sank into a chair overwhelmed with confusion. His heart began to throb ... Did he realize at that moment the inevitable strangeness of his future relations with his son? Was he aware that Arkady might have shown him more respect if he had never mentioned that subject at all? Did he reproach himself for weakness? It is hard to say. All these feelings moved within him, though in the state of vague sensations only, but the flush remained on his face, and his heart beat rapidly.

Then came the sound of hurrying footsteps and Arkady appeared on the terrace. "We have introduced ourselves, Daddy!" he cried with an expression of affectionate and good-natured triumph on his face. "Fedosya Nikolayevna is really not very well today, and she will come out a little later. But why didn't you tell me I have a brother? I should have kissed him last night as I kissed him just now!"

Nikolai Petrovich tried to say something, tried to rise and open wide his arms. Arkady flung himself on his neck.

"What's this? Embracing again!" sounded the voice of Pavel Petrovich behind them.

Father and son were both equally glad to see him at that moment; there are situations, however touching, from which one nevertheless wants to escape as quickly as possible.

"Why are you surprised at that?" said Nikolai Petrovich gaily. "What ages I've been waiting for Arkasha. I haven't had time to look at him properly since yesterday."

Arkady went up to his uncle and again felt on his cheeks the touch of that perfumed mustache. Pavel Petrovich sat down at the table. He was wearing another elegant English suit with a bright little fez on his head. That fez and the carelessly tied little cravat suggested the freedom of country life, but the stiff collar of his shirt – not white, it is true, but striped, as is correct with morning dress – stood up as inexorably as ever against his well-shaved chin.

"Where is your new friend?" he asked Arkady.

"He's not in the house; he usually gets up early and goes off somewhere. The main thing is not to pay any attention to him; he dislikes ceremony."

"Yes, that's obvious," Pavel Petrovich began, slowly spreading butter on his bread. "Is he going to stay long with us?"

"Possibly. He came here on his way to his father's."

"And where does his father live?"

"In our province, about sixty-five miles from here. He has a small property there. He used to be an army doctor."

"Tut, tut, tut! Of course. I kept on asking myself, 'Where have I heard that name before, Bazarov?' Nikolai, don't you remember, there was a surgeon called Bazarov in our father's division."

"I believe there was."

"Exactly. So that surgeon is his father. Hm!" Pavel Petrovich pulled his mustache. "Well, and Monsieur Bazarov, what is he?" he asked in a leisurely tone.

"What is Bazarov?" Arkady smiled. "Would you like me to tell you, uncle, what he really is?"

"Please do, nephew."

"He is a nihilist!"

"What?" asked Nikolai Petrovich, while Pavel Petrovich lifted his knife in the air with a small piece of butter on the tip and remained motionless.

"He is a nihilist," repeated Arkady.

"A nihilist," said Nikolai Petrovich. "That comes from the Latin nihil, nothing, as far as I can judge; the word must mean a man who ... who recognizes nothing?"

"Say – who respects nothing," interposed Pavel Petrovich and lowered his knife with the butter on it.

"Who regards everything from the critical point of view," said Arkady.

"Isn't that exactly the same thing?" asked Pavel Petrovich.

"No, it's not the same thing. A nihilist is a person who does not bow down to any authority, who does not accept any principle on faith, however much that principle may be revered."

"Well, and is that good?" asked Pavel Petrovich. "That depends, uncle dear. For some it is good, for others very bad."

"Indeed. Well, I see that's not in our line. We old-fashioned people think that without principles, taken as you say on faith, one can't take a step or even breathe. *Vous avez changé tout cela;* may God grant you health and a general's rank, and we shall be content to look on and admire your ... what was the name?"

"Nihilists," said Arkady, pronouncing very distinctly.

"Yes, there used to be Hegelists and now there are nihilists. We shall see how you will manage to exist in the empty airless void; and now ring, please, brother Nikolai, it's time for me to drink my cocoa."

Nikolai Petrovich rang the bell and called, "Dunyasha!" But instead of Dunyasha, Fenichka herself appeared on the terrace. She was a young woman of about twenty-three with a soft white skin, dark hair and eyes, childishly pouting lips and plump little hands. She wore a neat cotton dress; a new blue kerchief lay lightly over her soft shoulders. She carried a large cup of cocoa and setting it down in front of Pavel Petrovich, she was overcome with confusion; the hot blood rushed in a wave of crimson under the delicate skin of her charming face. She lowered her eyes and stood by the table slightly pressing it with her finger tips. She looked as if she were ashamed of having come in and somehow felt at the same time that she had a right to come.

Pavel Petrovich frowned and Nikolai Petrovich looked embarrassed. "Good morning, Fenichka," he muttered through his teeth.

"Good morning," she replied in a voice not loud but resonant, and casting a quick glance at Arkady, who gave her a friendly smile, she went quietly away. She had a slightly swaying walk, but that also suited her.

For some minutes silence reigned on the terrace. Pavel Petrovich was sipping his cocoa; suddenly he raised his head. "Here is Mr. Nihilist coming over to visit us," he murmured.

Bazarov was in fact approaching through the garden, striding over the flower beds. His linen coat and trousers were bespattered with mud; a clinging marsh plant was twined round the crown of his old round hat, in his right hand he held a small bag in which something alive was wriggling. He walked quickly up to the terrace and said with a nod, "Good morning, gentlemen; sorry I was late for tea; I'll join you in a moment. I just have to put these prisoners away."

"What have you there, leeches?" asked Pavel Petrovich.

"No, frogs."

"Do you eat them or keep them for breeding?"

"For experiments," answered Bazarov indifferently, and went into the house.

"So he's going to cut them up," observed Pavel Petrovich; "he has no faith in principles, but he has faith in frogs."

Arkady looked sadly at his uncle; Nikolai Petrovich almost imperceptibly shrugged his shoulders. Pavel Petrovich himself felt that his epigram had misfired and he began to talk about farming and the new bailiff who had come to him the evening before to complain that a laborer, Foma, was "debauched," and had become unmanageable. "He's such an Æsop," he remarked. "He announces to everyone that he's a worthless fellow; he wants to have a good time and then he'll suddenly leave his job on account of some stupidity."

Chapter 6

Bazarov came back, sat down at the table and began to drink tea hurriedly. Both brothers watched him in silence, and Arkady glanced furtively from one to the other.

"Did you walk far this morning?" asked Nikolai Petrovich at last.

"To where you've got a little marsh near an aspen wood. I scared away five snipe. You might shoot them, Arkady."

"So you're not a sportsman yourself?"

"No."

"Isn't physics your special subject?" asked Pavel Petrovich in his turn.

"Yes, physics, and natural science in general."

"They say the Teutons have lately had great success in that line."

"Yes, the Germans are our teachers in it," Bazarov answered carelessly.

Pavel Petrovich had used the word "Teutons" instead of "Germans" with an ironical intention, which, however, no one noticed.

"Have you such a high opinion of Germans?" asked Pavel Petrovich with exaggerated politeness. He was beginning to feel a concealed irritation. Bazarov's complete nonchalance disgusted his aristocratic nature. This surgeon's son was not only self-assured, he even answered abruptly and unwillingly and there was something coarse and almost insolent in the tone of his voice.

"Their scientists are a clever lot."

"Ah, yes. I expect you hold a less flattering opinion about Russian scientists."

"Very likely."

"That is very praiseworthy self-denial," said Pavel Petrovich, drawing himself up and throwing back his head. "But how is it that Arkady Nikolaich was telling us just now that you acknowledge no authorities? Don't you even believe in them?"

"Why should I acknowledge them, or believe in them? If they tell me the truth, I agree – that's all."

"And do all Germans tell the truth?" murmured Pavel Petrovich, and his face took on a distant, detached expression, as if he had withdrawn to some misty height.

"Not all," answered Bazarov with a short yawn, obviously not wanting to prolong the discussion.

Pavel Petrovich looked at Arkady, as if he wanted to say, "How polite your friend is."

"As far as I'm concerned," he began again with some effort, "I plead guilty of not liking Germans. There's no need to mention Russian Germans, we all know what sort of creatures they are. But even German Germans don't appeal to me. Formerly there were a few Germans here and there; well, Schiller for instance, or Goethe – my brother is particularly fond of them – but nowadays they all seem to have turned into chemists and materialists..."

"A decent chemist is twenty times more useful than any poet," interrupted Bazarov.

"Oh, indeed!" remarked Pavel Petrovich, and as if he were falling asleep he slightly raised his eyebrows. "So you don't acknowledge art?"

"The art of making money or of advertising pills!" cried Bazarov, with a contemptuous laugh.

"Ah, just so; you like joking, I see. So you reject all that Very well. So you believe in science only?"

"I have already explained to you that I don't believe in anything; and what is science – science in the abstract? There are sciences, as there are trades and professions, but abstract science just doesn't exist."

"Excellent. Well, and do you maintain the same negative attitude towards other traditions which have become generally accepted for human conduct?"

"What is this, a cross-examination?" asked Bazarov.

Pavel Petrovich turned a little pale ... Nikolai Petrovich felt that the moment had come for him to intervene in the conversation.

"Sometime we should discuss this subject with you in greater detail, my dear Evgeny Vassilich; we will hear your views and express our own. I must say I'm personally very glad you are studying natural science. I heard that Liebig made some wonderful discoveries about improving the soil. You can help me in my agricultural work and give me some useful advice."

"I'm at your service, Nikolai Petrovich, but Liebig is quite above our heads. We must first learn the alphabet and only then begin to read, and we haven't yet grasped the a b c."

"You are a nihilist all right," thought Nikolai Petrovich, and added aloud, "All the same I hope you will let me apply to you occasionally. And now, brother, I think it's time for us to go and have our talk with the bailiff."

Pavel Petrovich rose from his seat. "Yes," he said, without looking at anyone; "it's sad to have lived like this for five years in the country, far from mighty intellects! You turn into a fool straight away. You try not to forget what you have learned – and then one fine day it turns out to be all rubbish, and they tell you that experienced people have nothing to do with such nonsense, and that you, if you please, are an antiquated old simpleton. What's to be done? Obviously young people are cleverer than we."

Pavel Petrovich turned slowly on his heels and went out; Nikolai Petrovich followed him.

"Is he always like that?" Bazarov coolly asked Arkady directly the door had closed behind the two brothers.

"I must say, Evgeny, you were unnecessarily rude to him," remarked Arkady. "You hurt his feelings."

"Well, am I to humor them, these provincial aristocrats? Why, it's all personal vanity, smart habits, and foppery. He should have continued his career in Petersburg if that's his turn of mind ... But enough of him! I've found a rather rare specimen of water beetle, Dytiscus marginatus – do you know it? I'll show you."

"I promised to tell you his story..." began Arkady.

"The story of the beetle?"

"Come, come, Evgeny – the story of my uncle. You'll see he's not the kind of man you take him for. He deserves pity rather than ridicule."

"I don't dispute, but why do you worry about him?"

"One should be just, Evgeny."

"How does that follow?"

"No, listen..."

And Arkady told him his uncle's story. The reader will find it in the following chapter.

Chapter 7

Pavel Petrovich Kirsanov was educated first at home, like his younger brother, and afterwards in the Corps of Pages. From childhood he was distinguished by his remarkable beauty; he was self-confident, rather ironical, and had a biting sense of humor; he could not fail to please people. He began to be received everywhere directly he had obtained his commission as an officer. He was pampered by society, and indulged in every kind of whim and folly, but that did not make him any less attractive. Women went crazy about him, men called him a fop and secretly envied him. He shared a flat with his brother, whom he loved sincerely although he was most unlike him. Nikolai Petrovich was rather lame, had small, agreeable but somewhat melancholy features, little black eyes and soft thin hair; he enjoyed being lazy, but he also liked reading and was shy in society. Pavel Petrovich did not spend a single evening at home, prided himself on his boldness and agility (he was just bringing gymnastics into fashion among the young men of his set), and had read in all five or six French books. At twenty-eight he was already a captain; a brilliant career lay before him. Suddenly all that was changed.

In those days there used to appear occasionally in Petersburg society a woman who has even now not been forgotten – Princess R. She had a well-educated and respectable, but rather stupid husband, and no children. She used suddenly to travel abroad and equally suddenly return to Russia, and in general she led an eccentric life. She was reputed to be a frivolous coquette, abandoned herself keenly to every kind of pleasure, danced to exhaustion, laughed and joked with young men whom she used to receive before dinner in a dimly lit drawing room, but at night she wept and said prayers, finding no peace anywhere, and often paced her room till morning, wringing her hands in anguish, or sat, pale and cold, reading a Psalter. Day came and she turned again into a lady of fashion, she went about again, laughed, chatted and literally flung herself into any activity which could afford her the slightest distraction. She had a wonderful figure; her hair, golden in color and heavy like gold, fell below her knees, yet no one would have called her a beauty; the only striking feature in her whole face was her eyes – and even her eyes were grey and not large – but their glance was swift and deeply penetrating, carefree to the point of audacity and thoughtful to the verge of melancholy – an enigmatic glance. Something extraordinary shone in those eyes even when her tongue was chattering the emptiest gossip. She dressed exquisitely. Pavel Petrovich met her at a ball, danced a mazurka with her, in the course of which she did not utter a single sensible word, and fell passionately in love with her. Accustomed to making conquests, he succeeded with her also, but his easy triumph did not damp his enthusiasm. On the contrary, he found himself in a still closer and more tormenting bondage to this woman, in whom, even when she surrendered herself without reserve, there seemed always to remain something mysterious and unattainable, to which no one could penetrate. What was hidden in that soul – God alone knows! It seemed as if she were in the grip of some strange powers, unknown even to herself; they seemed to play with her at will and her limited mind was not strong enough to master their caprices. Her whole behavior was a maze of inconsistencies; the only letters which could have aroused her husband's just suspicions she wrote to a man who was almost a stranger to her, and her love had always an element of sadness; she no longer laughed and joked with the man whom she had chosen, but listened to him and looked at him in bewilderment. Sometimes this bewilderment would change suddenly into a cold horror; her face would take on a wild, deathlike expression and she would lock herself up in her bedroom; her maid, putting her ear to the keyhole, could hear her smothered sobs. More than once, as he returned home after a tender meeting, Kirsanov felt within him that heart-rending, bitter gloom which follows the consciousness of total failure. "What more do I want?" he asked himself, but his heart was heavy. He once gave her a ring which had a sphinx engraved in the stone.

"What is this?" she asked. "A sphinx?"

"Yes," he answered, "and that sphinx is – you."

"Me?" she asked, and slowly looked at him with her enigmatic eyes. "Do you know, that is very flattering," she added with a meaningless smile, while her eyes still looked as strangely as before.

Pavel Petrovich suffered even while Princess R. loved him, but when she became cold to him, and that happened quite soon, he almost went out of his mind. He tortured himself, he was jealous, he gave her no rest but followed her everywhere. She grew sick of his persistent pursuit of her and went abroad. He resigned from his regiment in spite of the entreaties of his friends and the advice of his superior officers, and he followed the princess abroad; four years he spent in foreign countries, at one time pursuing her, at other times trying to lose sight of her; he was ashamed of himself, he was indignant at his own lack of resolution – but nothing helped. Her image – that incomprehensible, almost meaningless, but fascinating image – was too deeply rooted in his heart. In Baden he once more revived his former relationship with her; it seemed as though she had never before loved him so passionately ... but in a month it was all over; the flame flared up for the last time and then died out forever. Foreseeing the inevitable separation, he wanted at least to remain her friend, as if lasting friendship with such a woman were possible ... She left Baden secretly and from that time permanently avoided meeting Kirsanov. He returned to Russia and tried to live as before, but he could not adapt himself to his old routine. He wandered from place to place like one possessed; he still went out to parties and retained the habits of a man of the world; he could boast of two or three more conquests; but he no longer expected anything from himself or from others, and he undertook nothing new. He grew old and grey, spending all his evenings at the club, embittered and bored – arguing indifferently in bachelor society became a necessity for him, and that was a bad sign. Of course the thought of marriage never even occurred to him. Ten years passed in this way, grey and fruitless years, but they sped by terribly quickly. Nowhere does time fly as it does in Russia; in prison, they say, it flies even faster. One day when he was dining at his club, Pavel Petrovich heard that Princess R. was dead. She had died in Paris in a state bordering on insanity. He rose from the table and paced about the rooms for a long time, occasionally standing motionless behind the card-players, but he returned home no earlier than usual. A few weeks later he received a packet on which his name had been written; it contained the ring which he had given to the princess. She had drawn lines in the shape of a cross over the sphinx and sent him a message to say that the solution of the enigma was the cross.

This happened at the beginning of the year 1848, at the same time as Nikolai Petrovich came to Petersburg after the death of his wife. Pavel Petrovich had hardly seen his brother since the latter had settled in the country; Nikolai Petrovich's marriage had coincided with the very first days of Pavel Petrovich's acquaintance with the princess. When he returned from abroad, he went to the country, intending to stay two months with his brother and to take pleasure in his happiness, but he could stand it for only a week. The difference between them was too great. In 1848 this difference had diminished; Nikolai Petrovich had lost his wife, Pavel Petrovich had abandoned his memories; after the death of the princess he tried not to think about her. But for Nikolai there remained the feeling of a well-spent life, and his son was growing up under his eyes; Pavel, on the contrary, a lonely bachelor, was entering into that indefinite twilight period of regrets which resemble hopes and of hopes which are akin to regrets, when youth is over and old age has not yet started.

This time was harder for Pavel Petrovich than for other people, for in losing his past he lost everything he had.

"I won't ask you to come to Maryino now," Nikolai Petrovich said to him one day (he had called his property by that name in honor of his wife); "you found it dull there even when my dear wife was alive, and now, I fear, you would be bored to death."

"I was stupid and fidgety then," answered Pavel Petrovich. "Since then I have calmed down, if not grown wiser. Now, on the contrary, if you will let me, I am ready to settle down with you for good."

Instead of answering, Nikolai Petrovich embraced him; but a year and a half elapsed after this conversation before Pavel Petrovich finally decided to carry out his intention. Once he was settled in the country, however, he would not leave it, even during those three winters which Nikolai spent in Petersburg with his son. He began to read, chiefly in English; indeed he organized his whole life in an English manner, rarely met his neighbors and went only out to the local elections, and then he was usually silent, though he occasionally teased and alarmed landowners of the old school by his liberal sallies, and he held himself aloof from members of the younger generation. Both generations regarded him as "stuck up," and both respected him for his excellent aristocratic manners, for his reputation as a lady killer, for the fact that he was always perfectly dressed and always stayed in the best room in the best hotel; for the fact that he knew about good food and had once even dined with the Duke of Wellington at Louis Philippe's table; for the fact that he took with him everywhere a real silver dressing case and a portable bath; for the fact that he smelt of some unusual and strikingly "distinguished" perfume; for the fact that he played whist superbly and always lost; lastly they respected him for his incorruptible honesty. Ladies found him enchantingly romantic, but he did not cultivate the society of ladies...

"So you see, Evgeny," remarked Arkady, as he finished his story, "how unjustly you judge my uncle. Not to mention that he has more than once helped my father out of financial troubles, given him all his money – perhaps you don't know, the property was never divided up – he's happy to help anyone; incidentally he is always doing something for the peasants; it is true, when he talks to them, he screws up his face and sniffs eau de Cologne..."

"Nerves, obviously," interrupted Bazarov.

"Perhaps, but his heart is in the right place. And he's far from stupid. What a lot of useful advice he has given me ... especially ... especially about relations with women."

"Aha! If you burn your mouth with hot milk, you'll even blow on water – we know that!"

"Well," continued Arkady, "in a word, he's profoundly unhappy – it's a crime to despise him."

"And who is despising him?" retorted Bazarov. "Still, I must say that a man who has staked his whole life on the one card of a woman's love, and when that card fails, turns sour and lets himself drift till he's fit for nothing, is not really a man. You say he's unhappy; you know better than I do; but he certainly hasn't got rid of all his foibles. I'm sure that he imagines he is busy and useful because he reads *Galignani* and once a month saves a peasant from being flogged."

"But remember his education, the age in which he grew up," said Arkady.

"Education?" ejaculated Bazarov. "Everyone should educate himself, as I've done, for instance ... And as for the age, why should I depend upon it? Let it rather depend on me. No, my dear fellow, that's all emptiness and loose living. And what are these mysterious relations between a man and a woman? We physiologists know what they are. You study the anatomy of the eye; and where does it come in, that enigmatic look you talk about? That's all romanticism, rubbish, and moldy æsthetics. We had much better go and examine the beetle."

And the two friends went off to Bazarov's room, which was already pervaded by a kind of medical surgical smell, mixed with the reek of cheap tobacco.

Chapter 8

Pavel Petrovich did not stay long at his brother's interview with the bailiff, a tall, thin man with the soft voice of a consumptive and cunning eyes, who to all Nikolai Petrovich's remarks answered, "Indeed, certainly, sir," and tried to show up the peasants as thieves and drunkards. The estate had only just started to be run on the new system, whose mechanism still creaked like an ungreased wheel and cracked in places like homemade furniture of raw, unseasoned wood. Nikolai Petrovich did not lose heart but he often sighed and felt discouraged; he realized that things could not be improved without more money, and his money was almost all spent. Arkady had spoken the truth; Pavel Petrovich had helped his brother more than once; several times, seeing him perplexed, racking his brains, not knowing which way to turn, Pavel Petrovich had moved towards the window, and with his hands thrust into his pockets had muttered between his teeth, *"Mais je puis vous donner de l'argent,"* and gave him money; but today he had none left himself and he preferred to go away. The petty disputes of agricultural management wearied him; besides, he could not help feeling that Nikolai Petrovich, with all his zeal and hard work, did not set about things in the right way, although he could not point out exactly what were his brother's mistakes. "My brother is not practical enough," he would say to himself; "they cheat him." On the other hand, Nikolai Petrovich had the highest opinion of Pavel Petrovich's practical capacity and was always asking for his advice. "I'm a mild, weak person, I've spent my life in the depths of the country," he used to say, "while you haven't seen so much of the world for nothing; you understand people, you see through them with an eagle's eye." In answer to such words, Pavel Petrovich only turned aside but did not contradict his brother.

Leaving Nikolai Petrovich in the study, he walked along the corridor which separated the front portion of the house from the back; on reaching a low door he stopped and hesitated for a moment, then, pulling at his mustache, he knocked on it.

"Who is there? Come in," called out Fenichka's voice.

"It is me," said Pavel Petrovich, and opened the door. Fenichka jumped up from the chair on which she was sitting with her baby, and putting him into the arms of a girl who at once carried him out of the room, she hastily straightened her kerchief.

"Excuse me for disturbing you," began Pavel Petrovich without looking at her; "I only wanted to ask you ... as they are sending into the town today ... to see that they buy some green tea for me."

"Certainly," answered Fenichka, "how much tea do you want?"

"Oh, half a pound will be enough, I should think. I see you have made some changes here," he added, casting a rapid look around and at Fenichka's face. "Those curtains," he went on, seeing that she did not understand him.

"Oh, yes, the curtains; Nikolai Petrovich kindly gave them to me, but they've been hung up for quite a long time."

"Yes, and I haven't been to see you for a long time. Now it is all very nice here."

"Thanks to Nikolai Petrovich's kindness," murmured Fenichka.

"You are more comfortable here than in the little side-wing where you used to be?" inquired Pavel Petrovich politely but without any trace of a smile.

"Certainly, it is better here."

"Who has been put in your place now?"

"The laundry-maids are there now."

"Ah!"

Pavel Petrovich was silent. "Now he will go," thought Fenichka; but he did not go and she stood in front of him rooted to the spot, moving her fingers nervously.

"Why did you send your little one away?" said Pavel Petrovich at last. "I love children; do let me see him."

Fenichka blushed all over with confusion and joy. She was frightened of Pavel Petrovich; he hardly ever spoke to her.

"Dunyasha," she called. "Will you bring Mitya, please?" (Fenichka was polite to every member of the household.) "But wait a moment; he must have a frock on." Fenichka was going towards the door.

"That doesn't matter," remarked Pavel Petrovich.

"I shall be back in a moment," answered Fenichka, and she went out quickly.

Pavel Petrovich was left alone and this time he looked round with special attention. The small, low room in which he found himself was very clean and cosy. It smelt of the freshly painted floor and of chamomile flowers. Along the walls stood chairs with lyre-shaped backs, bought by the late General Kirsanov in Poland during a campaign; in one corner was a little bedstead under a muslin canopy alongside a chest with iron clamps and a curved lid. In the opposite corner a little lamp was burning in front of a big, dark picture of St. Nicholas the Miracle-Worker; a tiny porcelain egg hung over the saint's breast suspended by a red ribbon from his halo; on the window sills stood carefully tied greenish glass jars filled with last year's jam; Fenichka had herself written in big letters on their paper covers the word "Gooseberry;" it was the favorite jam of Nikolai Petrovich. A cage containing a short-tailed canary hung on a long cord from the ceiling; he constantly chirped and hopped about, and the cage kept on swinging and shaking, while hemp seeds fell with a light tap onto the floor. On the wall just above a small chest of drawers hung some rather bad photographs of Nikolai Petrovich taken in various positions; there, too, was a most unsuccessful photograph of Fenichka; it showed an eyeless face smiling with effort in a dingy frame – nothing more definite could be distinguished – and above Fenichka, General Yermolov, in a Caucasian cloak, scowled menacingly at distant mountains, from under a little silk shoe for pins which fell right over his forehead.

Five minutes passed; a sound of rustling and whispering could be heard in the next room. Pavel Petrovich took from the chest of drawers a greasy book, an odd volume of Masalsky's *Musketeer,* and turned over a few pages ... The door opened and Fenichka came in with Mitya in her arms. She bad dressed him in a little red shirt with an embroidered collar, had combed his hair and washed his face; he was breathing heavily, his whole body moved up and down, and he waved his little hands in the air as all healthy babies do; but his smart shirt obviously impressed him and his plump little person radiated delight. Fenichka had also put her own hair in order and rearranged her kerchief; but she might well have remained as she was. Indeed, is there anything more charming in the world than a beautiful young mother with a healthy child in her arms?

"What a chubby little fellow," said Pavel Petrovich, graciously tickling Mitya's double chin with the tapering nail of his forefinger; the baby stared at the canary and laughed.

"That's uncle," said Fenichka, bending her face over him and slightly rocking him, while Dunyasha quietly set on the window sill a smoldering candle, putting a coin under it.

"How many months old is he?" asked Pavel Petrovich.

"Six months, it will be seven on the eleventh of this month."

"Isn't it eight, Fedosya Nikolayevna?" Dunyasha interrupted timidly.

"No, seven. What an idea!"

The baby laughed again, stared at the chest and suddenly seized his mother's nose and mouth with all his five little fingers. "Naughty little one," said Fenichka without drawing her face away.

"He's like my brother," said Pavel Petrovich.

"Who else should he be like?" thought Fenichka.

"Yes," continued Pavel Petrovich as though speaking to himself. "An unmistakable likeness." He looked attentively, almost sadly at Fenichka.

"That's uncle," she repeated, this time in a whisper.

"Ah, Pavel, there you are!" suddenly resounded the voice of Nikolai Petrovich.

Pavel Petrovich turned hurriedly round with a frown on his face, but his brother looked at him with such delight and gratitude that he could not help responding to his smile.

"You've got a splendid little boy," he said, and looked at his watch. "I came in here to ask about some tea..."

Then, assuming an expression of indifference, Pavel Petrovich at once left the room.

"Did he come here of his own accord?" Nikolai Petrovich asked Fenichka.

"Yes, he just knocked and walked in."

"Well, and has Arkasha come to see you again?"

"No. Hadn't I better move into the side-wing again, Nikolai Petrovich?"

"Why should you?"

"I wonder whether it wouldn't be better just at first."

"No," said Nikolai Petrovich slowly, and rubbed his forehead. "We should have done it sooner ... How are you, little balloon?" he said, suddenly brightening, and went up to the child and kissed him on the cheek; then he bent lower and pressed his lips to Fenichka's hand, which lay white as milk on Mitya's little red shirt.

"Nikolai Petrovich, what are you doing?" she murmured, lowering her eyes, then quietly looked up again; her expression was charming as she peeped from under her eyelids and smiled tenderly and rather stupidly.

Nikolai Petrovich had made Fenichka's acquaintance in the following way. Three years ago he had once stayed the night at an inn in a remote provincial town. He was pleasantly surprised by the cleanliness of the room assigned to him and the freshness of the bed linen; surely there must be a German woman in charge, he thought at first; but the housekeeper turned out to be a Russian, a woman of about fifty, neatly dressed, with a good-looking, sensible face and a measured way of talking. He got into conversation with her at tea and liked her very much. Nikolai Petrovich at that time had only just moved into his new home, and not wishing to keep serfs in the house, he was looking for wage servants; the housekeeper at the inn complained about the hard times and the small number of visitors to that town; he offered her the post of housekeeper in his home and she accepted it. Her husband had long been dead; he had left her with an only daughter, Fenichka. Within a fortnight Arina Savishna (that was the new housekeeper's name) arrived with her daughter at Maryino and was installed in the side-wing. Nikolai Petrovich had made a good choice. Arina brought order into the household. No one talked about Fenichka, who was then seventeen, and hardly anyone saw her; she lived in quiet seclusion and only on Sundays Nikolai Petrovich used to notice the delicate profile of her pale face somewhere in a corner of the church. Thus another year passed.

One morning Arina came into his study, and after bowing low as usual, asked him if he could help her daughter, as a spark from the stove had flown into her eye. Nikolai Petrovich, like many home-loving country people, had studied simple remedies and had even procured a homeopathic medicine chest. He at once told Arina to bring the injured girl to him. Fenichka was much alarmed when she heard that the master had sent for her, but she followed her mother. Nikolai Petrovich led her to the window and took her head between his hands. After thoroughly examining her red and swollen eye, he made up a poultice at once, and tearing his handkerchief in strips showed her how it should be applied. Fenichka listened to all he said and turned to go out. "Kiss the master's hand, you silly girl," said Arina. Nikolai Petrovich did not hold out his hand and in confusion himself kissed her bent head on the parting of the hair. Fenichka's eye soon healed, but the impression she had made on Nikolai Petrovich did not pass away so quickly. He had constant visions of that pure, gentle, timidly raised face; he felt that soft hair under the palms of his hands, and saw those innocent, slightly parted lips, through which pearly teeth gleamed with moist brilliance in the sunshine. He began to watch her very attentively in church and tried to get into conversation with her. At first she was extremely shy with him, and one day, meeting him towards evening on a narrow footpath crossing a rye field, she ran into the tall, thick rye, overgrown with cornflowers and wormwood, to avoid meeting him face to face. He caught sight of her small head through the golden network of ears of rye, from which she was peering out like a wild animal, and called out to her affectionately, "Good evening, Fenichka. I won't bite."

"Good evening," murmured Fenichka, without emerging from her hiding place.

By degrees she began to feel more at ease with him, but she was still a shy girl when suddenly her mother, Arina, died of cholera. What was to become of Fenichka? She had inherited from her mother a love of order, tidiness and regularity, but she was so young, so alone in the world; Nikolai Petrovich was so genuinely kind and considerate ... There is no need to describe what followed...

"So my brother came to see you?" Nikolai Petrovich asked her. "He just knocked and came in?"

"Yes."

"Well, that's good. Let me give Mitya a swing."

And Nikolai Petrovich began to toss him almost up to the ceiling, to the vast delight of the baby, and to the considerable anxiety of his mother, who each time he flew upwards stretched out her arms towards his little bare legs.

Meanwhile Pavel Petrovich had gone back to his elegant study, which was decorated with handsome blue wallpaper, and with weapons hanging from a multicolored Persian carpet fixed to the wall; it had walnut furniture, upholstered in dark green velvet, a Renaissance bookcase of ancient black oak, bronze statuettes on the magnificent writing desk, an open hearth ... He threw himself on the sofa, clasped his hands behind his head and remained motionless, looking at the ceiling with an expression verging on despair. Perhaps because he wanted to hide even from the walls whatever was reflected in his face, or for some other reason, he rose, drew the heavy window curtains and again threw himself on the sofa.

Chapter 9

On that same day Bazarov met Fenichka. He was walking with Arkady in the garden and explaining to him why some of the trees, particularly the oaks, were growing badly.

"You would do better to plant silver poplars here, or firs and perhaps limes, with some extra black earth. The arbor there has grown up well," he added, "because it's acacia and lilac; they're good shrubs, they don't need looking after. Ah! there's someone inside."

In the arbor Fenichka was sitting with Dunyasha and Mitya. Bazarov stopped and Arkady nodded to Fenichka like an old friend.

"Who's that?" Bazarov asked him directly they had passed by. "What a pretty girl!"

"Whom do you mean?"

"You must know; only one of them is pretty."

Arkady, not without embarrassment, explained to him briefly who Fenichka was.

"Aha!" remarked Bazarov. "That shows your father's got good taste. I like your father; ay, ay! He's a good fellow. But we must make friends," he added, and turned back towards the arbor.

"Evgeny," cried Arkady after him in bewilderment, "be careful what you do, for goodness' sake."

"Don't worry," said Bazarov. "I'm an experienced man, not a country bumpkin."

Going up to Fenichka, he took off his cap. "May I introduce myself?" he began, making a polite bow. "I'm a friend of Arkady Nikolayevich and a harmless person."

Fenichka got up from the garden seat and looked at him without speaking.

"What a wonderful baby," continued Bazarov. "Don't be uneasy, my praises have never brought the evil eye. Why are his cheeks so flushed? Is he cutting his teeth?"

"Yes," murmured Fenichka, "he has cut four teeth already and now the gums are swollen again."

"Show me ... don't be afraid, I'm a doctor." Bazarov took the baby in his arms, and to the great astonishment of both Fenichka and Dunyasha the child made no resistance and was not even frightened.

"I see, I see ... It's nothing, he'll have a good set of teeth. If anything goes wrong you just tell me. And are you quite well yourself?"

"Very well, thank God."

"Thank God, that's the main thing. And you?" he added, turning to Dunyasha.

Dunyasha, who behaved very primly inside the house and was frivolous out of doors, only giggled in reply.

"Well, that's all right. Here's your young hero."

Fenichka took back the baby in her arms.

"How quiet he was with you," she said in an undertone. "Children are always good with me," answered Bazarov. "I have a way with them."

"Children know who loves them," remarked Dunyasha. "Yes, they certainly do," Fenichka added. "Mitya won't allow some people to touch him, not for anything."

"Will he come to me?" asked Arkady, who after standing at a distance for some time had come to join them. He tried to entice Mitya into his arms, but Mitya threw back his head and screamed, much to Fenichka's confusion.

"Another day, when he's had time to get accustomed to me," said Arkady graciously, and the two friends walked away.

"What's her name?" asked Bazarov.

"Fenichka ... Fedosya," answered Arkady.

"And her father's name? One must know that, too."

"Nikolayevna."

"Good. What I like about her is that she's not too embarrassed. Some people, I suppose, would think ill of her on that account. But what rubbish! Why should she be embarrassed? She's a mother and she's quite right."

"She is in the right," observed Arkady, "but my father..."

"He's right, too," interposed Bazarov.

"Well, no, I don't think so."

"I suppose an extra little heir is not to your liking."

"You ought to be ashamed to attribute such thoughts to me!" retorted Arkady hotly. "I don't consider my father in the wrong from that point of view; as I see it, he ought to marry her."

"Well, well," said Bazarov calmly, "how generous-minded we are! So you still attach significance to marriage; I didn't expect that from you."

The friends walked on a few steps in silence.

"I've seen all round your father's place," began Bazarov again. "The cattle are bad, the horses are broken down, the buildings aren't up to much, and the workmen look like professional loafers; and the bailiff is either a fool or a knave, I haven't yet found out which."

"You are very severe today, Evgeny Vassilich."

"And the good peasants are taking your father in properly; you know the proverb 'the Russian peasant will cheat God himself.'"

"I begin to agree with my uncle," remarked Arkady. "You certainly have a poor opinion of Russians."

"As if that mattered! The only good quality of a Russian is to have the lowest possible opinion about himself. What matters is that twice two make four and the rest is all rubbish."

"And is nature rubbish?" said Arkady, gazing pensively at the colored fields in the distance, beautifully lit up in the mellow rays of the sinking sun.

"Nature, too, is rubbish in the sense you give to it. Nature is not a temple but a workshop, and man is the workman in it."

At that moment the long drawn-out notes of a cello floated out to them from the house. Someone was playing Schubert's *Expectation* with feeling, though with an untrained hand, and the sweet melody flowed like honey through the air.

"What is that?" exclaimed Bazarov in amazement.

"My father."

"Your father plays the cello?"

"Yes."

"And how old is your father?"

"Forty-four."

Bazarov suddenly roared with laughter.

"What are you laughing at?"

"My goodness! A man of forty-four, a father of a family, in this province, plays on the cello!"

Bazarov went on laughing, but, much as he revered his friend's example, this time Arkady did not even smile.

Chapter 10

A fortnight passed by. Life at Maryino pursued its normal course, while Arkady luxuriously enjoyed himself and Bazarov worked. Everyone in the house had grown accustomed to Bazarov, to his casual behavior, to his curt and abrupt manner of speaking. Fenichka indeed, felt so much at ease with him that one night she had him awakened; Mitya had been seized by convulsions; Bazarov had gone, half-joking and half-yawning as usual, had sat with her for two hours and relieved the child. On the other hand, Pavel Petrovich had grown to hate Bazarov with all the strength of his soul; he regarded him as conceited, impudent, cynical and vulgar, he suspected that Bazarov had no respect for him, that he all but despised him – him, Pavel Kirsanov! Nikolai Petrovich was rather frightened of the young "Nihilist" and doubted the benefit of his influence on Arkady, but he listened keenly to what he said and was glad to be present during his chemical and scientific experiments. Bazarov had brought a microscope with him and busied himself with it for hours. The servants also took to him, though he made fun of them; they felt that he was more like one of themselves, and not a master. Dunyasha was always ready to giggle with him and used to cast significant sidelong glances at him when she skipped past like a squirrel. Pyotr, who was vain and stupid to the highest degree, with a constant forced frown on his brow, and whose only merit consisted in the fact that he looked polite, could spell out a page of reading and assiduously brushed his coat – even he grinned and brightened up when Bazarov paid any attention to him; the farm boys simply ran after "the doctor" like puppies. Only old Prokovich disliked him; at table he handed him dishes with a grim expression; he called him "butcher" and "upstart" and declared that with his huge whiskers he looked like a pig in a sty. Prokovich in his own way was quite as much of an aristocrat as Pavel Petrovich.

The best days of the year had come – the early June days. The weather was lovely; in the distance, it is true, cholera was threatening, but the inhabitants of that province had grown used to its periodic ravages. Bazarov used to get up very early and walk for two or three miles, not for pleasure – he could not bear walking without an object – but in order to collect specimens of plants and insects. Sometimes he took Arkady with him. On the way home an argument often sprang up, in which Arkady was usually defeated in spite of talking more than his companion.

One day they had stayed out rather late. Nikolai Petrovich had gone into the garden to meet them, and as he reached the arbor he suddenly heard the quick steps and voices of the two young men; they were walking on the other side of the arbor and could not see him.

"You don't know my father well enough," Arkady was saying. "Your father is a good fellow," said Bazarov, "but his day is over; his song has been sung to extinction."

Nikolai Petrovich listened intently ... Arkady made no reply.

The man whose day was over stood still for a minute or two, then quietly returned to the house.

"The day before yesterday I saw him reading Pushkin," Bazarov went on meanwhile. "Please explain to him how utterly useless that is. After all he's not a boy, it's high time he got rid of such rubbish. And what an idea to be romantic in our times! Give him something sensible to read."

"What should I give him?" asked Arkady.

"Oh, I think Büchner's *Stoff und Kraft* to start with."

"I think so too," remarked Arkady approvingly. "*Stoff und Kraft* is written in popular language..."

"So it seems," said Nikolai Petrovich the same day after dinner to his brother, as they sat in his study, "you and I are behind the times, our day is over. Well ... perhaps Bazarov is right; but one thing, I must say, hurts me; I was so hoping just now to get on really close and friendly terms with Arkady, and it turns out that I've lagged behind while he has gone forward, and we simply can't understand one another."

"But how has he gone forward? And in what way is he so different from us?" exclaimed Pavel Petrovich impatiently. "It's that *grand seigneur* of a nihilist who has knocked such ideas into his head. I loathe that doctor fellow; in my opinion he's nothing but a charlatan; I'm sure that in spite of all his tadpoles he knows precious little even in medicine."

"No, brother, you mustn't say that; Bazarov is clever and knows his subject."

"And so disagreeably conceited," Pavel Petrovich broke in again.

"Yes," observed Nikolai Petrovich, "he is conceited. Evidently one can't manage without it, that's what I failed to take into account. I thought I was doing everything to keep up with the times; I divided the land with the peasants, started a model farm, so that I'm even described as a 'Rebel' all over the province; I read, I study, I try in every way to keep abreast of the demands of the day – and they say my day is over. And brother, I really begin to think that it is."

"Why is that?"

"I'll tell you why. I was sitting and reading Pushkin today ... I remember, it happened to be *The Gypsies* ... Suddenly Arkady comes up to me and silently, with such a kind pity in his face, as gently as if I were a baby, takes the book away from me and puts another one in front of me instead ... a German book ... smiles and goes out, carrying Pushkin off with him."

"Well, really! What book did he give you?"

"This one."

And Nikolai Petrovich pulled out of his hip pocket the ninth edition of Büchner's well-known treatise.

Pavel Petrovich turned it over in his hands. "Hm!" he growled, "Arkady Nikolayevich is taking your education in hand. Well, have you tried to read it?"

"Yes, I tried."

"What did you think of it?"

"Either I'm stupid, or it's all nonsense. I suppose I must be stupid."

"But you haven't forgotten your German?" asked Pavel Petrovich.

"Oh, I understand the language all right."

Pavel Petrovich again fingered the book and glanced across at his brother. Both were silent.

"Oh, by the way," began Nikolai Petrovich, evidently wanting to change the subject – "I've had a letter from Kolyazin."

"From Matvei Ilyich?"

"Yes. He has come to inspect the province. He's quite a bigwig now, he writes to say that as a relation he wants to see us again, and invites you, me and Arkady to go to stay in the town."

"Are you going?" asked Pavel Petrovich.

"No. Are you?"

"No. I shan't go. What is the sense of dragging oneself forty miles on a wild-goose chase. Mathieu wants to show off to us in all his glory. Let him go to the devil! He'll have the whole province at his feet, so he can get on without us. It's a grand honor – a privy councilor! If I had continued in the service, drudging along in that dreary routine, I should have been a general-adjutant by now. Besides, you and I are behind the times."

"Yes, brother; it seems the time has come to order a coffin, and to cross the arms over one's chest," remarked Nikolai Petrovich with a sigh.

"Well, I shan't give in quite so soon," muttered his brother. "I've got a quarrel with this doctor creature in front of me, I'm sure of that."

The quarrel materialized that very evening at tea. Pavel Petrovich came into the drawing room all keyed up, irritable and determined. He was only waiting for a pretext to pounce upon his enemy, but for some time no such pretext arose. As a rule Bazarov spoke little in the presence of the "old Kirsanovs" (that was what he called the brothers), and that evening he felt in a bad humor and drank cup after cup of tea without saying a word. Pavel Petrovich was burning with impatience; his wishes were fulfilled at last.

The conversation turned to one of the neighboring landowners. "Rotten aristocratic snob," observed Bazarov casually; he had met him in Petersburg.

"Allow me to ask you," began Pavel Petrovich, and his lips were trembling, "do you attach an identical meaning to the words 'rotten' and 'aristocrat'?"

"I said 'aristocratic snob,'" replied Bazarov, lazily swallowing a sip of tea.

"Precisely, but I imagine you hold the same opinion of aristocrats as of aristocratic snobs. I think it my duty to tell you that I do not share that opinion. I venture to say that I am well known to be a man of liberal views and devoted to progress, but for that very reason I respect aristocrats – real aristocrats. Kindly remember, sir," (at these words Bazarov lifted his eyes and looked at Pavel Petrovich) "kindly remember, sir," he repeated sharply, "the English aristocracy. They did not abandon one iota of their rights, and for that reason they respect the rights of others; they demand the fulfillment of what is due to them, and therefore they respect their own duties. The aristocracy gave freedom to England, and they maintain it for her."

"We've heard that story many times; what are you trying to prove by it?"

"I am tryin' to prove by that, sir," (when Pavel Petrovich became angry he intentionally clipped his words, though of course he knew very well that such forms are not strictly grammatical. This whim indicated a survival from the period of Alexander I. The great ones of that time, on the rare occasions when they spoke their own language, made use of such distortions as if seeking to show thereby that though they were genuine Russians, yet at the same time as grand seigneurs they could afford to ignore the grammatical rules of scholars) "I am tryin' to prove by that, sir, that without a sense of personal dignity, without self-respect – and these two feelings are developed in the aristocrat – there is no firm foundation for the social ... *bien public* ... for the social structure. Personal character, my good sir, that is the chief thing; a man's personality must be as strong as a rock since everything else is built up on it. I am well aware, for instance, that you choose to consider my habits, my dress, even my tidiness, ridiculous; but all this comes from a sense of self-respect and of duty – yes, from a sense of duty. I live in the wilds of the country, but I refuse to lower myself. I respect the dignity of man in myself."

"Let me ask you, Pavel Petrovich," muttered Bazarov, "you respect yourself and you sit with folded hands; what sort of benefit does that do to the *bien public?* If you didn't respect yourself, you'd do just the same."

Pavel Petrovich turned pale. "That is quite another question. There is absolutely no need for me to explain to you now why I sit here with folded hands, as you are pleased to express yourself. I wish only to tell you that aristocracy – is a principle, and that only depraved or stupid people can live in our time without principles. I said as much to Arkady the day after he came home, and I repeat it to you now. Isn't that so, Nikolai?"

Nikolai Petrovich nodded his head.

"Aristocracy, liberalism, progress, principles," said Bazarov. "Just think what a lot of foreign ... and useless words! To a Russian they're no good for anything!"

"What is good for Russians according to you? If we listen to you, we shall find ourselves beyond the pale of humanity, outside human laws. Doesn't the logic of history demand..."

"What's the use of that logic to us? We can get along without it."

"What do you mean?"

"Why, this. You don't need logic, I suppose, to put a piece of bread in your mouth when you're hungry. For what do we need those abstractions?"

Pavel Petrovich raised his hands. "I simply don't understand you after all that. You insult the Russian people. I fail to understand how it is possible not to acknowledge principles, rules! By virtue of what can you act?"

"I already told you, uncle dear, that we don't recognize any authorities," interposed Arkady.

"We act by virtue of what we recognize as useful," went on Bazarov. "At present the most useful thing is denial, so we deny—"

"Everything?"

"Everything."

"What? Not only art, poetry ... but ... the thought is appalling..."

"Everything," repeated Bazarov with indescribable composure.

Pavel Petrovich stared at him. He had not expected this, and Arkady even blushed with satisfaction.

"But allow me," began Nikolai Petrovich. "You deny everything, or to put it more precisely, you destroy everything ... But one must construct, too, you know."

"That is not our business ... we must first clear the ground."

"The present condition of the people demands it," added Arkady rather sententiously; "we must fulfill those demands, we have no right to yield to the satisfaction of personal egotism."

That last phrase obviously displeased Bazarov; it smacked of philosophy, or romanticism, for Bazarov called philosophy a kind of romanticism – but he did not judge it necessary to correct his young disciple.

"No, no!" cried Pavel Petrovich with sudden vehemence. "I can't believe that you young men really know the Russian people, that you represent their needs and aspirations! No, the Russian people are not what you imagine them to be. They hold tradition sacred, they are a patriarchal people, they cannot live without faith..."

"I'm not going to argue with you," interrupted Bazarov. "I'm even ready to agree that there you are right."

"And if I am right..."

"It proves nothing, all the same."

"Exactly, it proves nothing," repeated Arkady with the assurance of an experienced chess player who, having foreseen an apparently dangerous move on the part of his adversary, is not in the least put out by it.

"How can it prove nothing?" mumbled Pavel Petrovich in consternation. "In that case you must be going against your own people."

"And what if we are?" exclaimed Bazarov. "The people imagine that when it thunders the prophet Ilya is riding across the sky in his chariot. What then? Are we to agree with them? Besides, if they are Russian, so am I."

"No, you are not a Russian after what you have said. I can't admit you have any right to call yourself a Russian."

"My grandfather ploughed the land," answered Bazarov with haughty pride. "Ask any one of your peasants which of us – you or me – he would more readily acknowledge as a fellow countryman. You don't even know how to talk to them."

"While you talk to them and despise them at the same time."

"What of that, if they deserve contempt! You find fault with my point of view, but what makes you think it came into being by chance, that it's not a product of that very national spirit which you are championing?"

"What an idea! How can we need nihilists?"

"Whether they are needed or not – is not for us to decide. Why, even you imagine you're not a useless person."

"Gentlemen, gentlemen, no personalities, please!" cried Nikolai Petrovich, getting up.

Pavel Petrovich smiled, and laying his hand on his brother's shoulder, made him sit down again.

"Don't be alarmed," he said, "I shan't forget myself, thanks to that sense of dignity which is so cruelly ridiculed by our friend – our friend, the doctor. Allow me to point out," he resumed, turning again to Bazarov, "you probably think that your doctrine is a novelty? That is an illusion of yours. The materialism which you preach, was more than once in vogue before and has always proved inadequate...."

"Yet another foreign word!" broke in Bazarov. He was beginning to feel angry and his face looked peculiarly copper-colored and coarse. "In the first place, we preach nothing; that's not in our line..."

"What do you do, then?"

"This is what we do. Not long ago we used to say that our officials took bribes, that we had no roads, no commerce, no real justice...."

"Oh, I see, you are reformers – that's the right name, I think. I, too, should agree with many of your reforms, but..."

"Then we suspected that talk and only talk about our social diseases was not worth while, that it led to nothing but hypocrisy and pedantry; we saw that our leading men, our so-called advanced people and reformers, are worthless; that we busy ourselves with rubbish, talk nonsense about art, about unconscious creation, parliamentarianism, trial by jury, and the devil knows what – when the real question is daily bread, when the grossest superstitions are stifling us, when all our business enterprises crash simply because there aren't enough honest men to carry them on, while the very emancipation which our government is struggling to organize will hardly come to any good, because our peasant is happy to rob even himself so long as he can get drunk at the pub."

"Yes," broke in Pavel Petrovich, "indeed, you were convinced of all this and you therefore decided to undertake nothing serious yourselves."

"We decided to undertake nothing," repeated Bazarov grimly. He suddenly felt annoyed with himself for having been so expansive in front of this gentleman.

"But to confine yourselves to abuse."

"To confine ourselves to abuse."

"And that is called nihilism?"

"And that is called nihilism," Bazarov repeated again, this time in a particularly insolent tone.

Pavel Petrovich screwed up his eyes a little. "So that's it," he murmured in a strangely composed voice. "Nihilism is to cure all our woes, and you – you are our saviors and heroes. Very well – but why do you find fault with others, including the reformers? Don't you do as much talking as anyone else?"

"Whatever faults we may have, that is not one of them," muttered Bazarov between his teeth.

"What then, do you act? Are you preparing for action?"

Bazarov made no reply. A tremor passed through Pavel Petrovich, but he at once regained control of himself.

"Hm! ... Action, destruction..." he went on. "But how can you destroy without even knowing why?"

"We shall destroy because we are a force," remarked Arkady.

Pavel Petrovich looked at his nephew and laughed.

"Yes, a force can't be called to account for itself," said Arkady, drawing himself up.

"Unhappy boy," groaned Pavel Petrovich, who could no longer maintain his show of firmness. "Can't you realize the kind of thing you are encouraging in Russia with your shallow doctrine! No, it's enough to try the patience of an angel! Force! There's force in the savage Kalmuk, in the Mongol, but what is that to us? What is dear to us is civilization, yes, yes, my good sir, its fruits are precious to us. And don't you tell me these fruits are worthless; the poorest dauber, *un barbouilleur,* the man who plays dance music for five farthings an evening, even they are of more use than you because they stand for civilization and not for brute Mongolian force! You fancy yourselves as advanced people, and yet you're only fit for the Kalmuk's dirty hovel! Force! And remember, you forceful gentlemen, that you're only four men and a half, and the others – are millions, who won't let you trample their sacred beliefs under foot, but will crush you instead!"

"If we're crushed, that's in store for us," said Bazarov. "But it's an open question. We're not so few as you suppose."

"What? You seriously suppose you can set yourself up against a whole people?"

"All Moscow was burnt down, you know, by a penny candle," answered Bazarov.

"Indeed! First comes an almost Satanic pride, then cynical jeers – so that is what attracts the young, what takes by storm the inexperienced hearts of boys! Here is one of them sitting beside you, ready to worship the ground beneath your feet. Look at him. (Arkady turned aside and frowned.) And this plague has already spread far and wide. I am told that in Rome our artists don't even enter the Vatican. Raphael they regard as a fool, because, of course, he is an authority; and these artists are themselves disgustingly sterile and weak, men whose imagination can soar no higher than *Girls at a Fountain* – and even the girls are abominably drawn! They are fine fellows in your view, I suppose?"

"To my mind," retorted Bazarov, "Raphael isn't worth a brass farthing, and they're no better than he."

"Bravo, bravo! Listen, Arkady ... that is how modern young men should express themselves! And if you come to think of it, they're bound to follow you. Formerly young men had to study. If they didn't want to be called fools they had to work hard whether they liked it or not. But now they need only say 'Everything in the world is rubbish!' and the trick is done. Young men are delighted. And, to be sure, they were only sheep before, but now they have suddenly turned into Nihilists."

"You have departed from your praiseworthy sense of personal dignity," remarked Bazarov phlegmatically, while Arkady had turned hot all over and his eyes were flashing. "Our argument has gone too far ... better cut it short, I think. I shall be quite ready to agree with you," he added, getting up, "when you can show me a single institution in our present mode of life, in the family or in society, which does not call for complete and ruthless destruction."

"I can show you millions of such institutions!" cried Pavel Petrovich – "millions! Well, take the commune, for instance."

A cold smile distorted Bazarov's lips. "Well, you had better talk to your brother about the commune. I should think he has seen by now what the commune is like in reality – its mutual guarantees, its sobriety and suchlike."

"Well, the family, the family as it exists among our peasants," cried Pavel Petrovich.

"On that subject, too, I think it will be better for you not to enter into too much detail. You know how the head of the family chooses his daughters-in-law? Take my advice, Pavel Petrovich, allow yourself a day or two to think it all over; you'll hardly find anything straight away. Go through the various classes of our society and examine them carefully, meanwhile Arkady and I will..."

"Will go on abusing everything," broke in Pavel Petrovich.

"No, we will go on dissecting frogs. Come, Arkady; good-by for the present, gentlemen!"

The two friends walked off. The brothers were left alone and at first only looked at each other.

"So that," began Pavel Petrovich, "that is our modern youth! Those young men are our heirs!"

"Our heirs!" repeated Nikolai Petrovich with a weary smile. He had been sitting as if on thorns throughout the argument, and only from time to time cast a sad furtive glance at Arkady. "Do you know what I was reminded of, brother? I once quarreled with our mother; she shouted and wouldn't listen to me. At last I said to her, 'Of course you can't understand me; we belong to two different generations.' She was terribly offended, but I thought, 'It can't be helped – a bitter pill, but she has to swallow it.' So now our turn has come, and our successors can tell us: 'You don't belong to our generation; swallow your pill.'"

"You are much too generous and modest," replied Pavel Petrovich. "I'm convinced, on the contrary, that you and I are far more in the right than these young gentlemen, although perhaps we express ourselves in more old-fashioned language – *vieilli* – and are not so insolently conceited ... and the airs these young people give themselves! You ask one 'Would you like white wine or red?' 'It is my custom to prefer red,' he answers in a deep voice and with a face as solemn as if the whole world were looking at him that moment..."

"Do you want any more tea?" asked Fenichka, putting her head in at the door; she had not wanted to come into the drawing room while the noisy dispute was going on.

"No, you can tell them to take away the samovar," answered Nikolai Petrovich, and he got up to meet her. Pavel Petrovich said *"bonsoir"* to him abruptly, and went to his own study.

Chapter 11

Half an hour later Nikolai Petrovich went into the garden to his favorite arbor. He was filled with melancholy thoughts. For the first time he saw clearly the distance separating him from his son and he foresaw that it would grow wider every day. So they were spent in vain, those winters in Petersburg, when sometimes he had pored for whole days on end over the latest books; in vain had he listened to the talk of the young men, and rejoiced when he succeeded in slipping a few of his own words into heated discussions.

"My brother says we are right," he thought, "and laying aside all vanity, it even seems to me that they are further from the truth than we are, though all the same I feel they have something behind them which we lack, some superiority over us ... is it youth? No, it can't only be that; their superiority may be that they show fewer traces of the slave-owner than we do."

Nikolai Petrovich's head sank despondently, and he passed his hand over his face.

"But to renounce poetry, to have no feeling for art, for nature..."

And he looked round, as though trying to understand how it was possible to have no feeling for nature. It was already evening; the sun was hidden behind a small clump of aspens which grew about a quarter of a mile from the garden; its shadow stretched indefinitely across the motionless fields. A little peasant on a white pony was riding along the dark narrow path near the wood; his whole figure was clearly visible even to the patch on his shoulder, although he was in the shade; the pony's hoofs rose and fell with graceful distinctness. The sun's rays on the farther side fell full on the clump of trees, and piercing through them threw such a warm light on the aspen trunks that they looked like pines, and their leaves seemed almost dark blue, while above them rose a pale blue sky, tinged by the red sunset glow. The swallows flew high; the wind had quite died down, some late bees hummed lazily among the lilac blossoms, a swarm of midges hung like a cloud over a solitary branch which stood out against the sky. "How beautiful, my God!" thought Nikolai Petrovich, and his favorite verses almost rose to his lips; then he remembered Arkady's *Stoff und Kraft* – and remained silent, but he still sat there, abandoning himself to the sad consolation of solitary thought. He was fond of dreaming, and his country life had developed that tendency in him. How short a time ago he had been dreaming like this, waiting for his son at the posting station, and how much had changed since that day; their relations, then indeterminate, had now been defined – and how defined! His dead wife came back to his imagination, but not as he had known her for so many years, not as a good domesticated housewife, but as a young girl with a slim waist, an innocent inquiring look and a tightly twisted pigtail on her childish neck. He remembered how he had seen her for the first time. He was still a student then. He had met her on the staircase of his lodgings, and running into her by accident he tried to apologize but could only mutter "Pardon, Monsieur," while she bowed, smiled, then suddenly seemed frightened and ran away, glanced quickly back at him, looked serious and blushed. Afterwards the first timid visits, the hints, the half-smiles and embarrassment; the uncertain sadness, the ups and downs and at last that overwhelming joy ... where had it all vanished away? She had been his wife, he had been happy as few on earth are happy ... "But," he mused, "those sweet fleeting moments, why could one not live an eternal undying life in them?"

He made no effort to clarify his thoughts, but he felt that he longed to hold that blissful time by something stronger than memory; he longed to feel his Marya near him, to sense her warmth and breathing; already he could fancy her actual presence...

"Nikolai Petrovich," came the sound of Fenichka's voice close by. "Where are you?"

He started. He felt no remorse, no shame. He never admitted even the possibility of comparison between his wife and Fenichka, but he was sorry that she had thought of coming to look for him. Her voice had brought back to him at once his grey hairs, his age, his daily existence...

The enchanted world arising out of the dim mists of the past, into which he had just stepped, quivered – and disappeared.

"I'm here," he answered; "I'm coming. You run along." "There they are, traces of the slave-owner," flashed through his mind. Fenichka peeped into the arbor without speaking to him and went away again; and he noticed with surprise that night had fallen while he was dreaming. Everything around was dark and hushed, and Fenichka's face had glimmered in front of him, so pale and slight. He got up and was about to go home, but the emotions stirring his heart could not be calmed so soon, and he began walking slowly about the garden, sometimes meditatively surveying the ground, then raising his eyes to the sky where multitudes of stars were twinkling. He went on walking till he was almost tired out, but the restlessness within him, a yearning vague melancholy excitement, was still not appeased. Oh, how Bazarov would have laughed at him if he had known what was happening to him then! Even Arkady would have condemned him. He, a man of forty-four, an agriculturist and a landowner, was shedding tears, tears without reason; it was a hundred times worse than playing the cello.

Nikolai Petrovich still walked up and down and could not make up his mind to go into the house, into the cosy peaceful nest, which looked at him so hospitably from its lighted windows; he had not the strength to tear himself away from the darkness, the garden, the sensation of fresh air on his face, and from that sad restless excitement.

At a turn in the path he met Pavel Petrovich. "What is the matter with you?" he asked Nikolai Petrovich. "You are as white as a ghost; you must be unwell. Why don't you go to bed?" Nikolai said a few words to his brother about his state of mind and moved away. Pavel Petrovich walked on to the end of the garden, also deep in thought, and he, too, raised his eyes to the sky – but his beautiful dark eyes reflected only the light of the stars. He was not born a romantic idealist, and his fastidiously dry though ardent soul, with its tinge of French scepticism, was not addicted to dreaming...

"Do you know what?" Bazarov was saying to Arkady that very night. "I've had a splendid idea. Your father was saying today that he had received an invitation from that illustrious relative of yours. Your father doesn't want to go, but why shouldn't we be off to X? You know the man invites you as well. You see what fine weather it is; we'll stroll around and look at the town. Let's have a jaunt for five or six days, no more."

"And you'll come back here afterwards?"

"No, I must go to my father's. You know he lives about twenty miles from X. I've not seen him or my mother for a long time; I must cheer the old people up. They've been good to me, my father particularly; he's awfully funny. I'm their only one."

"Will you stay long with them?"

"I don't think so. It will be dull, of course. "And you'll come to us again on your way back."

"I don't know ... we'll see. Well, what do you say? Shall we go?"

"If you like," answered Arkady languidly.

In his heart he was overjoyed by his friend's suggestion, but thought it a duty to conceal his feeling. He was not a nihilist for nothing!

The next day he set off with Bazarov to X. The younger members of the household at Maryino were sorry about their departure; Dunyasha even wept ... but the older people breathed more freely.

Chapter 12

The town of X. to which our friends set off was under the jurisdiction of a governor, who was still a young man, and who was at once progressive and despotic, as so often happens with Russians. Before the end of the first year of his governorship, he had managed to quarrel not only with the marshal of nobility, a retired guards-officer, who kept open house and a stud of horses, but even with his own subordinates. The resulting feuds at length grew to such proportions that the ministry in Petersburg found it necessary to send a trusted official with a commission to investigate everything on the spot. The choice of the authorities fell on Matvei Ilyich Kolyazin, the son of that Kolyazin under whose protection the brothers Kirsanov had been when they were students in Petersburg. He was also a "young man," that is to say, he was only just over forty, but he was well on the way to becoming a statesman and already wore two stars on his breast – admittedly, one of them was a foreign star and not of the first magnitude. Like the governor, upon whom he had come to pass judgment, he was considered a "progressive," and though he was already a bigwig he was not altogether like the majority of bigwigs. Of himself he had the highest opinion, his vanity knew no bounds, but his manners were simple, he had a friendly face, he listened indulgently and laughed so good-naturedly that on first acquaintance he might even have been taken for "a jolly good fellow." On important occasions, however, he knew, so to speak, how to make his authority felt. "Energy is essential," he used to say then; *"l'energie est la première qualité d'un homme d'état"* yet in spite of all that, he was habitually cheated, and any thoroughly experienced official could twist him round his finger. Matvei Ilyich used to speak with great respect about Guizot, and tried to impress everyone with the idea that he did not belong to the class of routine officials and old-fashioned bureaucrats, that not a single phenomenon of social life escaped his attention ... He was quite at home with phrases of the latter kind. He even followed (with a certain casual condescension, it is true) the development of contemporary literature – as a grown-up man who meets a crowd of street urchins will sometimes join them out of curiosity. In reality, Matvei Ilyich had not got much further than those politicians of the time of Alexander I, who used to prepare for an evening party at Madame Svyechin's by reading a page of Condillac; only his methods were different and more modern. He was a skillful courtier, and extremely cunning hypocrite, and little more; he had no aptitude for handling public affairs, and his intellect was scanty, but he knew how to manage his own affairs successfully; no one could get the better of him there, and of course, that is a most important thing.

Matvei Ilyich received Arkady with the amiability, or should we say playfulness, characteristic of the enlightened higher official. He was astonished, however, when he heard that both the cousins he had invited had stayed at home in the country. "Your father was always a queer fellow," he remarked, playing with the tassels of his magnificent velvet dressing gown, and turning suddenly to a young official in a faultlessly buttoned-up uniform, he shouted with an air of concern, "What?" The young man, whose lips were almost glued together from prolonged silence, came forward and looked in perplexity at his chief ... But having embarrassed his subordinate, Matvei Ilyich paid him no further attention. Our higher officials are fond of upsetting their subordinates, and they resort to quite varied means of achieving that end. The following method, among others, is often used, "is quite a favorite," as the English say: a high official suddenly ceases to understand the simplest words and pretends to be deaf; he asks, for instance, what day of the week it is.

He is respectfully informed, "Today's Friday, your Excellency."

"Eh? What? What's that? What do you say?" the great man repeats with strained attention.

"Today's Friday, your Excellency."

"Eh? What? What's Friday? What Friday?"

"Friday, your Excellency, the day of the week."

"What, are you presuming to teach me something?"

Matvei Ilyich remained a higher official, though he considered himself a liberal.

"I advise you, my dear boy, to go and call on the governor," he said to Arkady. "You understand I don't advise you to do so on account of any old-fashioned ideas about the necessity of paying respect to the authorities, but simply because the governor is a decent fellow; besides, you probably want to get to know the society here ... You're not a bear, I hope? And he's giving a large ball the day after tomorrow."

"Will you be at the ball?" inquired Arkady.

"He gives it in my honor," answered Matvei Ilyich, almost pityingly. "Do you dance?"

"Yes, I dance, but not well."

"That's a pity! There are pretty women here, and it's a shame for a young man not to dance. Of course I don't say that because of any old conventions; I would never suggest that a man's wit lies in his feet, but Byronism has become ridiculous – *il a fait son temps.*"

"But, uncle, it's not because of Byronism that I don't..."

"I'll introduce you to some of the local ladies and take you under my wing," interrupted Matvei Ilyich, and he laughed a self-satisfied laugh. "You'll find it warm, eh?"

A servant entered and announced the arrival of the superintendent of government institutions, an old man with tender eyes and deep lines round his mouth, who was extremely fond of nature, especially on summer days, when, to use his words, "every little busy bee takes a little bribe from every little flower." Arkady withdrew.

He found Bazarov at the inn where they were staying, and took a long time to persuade him to accompany him to the governor's.

"Well, it can't be helped," said Bazarov at last. "It's no good doing things by halves. We came to look at the landowners, so let us look at them!"

The governor received the young men affably, but he did not ask them to sit down, nor did he sit down himself. He was perpetually fussing and hurrying; every morning he put on a tight uniform and an extremely stiff cravat; he never ate or drank enough; he could never stop making arrangements. He invited Kirsanov and Bazarov to his ball, and within a few minutes he invited them a second time, taking them for brothers and calling them Kisarov.

They were on their way back from the governor's, when suddenly a short man in Slav national dress jumped out of a passing carriage and crying "Evgeny Vassilich," rushed up to Bazarov.

"Ah, it's you, Herr Sitnikov," remarked Bazarov, still walking along the pavement. "What chance brought you here?"

"Just fancy, quite by accident," the man replied, and returning to the carriage, he waved his arms several times and shouted, "Follow, follow us! My father had business here," he went on, jumping across the gutter, "and so he asked me to come ... I heard today you had arrived and have already been to visit you." (In fact on returning home the friends did find there a card with the corners turned down, bearing the name Sitnikov, in French on one side, and in Slavonic characters on the other.) "I hope you are not coming from the governor's."

"It's no use hoping. We've come straight from him."

"Ah, in that case I will call on him, too ... Evgeny Vassilich, introduce me to your ... to the...."

"Sitnikov, Kirsanov," mumbled Bazarov, without stopping.

"I am much honored," began Sitnikov, stepping sideways, smirking and pulling off his over-elegant gloves. "I have heard so much ... I am an old acquaintance of Evgeny Vassilich and I may say – his disciple. I owe to him my regeneration..."

Arkady looked at Bazarov's disciple. There was an expression of excited stupidity in the small but agreeable features of his well-groomed face; his little eyes, which looked permanently surprised, had a staring uneasy look, his laugh, too, was uneasy – an abrupt wooden laugh.

"Would you believe it," he continued, "when Evgeny Vassilich for the first time said before me that we should acknowledge no authorities, I felt such enthusiasm ... my eyes were opened! By the way, Evgeny Vassilich, you simply must get to know a lady here who is really capable of understanding you and for whom your visit would be a real treat; you may have heard of her?"

"Who is it?" grunted Bazarov unwillingly.

"Kukshina, Eudoxie, Evdoksya Kukshina. She's a remarkable nature, *émancipeé* in the true sense of the word, an advanced woman. Do you know what? Let us all go and visit her now. She lives only two steps from here ... We will have lunch there. I suppose you have not lunched yet?"

"No, not yet."

"Well, that's splendid. She has separated, you understand, from her husband; she is not dependent on anyone."

"Is she pretty?" Bazarov broke in.

"N-no, one couldn't say that."

"Then what the devil are you asking us to see her for?"

"Ha! You must have your joke ... she will give us a bottle of champagne."

"So that's it. The practical man shows himself at once. By the way, is your father still in the vodka business?"

"Yes," said Sitnikov hurriedly and burst into a shrill laugh. "Well, shall we go?"

"You wanted to meet people, go along," said Arkady in an undertone.

"And what do you say about it, Mr. Kirsanov?" interposed Sitnikov. "You must come too – we can't go without you."

"But how can we burst in upon her all at once?"

"Never mind about that. Kukshina is a good sort!"

"Will there be a bottle of champagne?" asked Bazarov.

"Three!" cried Sitnikov, "I'll answer for that."

"What with?"

"My own head."

"Better with your father's purse. However, we'll come along."

Chapter 13

The small detached house in Moscow style inhabited by Avdotya Nikitishna – or Evdoksya Kukshina, stood in one of those streets of X. which had been lately burnt down (it is well known that our Russian provincial towns are burnt down once every five years). At the door, above a visiting card nailed on at a slant, hung a bell handle, and in the hall the visitors were met by someone in a cap, not quite a servant nor quite a companion – unmistakable signs of the progressive aspirations of the lady of the house. Sitnikov asked if Avdotya Nikitishna was at home.

"Is that you, Viktor?" sounded a shrill voice from the other room. "Come in!"

The woman in the cap disappeared at once.

"I'm not alone," said Sitnikov, casting a sharp look at Arkady and Bazarov as he briskly pulled off his cloak, beneath which appeared something like a leather jacket.

"No matter," answered the voice. *"Entrez."*

The young men went in. The room which they entered was more like a working study than a drawing room. Papers, letters, fat issues of Russian journals, for the most part uncut, lay thrown about on dusty tables; white cigarette ends were scattered all over the place. A lady, still young, was half lying on a leather-covered sofa; her blonde hair was disheveled and she was wearing a crumpled silk dress, with heavy bracelets on her short arms and a lace kerchief over her head. She rose from the sofa, and carelessly drawing over her shoulders a velvet cape trimmed with faded ermine, she murmured languidly, "Good morning, Viktor," and held out her hand to Sitnikov.

"Bazarov, Kirsanov," he announced abruptly, successfully imitating Bazarov's manner.

"So glad to meet you," answered Madame Kukshina, fixing on Bazarov her round eyes, between which appeared a forlorn little turned-up red nose, "I know you," she added, and pressed his hand.

Bazarov frowned. There was nothing definitely ugly in the small plain figure of the emancipated woman; but her facial expression produced an uncomfortable effect on the spectator. One felt impelled to ask her, "What's the matter, are you hungry? Or bored? Or shy? Why are you fidgeting?" Both she and Sitnikov had the same nervous manner. Her movements and speech were very unconstrained and at the same time awkward; she evidently regarded herself as a good-natured simple creature, yet all the time, whatever she did, it always struck one that it was not exactly what she wanted to do; everything with her seemed, as children say, done on purpose, that is, not spontaneously or simply.

"Yes, yes, I know you, Bazarov," she repeated. (She had the habit – peculiar to many provincial and Moscow ladies – of calling men by their bare surnames from the moment she first met them.) "Would you like a cigar?"

"A cigar is all very well," interjected Sitnikov, who was already lolling in an arm-chair with his legs in the air, "but give us some lunch. We're frightfully hungry; and tell them to bring us up a little bottle of champagne."

"You sybarite," cried Evdoksya with a laugh. (When she laughed the gums showed over her upper teeth.) "Isn't it true, Bazarov, he's a sybarite?"

"I like comfort in life," pronounced Sitnikov gravely. "But that doesn't prevent me from being a liberal."

"It does, though, it does!" exclaimed Evdoksya, and nevertheless gave instructions to her maid both about the lunch and about the champagne. "What do you think about that?" she added, turning to Bazarov. "I'm sure you share my opinion."

"Well, no," retorted Bazarov; "a piece of meat is better than a piece of bread even from the point of view of chemistry."

"You are studying chemistry? That's my passion. I've invented a new sort of paste."

"A paste? You?"

"Yes. And do you know what it's for? To make dolls' heads, so that they can't break. I'm practical also, you see. But it's not quite ready yet. I've still got to read Liebig. By the way, have you read Kislyakov's article on female labor in the *Moscow News?* Please read it. Of course you're interested in the woman's question – and in the schools, too? What does your friend do? What is his name?"

Madame Kukshina poured out her questions one after another, with affected negligence, without waiting for the answers; spoilt children talk like that to their nurses.

"My name is Arkady Nikolaich Kirsanov, and I do nothing." Evdoksya giggled. "Oh, how charming! What, don't you smoke? Viktor, you know I'm very angry with you."

"What for?"

"They tell me you've begun praising George Sand. A backward woman and nothing else! How can people compare her with Emerson? She hasn't a single idea about education or physiology or anything. I'm sure she's never even heard of embryology and in these days what can be done without that?" (Evdoksya actually threw up her hands.) "Oh, what a wonderful article Elisyevich has written about it! He's a gentleman of genius." (Evdoksya constantly used the word "gentleman" instead of the word "man.") "Bazarov, sit by me on the sofa. You don't know, perhaps, but I'm awfully afraid of you."

"And why, may I ask?"

"You're a dangerous gentleman, you're such a critic. My God, how absurd! I'm talking like some provincial landowner – but I really am one. I manage my property myself, and just imagine, my bailiff Yerofay – he's a wonderful type, just like Fenimore Cooper's Pathfinder – there's something so spontaneous about him! I've come to settle down here; it's an intolerable town, isn't it? But what is one to do?"

"The town's like any other town," remarked Bazarov coolly.

"All its interests are so petty, that's what is so dreadful! I used to spend the winters in Moscow ... but now my lawful husband Monsieur Kukshin lives there. And besides, Moscow nowadays – I don't know, it's not what it was. I'm thinking of going abroad – I almost went last year."

"To Paris, I suppose," said Bazarov.

"To Paris and to Heidelberg."

"Why to Heidelberg?"

"How can you ask! Bunsen lives there!"

Bazarov could find no reply to that one.

" *Pierre* Sapozhnikov ... do you know him?"

"No, I don't."

"Not know *Pierre* Sapozhnikov ... he's always at Lydia Khostatov's."

"I don't know her either."

"Well, he undertook to escort me. Thank God I'm independent – I've no children ... what did I say? Thank God! Never mind though!"

Evdoksya rolled a cigarette between her fingers, brown with tobacco stains, put it across her tongue, licked it and started to smoke. The maid came in with a tray.

"Ah, here's lunch! Will you have an apéritif first? Viktor, open the bottle; that's in your line."

"Yes, it's in my line," mumbled Sitnikov, and again uttered a piercing convulsive laugh.

"Are there any pretty women here?" asked Bazarov, as he drank down a third glass.

"Yes, there are," answered Evdoksya, "but they're all so empty-headed. For instance, my friend Odintsova is nice looking. It's a pity she's got such a reputation ... Of course that wouldn't matter, but she has no independent views, no breadth of outlook, nothing ... of that kind. The whole system of education wants changing. I've thought a lot about it; our women are so badly educated."

"There's nothing to be done with them," interposed Sitnikov; "one ought to despise them and I do despise them utterly and completely." (The possibility of feeling and expressing contempt was the most agreeable sensation to Sitnikov; he attacked women in particular, never suspecting that it would be his fate a few months later to cringe to his wife merely because she had been born a princess Durdoleosov.) "Not one of them would be capable of understanding our conversation; not one of them deserves to be spoken about by serious men like us."

"But there's no need whatsoever for them to understand our conversation," remarked Bazarov.

"Whom do you mean?" sad Evdoksya.

"Pretty women."

"What? Do you then share the ideas of Proudhon?"

Bazarov drew himself up haughtily.

"I share no one's ideas; I have my own."

"Damn all authorities!" shouted Sitnikov, delighted to have an opportunity of expressing himself boldly in front of the man he slavishly admired.

"But even Macaulay...," Madame Kukshina was trying to say.

"Damn Macaulay!" thundered Sitnikov. "Are you going to stand up for those silly females?"

"Not for silly females, no, but for the rights of women which I have sworn to defend to the last drop of my blood."

"Damn...," but here Sitnikov stopped. "But I don't deny you that," he said.

"No, I see you're a Slavophil!"

"No, I'm not a Slavophil, though, of course...."

"No, no, no! You are a Slavophil. You're a supporter of patriarchal despotism. You want to have the whip in your hand!"

"A whip is a good thing," said Bazarov, "but we've got to the last drop...."

"Of what?" interrupted Evdoksya.

"Of champagne, most honored Avdotya Nikitishna, of champagne – not of your blood."

"I can never listen calmly when women are attacked," went on Evdoksya. "It's awful, awful. Instead of attacking them you should read Michelet's book *De l'Amour!* That's something exquisite! Gentlemen, let us talk about love," added Evdoksya, letting her arm rest on the crumpled sofa cushion.

A sudden silence followed.

"No, why should we talk of love?" said Bazarov. "But you mentioned just now a Madame Odintsov ... That was the name, I think – who is the lady?"

"She's charming, delightful," squeaked Sitnikov. "I'll introduce you. Clever, rich, a widow. It's a pity she's not yet advanced enough; she ought to see more of our Evdoksya. I drink to your health, *Eudoxie,* clink glasses! *Et toc et toc et tin-tin-tin! Et toc, et toc, et tin-tin-tin!"*

"Viktor, you're a rascal!"

The lunch was prolonged. The first bottle of champagne was followed by another, by a third, and even by a fourth ... Evdoksya chattered away without drawing breath; Sitnikov seconded her. They talked a lot about whether marriage was a prejudice or a crime, whether men were born equal or not, and precisely what constitutes individuality. Finally things went so far that Evdoksya, flushed from the wine she had drunk, began tapping with her flat finger tips on a discordant piano, and singing in a husky voice, first gipsy songs, then Seymour Schiff's song *Granada lies slumbering,* while Sitnikov tied a scarf round his head and represented the dying lover at the words

"And thy lips to mine
In burning kiss entwine..."

Arkady could stand no more. "Gentlemen, this is approaching bedlam," he remarked aloud.

Bazarov, who at rare intervals had thrown a sarcastic word or two into the conversation – he paid more attention to the champagne – yawned loudly, rose to his feet and without taking leave of their hostess, he walked off with Arkady. Sitnikov jumped up and followed them.

"Well, what do you think of her?" he asked, hopping obsequiously from one side to another. "As I told you, a remarkable personality! If only we had more women like that! She is, in her own way, a highly moral phenomenon."

"And is that establishment of your father's also a moral phenomenon?" muttered Bazarov, pointing to a vodka shop which they were passing at that moment.

Sitnikov again gave vent to his shrill laugh. He was much ashamed of his origin, and hardly knew whether to feel flattered or offended by Bazarov's unexpected familiarity.

Chapter 14

Two days later the Governor's ball took place. Matvei Ilyich was the real hero of the occasion. The marshal of nobility announced to all and sundry that he had come only out of respect for him, while the governor, even at the ball, and even while he was standing still, continued to "make arrangements." The amiability of Matvei Ilyich's manner was equaled only by his dignity. He behaved graciously to everyone, to some with a shade of disgust, to others with a shade of respect, he was gallant, "*en vrai chevalier français,*" to all the ladies, and was continually bursting into hearty resounding laughter, in which no one else joined, as befits a high official. He slapped Arkady on the back and called him "nephew" loudly, bestowed on Bazarov – who was dressed in a shabby frock coat – an absent-minded but indulgent sidelong glance, and an indistinct but affable grunt in which the words "I" and "very" were vaguely distinguishable; held out a finger to Sitnikov and smiled at him though his head had already turned round to greet someone else; even to Madame Kukshina, who appeared at the ball without a crinoline, wearing dirty gloves and a bird of paradise in her hair, he said "*enchanté.*" There were crowds of people and plenty of men dancers; most of the civilians stood in rows along the walls, but the officers danced assiduously, especially one who had spent six weeks in Paris, where he had mastered several daring exclamations such as – *zut, Ah fichtre, pst, pst, mon bibi,* and so on. He pronounced them perfectly with real genuine Parisian chic, and at the same time he said *"si j'aurais"* instead of *"si j'avais,"* and *"absolument"* in the sense of "absolutely," expressed himself in fact in that Great Russo-French jargon which the French laugh at when they have no reason to assure us that we speak French like angels – *"comme des anges."*

Arkady danced badly, as we already know, and Bazarov did not dance at all. They both took up their position in a corner, where Sitnikov joined them. With an expression of contemptuous mockery on his face, he uttered one spiteful remark after another, looked insolently around him, and appeared to be thoroughly enjoying himself. Suddenly his face changed, and turning to Arkady he said in a rather embarrassed tone, "Odintsova has arrived."

Arkady looked round and saw a tall woman in a black dress standing near the door. He was struck by her dignified bearing. Her bare arms lay gracefully across her slim waist; light sprays of fuchsia hung from her shining hair over her sloping shoulders; her clear eyes looked out from under a prominent white forehead; their expression was calm and intelligent – calm but not pensive – and her lips showed a scarcely perceptible smile. A sort of affectionate and gentle strength emanated from her face.

"Do you know her?" Arkady asked Sitnikov.

"Very well. Would you like me to introduce you?"

"Please ... after this quadrille."

Bazarov also noticed Madame Odintsov.

"What a striking figure," he said. "She's not like the other females."

When the quadrille was over, Sitnikov led Arkady over to Madame Odintsov. But he hardly seemed to know her at all, and stumbled over his words, while she looked at him in some surprise. But she looked pleased when she heard Arkady's family name, and she asked him whether he was not the son of Nikolai Petrovich.

"Yes!"

"I have seen your father twice and heard a lot about him," she went on. "I am very glad to meet you."

At this moment some adjutant rushed up to her and asked her for a quadrille. She accepted.

"Do you dance then?" asked Arkady respectfully.

"Yes, and why should you suppose I don't dance? Do you think I'm too old?"

"Please, how could I possibly ... but in that case may I ask you for a mazurka?"

Madame Odintsov smiled graciously. "Certainly," she said, and looked at Arkady, not exactly patronizingly but in the way married sisters look at very young brothers. She was in fact not much older than Arkady – she was twenty-nine – but in her presence he felt like a schoolboy, so that the difference in their ages seemed to matter much more. Matvei Ilyich came up to her in a majestic manner and started to pay her compliments. Arkady moved aside, but he still watched her; he could not take his eyes off her even during the quadrille. She talked to her partner as easily as she had to the grand official, slightly turning her head and eyes, and once or twice she laughed softly. Her nose – like most Russian noses – was rather thick, and her complexion was not translucently clear; nevertheless Arkady decided that he had never before met such a fascinating woman. The sound of her voice clung to his ears, the very folds of her dress seemed to fall differently – more gracefully and amply than on other women – and her movements were wonderfully flowing and at the same time natural.

Arkady was overcome by shyness when at the first sounds of the mazurka he took a seat beside his partner; he wanted to talk to her, but he only passed his hand through his hair and could not find a single word to say. But his shyness and agitation soon passed; Madame Odintsov's tranquillity communicated itself to him; within a quarter of an hour he was telling her freely about his father, his uncle, his life in Petersburg and in the country. Madame Odintsov listened to him with courteous sympathy, slowly opening and closing her fan. The conversation was broken off when her partners claimed her; Sitnikov, among others, asked her to dance twice. She came back, sat down again, took up her fan, and did not even breathe more rapidly, while Arkady started talking again, penetrated through and through by the happiness of being near her, talking to her, looking at her eyes, her lovely forehead and her whole charming, dignified and intelligent face. She said little, but her words showed an understanding of life; judging by some of her remarks Arkady came to the conclusion that this young woman had already experienced and thought a great deal...

"Who is that you were standing with?" she asked him, "when Mr. Sitnikov brought you over to me?"

"So you noticed him?" asked Arkady in his turn. "He has a wonderful face, hasn't he? That's my friend Bazarov."

Arkady went on to discuss "his friend." He spoke of him in such detail and with so much enthusiasm that Madame Odintsov turned round and looked at him attentively. Meanwhile the mazurka was drawing to a close. Arkady was sorry to leave his partner, he had spent almost an hour with her so happily! Certainly he had felt the whole time as though she were showing indulgence to him, as though he ought to be grateful to her ... but young hearts are not weighed down by that feeling.

The music stopped.

"Merci," murmured Madame Odintsov, rising. "You promised to pay me a visit; bring your friend with you. I am very curious to meet a man who has the courage to believe in nothing."

The governor came up to Madame Odintsov, announced that supper was ready, and with a worried look offered her his arm. As she went out, she turned to smile once more at Arkady. He bowed low, followed her with his eyes (how graceful her figure seemed to him, how radiant in the sober luster of the black silk folds!) and he was conscious of some kind of refreshing humility of soul as he thought, "This very minute she has forgotten my existence."

"Well?" Bazarov asked Arkady as soon as he had returned to the corner. "Did you have a good time? A man has just told me that your lady is – oh never mind what – but the fellow is probably a fool. What do you think? Is she?"

"I don't understand what you mean," said Arkady.

"My goodness, what innocence!"

"In that case I don't understand the man you quote. Madame Odintsov is very charming, but she is so cold and reserved that...."

"Still waters run deep, you know," interposed Bazarov. "You say she is cold; that just adds to the flavor. You like ices, I expect."

"Perhaps," muttered Arkady. "I can't express any opinion about that. She wants to meet you and asked me to bring you over to visit her."

"I can imagine how you described me! Never mind, you did well. Take me along. Whoever she may be, whether she's just a provincial climber or an 'emancipated' woman like Kukshina – anyhow she's got a pair of shoulders the like of which I haven't seen for a long time."

Arkady was hurt by Bazarov's cynicism, but – as often happens – he did not blame his friend for those particular things which he disliked in him...

"Why do you disagree with free thought for women?" he asked in a low voice.

"Because, my lad, as far as I can see, free-thinking women are all monsters."

The conversation was cut short at this point. Both young men left immediately after supper. They were pursued by a nervously angry but fainthearted laugh from Madame Kukshina, whose vanity had been deeply wounded by the fact that neither of them had paid the slightest attention to her. She stayed later than anyone else at the ball, and at four o'clock in the morning she was dancing a polka-mazurka in Parisian style with Sitnikov. The governor's ball culminated in this edifying spectacle.

Chapter 15

"We'll soon see to what species of mammal this specimen belongs," Bazarov said to Arkady the following day as they mounted the staircase of the hotel where Madame Odintsov was staying. "I can smell something wrong here."

"I'm surprised at you," cried Arkady. "What? You, of all people, Bazarov, clinging to that narrow morality which...."

"What a funny fellow you are!" said Bazarov carelessly, cutting him short. "Don't you know that in my dialect and for my purpose 'something wrong' means 'something right'? That's just my advantage. Didn't you tell me yourself this morning that she made a strange marriage, though, to my mind to marry a rich old man is far from a strange thing to do – but on the contrary, sensible enough. I don't believe the gossip of the town, but I should like to think, as our enlightened governor says, that it's just."

Arkady made no answer, and knocked at the door of the apartment. A young servant in livery ushered the two friends into a large room, furnished in bad taste like all Russian hotel rooms, but filled with flowers. Madame Odintsov soon appeared in a simple morning dress. In the light of the spring sunshine she looked even younger than before. Arkady introduced Bazarov, and noticed with concealed astonishment that he seemed embarrassed, while Madame Odintsov remained perfectly calm, as she had been on the previous day. Bazarov was himself conscious of feeling embarrassed and was annoyed about it. "What an idea! Frightened of a female," he thought, and lolling in an arm-chair, quite like Sitnikov, he began to talk in an exaggeratedly casual manner, while Madame Odintsov kept her clear eyes fixed on him.

Anna Sergeyevna Odintsova was the daughter of Sergei Nikolayevich Loktev, notorious for his personal beauty, speculations and gambling, who after fifteen years of a stormy and sensational life in Petersburg and Moscow, ended by ruining himself completely at cards and was obliged to retire to the country, where soon afterwards he died, leaving a very small property to his two daughters – Anna, a girl of twenty at that time, and Katya, a child of twelve. Their mother, who belonged to an impoverished princely family, had died in Petersburg while her husband was still in his heyday. Anna's position after her father's death was a very difficult one. The brilliant education which she had received in Petersburg had not fitted her for the cares of domestic and household economy – nor for an obscure life buried in the country. She knew no one in the whole neighborhood, and there was no one she could consult. Her father had tried to avoid all contact with his neighbors; he despised them in his way and they despised him in theirs. However, she did not lose her head, and promptly sent for a sister of her mother's, Princess Avdotya Stepanovna X. – a spiteful, arrogant old lady who, on installing herself in her niece's house, appropriated the best rooms for herself, grumbled and scolded from morning till night and refused to walk a step, even in the garden, without being attended by her one and only serf, a surly footman in a threadbare pea-green livery with light-blue trimming and a three-cornered hat. Anna patiently put up with all her aunt's caprices, gradually set to work on her sister's education and, it seemed, was already reconciled to the idea of fading away in the wilderness ... But fate had decreed otherwise. She happened to be seen by a certain Odintsov, a wealthy man of forty-six, an eccentric hypochondriac, swollen, heavy and sour, but not stupid and quite good-natured; he fell in love with her and proposed marriage. She agreed to become his wife, and they lived together for six years; then he died, leaving her all his property. For nearly a year after his death Anna Sergeyevna remained in the country; then she went abroad with her sister, but stayed only in Germany; she soon grew tired of it and came back to live at her beloved Nikolskoe, nearly thirty miles from the town of X. Her house was magnificent, luxuriously furnished and had a beautiful garden with conservatories; her late husband had spared no expense to gratify his wishes. Anna Sergeyevna rarely visited the town, and as a rule only on business; even then she did not stay long. She was not popular in the province; there had been a fearful outcry when she married Odintsov; all sorts of slanderous stories were invented about her; it was asserted that she had helped her father in his gambling escapades and even that she had gone abroad for a special reason to conceal some unfortunate consequences ... "You understand?" the indignant gossips would conclude. "She has been through fire and water," they said of her, to which a noted provincial wit added "And through the brass instruments." All this talk reached her, but she turned a deaf ear to it; she had an independent and sufficiently determined character.

Madame Odintsov sat leaning back in her armchair, her hands folded, and listened to Bazarov. Contrary to his habit, he was talking a lot and was obviously trying to interest her – which also surprised Arkady. He could not be sure whether Bazarov had achieved his object, for it was difficult to learn from Anna Sergeyevna's face what impression was being made on her; it retained the same gracious refined look; her bright eyes shone with attention, but it was an unruffled attention. During the first minutes of the visit, Bazarov's awkward manners had impressed her disagreeably, like a bad smell, or a discordant sound; but she saw at once that he was nervous and that flattered her. Only the commonplace was repulsive to her, and no one would have accused Bazarov of being commonplace. Arkady had several surprises in store for him that day. He had expected that Bazarov would talk to an intelligent woman like Madame Odintsov about his convictions and views; she herself had expressed a desire to hear the man "who dares to believe in nothing," but instead of that Bazarov talked about medicine, about homeopathy and about botany. It turned out that Madame Odintsov had not wasted her time in solitude; she had read a number of good books and herself spoke an excellent Russian. She turned the conversation to music, but, observing that Bazarov had no appreciation of art, quietly turned it back to botany, although Arkady was just launching out on a discourse about the significance of national melodies. Madame Odintsov continued to treat him as though he were a younger brother; she seemed to appreciate his good nature and youthful simplicity – and that was all. A lively conversation went on for over three hours, ranging freely over a variety of subjects.

At last the friends got up and began to take their leave. Anna Sergeyevna looked at them kindly, held out her beautiful white hand to each in turn, and after a moment's thought, said with a diffident but delightful smile, "If you are not afraid of being bored, gentlemen, come and see me at Nikolskoe."

"Oh, Anna Sergeyevna," cried Arkady, "that will be the greatest happiness for me."

"And you, Monsieur Bazarov?"

Bazarov only bowed – and Arkady had yet another surprise; he noticed that his friend was blushing.

"Well," he said to him in the street, "do you still think she's...."

"Who can tell! Just see how frozen she is!" answered Bazarov; then after a short pause he added, "She's a real Grand Duchess, a commanding sort of person; she only needs a train behind her, and a crown on her head."

"Our Grand Duchesses can't talk Russian like that," observed Arkady.

"She has known ups and downs, my lad; she's been hard up."

"Anyhow, she's delightful," said Arkady.

"What a magnificent body," went on Bazarov. "How I should like to see it on the dissecting table."

"Stop, for heaven's sake, Evgeny! You go too far!"

"Well, don't get angry, you baby! I meant it's first-rate. We must go to stay with her."

"When?"

"Well, why not the day after tomorrow. What is there to do here? Drink champagne with Kukshina? Listen to your cousin, the liberal statesman? ... Let's be off the day after tomorrow. By the way – my father's little place is not far from there. This Nikolskoe is on the X. road, isn't it?"

"Yes."

"Excellent. Why hesitate? Leave that to fools – and intellectuals. I say – what a splendid body!"

Three days later the two friends were driving along the road to Nikolskoe. The day was bright and not too hot, and the plump post horses trotted smartly along, flicking their tied and plaited tails. Arkady looked at the road, and, without knowing why, he smiled.

"Congratulate me," exclaimed Bazarov suddenly. "Today's the 22nd of June, my saint's day. Let us see how he will watch over me. They expect me home today," he added, dropping his voice ... "Well, they can wait – what does it matter!"

Chapter 16

The country house in which Anna Sergeyevna lived stood on the slope of a low hill not far from a yellow stone church with a green roof, white columns, and decorated with a fresco over the main entrance, representing *The Resurrection of Christ* in the Italian style. Especially remarkable for its voluminous contours was the figure of a swarthy soldier in a helmet, sprawling in the foreground of the picture. Behind the church stretched a long village street with chimneys peeping out here and there from thatched roofs. The manor house was built in the same style as the church, the style now famous as that of Alexander I; the whole house was painted yellow, and it had a green roof, white columns and a pediment with a coat of arms carved on it. The provincial architect had designed both buildings according to the instructions of the late Odintsov, who could not endure – as he expressed it – senseless and arbitrary innovations. The house was flanked on both sides by the dark trees of an old garden; an avenue of clipped pines led up to the main entrance.

Our friends were met in the hall by two tall footmen in livery; one of them ran at once to fetch the butler. The butler, a stout man in a black tail coat, promptly appeared and led the visitors up a staircase covered with rugs into a specially prepared room in which two beds had been arranged with every kind of toilet accessory. It was evident that order reigned in the house; everything was clean, and there was everywhere a peculiar dignified fragrance such as one encounters in ministerial reception rooms.

"Anna Sergeyevna asks you to come to see her in half an hour," the butler announced. "Have you any orders to give meanwhile?"

"No orders, my good sir," answered Bazarov, "but perhaps you will kindly trouble yourself to bring a glass of vodka."

"Certainly, sir," said the butler, looking rather surprised, and went out, his boots creaking.

"What *grand genre*," remarked Bazarov, "that's what you call it in your set, I think. A Grand Duchess complete."

"A nice Grand Duchess," answered Arkady, "to invite straight away such great aristocrats as you and me to stay with her."

"Especially me, a future doctor and a doctor's son, and grandson of a village priest ... you know that, I suppose ... a village priest's grandson, like the statesman Speransky," added Bazarov, after a brief silence, pursing his lips. "Anyhow, she gives herself the best of everything, this pampered lady! Shan't we soon find ourselves wearing tail coats?"

Arkady only shrugged his shoulders ... but he, too, felt a certain embarrassment.

Half an hour later Bazarov and Arkady made their way together into the drawing room. It was a large lofty room, luxuriously furnished but with little personal taste. Heavy expensive furniture stood in a conventional stiff arrangement along the walls, which were covered in a buff wall paper decorated with golden arabesques. Odintsov had ordered the furniture from Moscow through a wine merchant who was a friend and agent of his. Over a sofa in the center of one wall hung a portrait of a flabby fair-haired man, which seemed to look disapprovingly at the visitors. "It must be the late husband," whispered Bazarov to Arkady. "Shall we dash off?" But at that moment the hostess entered. She wore a light muslin dress; her hair, smoothly brushed back behind her ears, imparted a girlish expression to her pure, fresh face.

"Thank you for keeping your promise," she began. "You must stay a little while; you won't find it so bad here. I will introduce you to my sister; she plays the piano well. That's a matter of indifference to you, Monsieur Bazarov, but you, Monsieur Kirsanov, are fond of music, I believe. Apart from my sister, an old aunt lives with me, and a neighbor sometimes comes over to play cards. That makes up our whole circle. And now let us sit down."

Madame Odintsov delivered this whole little speech very fluently and distinctly, as if she had learned it by heart; then she turned to Arkady. It appeared that her mother had known Arkady's mother and had even been her confidante in her love for Nikolai Petrovich. Arkady began to talk with warm feeling about his dead mother; meanwhile Bazarov sat and looked through some albums. "What a tame cat I've become," he thought.

A beautiful white wolfhound with a blue collar ran into the drawing room and tapped on the floor with its paws; it was followed by a girl of eighteen with a round and pleasing face and small dark eyes. In her hands she held a basket filled with flowers.

"This is my Katya," said Madame Odintsov, nodding in her direction.

Katya made a slight curtsey, sat down beside her sister and began arranging the flowers. The wolfhound, whose name was Fifi, went up to both visitors in turn, wagging its tail and thrusting its cold nose into their hands.

"Did you pick them all yourself?" asked Madame Odintsov.

"Yes," answered Katya.

"Is auntie coming down for tea?"

"She's coming."

When Katya spoke, her face had a charming smile, at once bashful and candid, and she looked up from under her eyebrows with a kind of amusing severity. Everything about her was naive and undeveloped, her voice, the downy bloom on her face, the rosy hands with white palms and the rather narrow shoulders ... she was constantly blushing and she breathed quickly.

Madame Odintsov turned to Bazarov. "You are looking at pictures out of politeness, Evgeny Vassilich," she began. "It doesn't interest you, so you had better come and join us, and we will have a discussion about something."

Bazarov moved nearer. "What have you decided to discuss?" he muttered.

"Whatever you like. I warn you, I am dreadfully argumentative."

"You?"

"Yes. That seems to surprise you. Why?"

"Because, so far as I can judge, you have a calm and cool temperament and to be argumentative one needs to get excited."

"How have you managed to sum me up so quickly? In the first place I am impatient and persistent – you should ask Katya; and secondly I am very easily carried away."

Bazarov looked at Anna Sergeyevna.

"Perhaps. You know best. Very well, if you want a discussion – so be it. I was looking at the views of Swiss mountains in your albums, and you remarked that they couldn't interest me. You said that because you suppose I have no artistic feeling – and it is true I have none; but those views might interest me from a geological standpoint, for studying the formation of mountains, for instance."

"Excuse me; but as a geologist, you would rather study a book, some special work on the subject and not a drawing."

"The drawing shows me at one glance what might be spread over ten pages in a book."

Anna Sergeyevna was silent for a few moments.

"So you have no feeling whatsoever for art?" she said, leaning her elbow on the table and by so doing bringing her face nearer to Bazarov. "How do you manage without it?"

"Why, what is it needed for, may I ask?"

"Well, at least to help one to know and understand people."

Bazarov smiled. "In the first place, experience of life does that, and in the second, I assure you the study of separate individuals is not worth the trouble it involves. All people resemble each other, in soul as well as in body; each of us has a brain, spleen, heart and lungs of similar construction; the so-called moral qualities are the same in all of us; the slight variations are insignificant. It is enough to have one single human specimen in order to judge all the others. People are like trees in a forest; no botanist would think of studying each individual birch tree."

Katya, who was arranging the flowers one by one in a leisurely way, raised her eyes to Bazarov with a puzzled expression, and meeting his quick casual glance, she blushed right up to her ears. Anna Sergeyevna shook her head.

"The trees in a forest," she repeated. "Then according to you there is no difference between a stupid and an intelligent person, or between a good and a bad one."

"No, there is a difference, as there is between the sick and the healthy. The lungs of a consumptive person are not in the same condition as yours or mine, although their construction is the same. We know more or less what causes physical ailments; but moral diseases are caused by bad education, by all the rubbish with which people's heads are stuffed from childhood onwards, in short, by the disordered state of society. Reform society, and there will be no diseases."

Bazarov said all this with an air as though he were all the while thinking to himself. "Believe me or not as you wish, it's all the same to me!" He slowly passed his long fingers over his whiskers and his eyes strayed round the room.

"And you suppose," said Anna Sergeyevna, "that when society is reformed there will be no longer any stupid or wicked people?"

"At any rate, in a properly organized society it will make no difference whether a man is stupid or clever, bad or good."

"Yes, I understand. They will all have the same spleen."

"Exactly, madam."

Madame Odintsov turned to Arkady. "And what is your opinion, Arkady Nikolayevich?"

"I agree with Evgeny," he answered.

Katya looked at him from under her eyelids.

"You amaze me, gentlemen," commented Madame Odintsov, "but we will talk about this again. I hear my aunt now coming in to tea – we must spare her."

Anna Sergeyevna's aunt, Princess X., a small shriveled woman with a pinched-up face like a fist, with staring bad-tempered eyes under her grey brows, came in, and scarcely bowing to the guests, sank into a broad velvet-covered arm-chair, in which no one except herself was privileged to sit. Katya put a stool under her feet; the old lady did not thank her or even look at her, only her hands shook under the yellow shawl which almost covered her decrepit body. The princess liked yellow, even her cap had yellow ribbons.

"How did you sleep, auntie?" asked Madame Odintsov, raising her voice.

"That dog here again," mumbled the old lady in reply, and noticing that Fifi was making two hesitating steps in her direction, she hissed loudly.

Katya called Fifi and opened the door for her. Fifi rushed out gaily, imagining she was going to be taken for a walk, but when she found herself left alone outside the door she began to scratch and whine. The princess frowned. Katya rose to go out...

"I expect tea is ready," said Madame Odintsov. "Come, gentlemen; auntie, will you go in to tea?"

The princess rose from her chair without speaking and led the way out of the drawing room. They all followed her into the dining room. A little Cossack page drew back noisily from the table a chair covered with cushions, also dedicated to the princess, who sank into it. Katya, who poured out tea, handed her first a cup decorated with a coat of arms. The old lady helped herself to honey, which she put in her cup (she considered it both sinful and extravagant to drink tea with sugar in it, although she never spent a penny of her own on anything), and suddenly asked in a hoarse voice, "And what does Prince Ivan write?"

No one made any reply. Bazarov and Arkady soon observed that the family paid no attention to her although they treated her respectfully. "They put up with her because of her princely family," thought Bazarov. After tea Anna Sergeyevna suggested that they should go out for a walk, but it began to rain a little, and the whole party, except the princess, returned to the drawing room. The neighbor arrived, the devoted card-player; his name was Porfiri Platonich, a plump greyish little man with short spindly legs, very polite and jocular. Anna Sergeyevna, who still talked principally to Bazarov, asked him whether he would like to play an old-fashioned game of preference with them. Bazarov accepted, saying that he certainly needed to prepare himself in advance for the duties in store for him as a country doctor.

"You must be careful," remarked Anna Sergeyevna; "Porfiri Platonich and I will defeat you. And you, Katya," she added, "play something to Arkady Nikolaich; he's fond of music, and we shall enjoy listening too."

Katya went unwillingly to the piano, and Arkady, although he was genuinely fond of music, unwillingly followed her; it seemed to him that Madame Odintsov was getting rid of him, and he felt already like most young men of his age, a vague and oppressive excitement, like a foretaste of love. Katya lifted the lid of the piano, and without looking at Arkady, asked in an undertone "What am I to play to you?"

"What you like," answered Arkady indifferently.

"What sort of music do you prefer?" went on Katya, without changing her attitude.

"Classical," answered Arkady in the same tone of voice.

"Do you like Mozart?"

"Yes, I like Mozart."

Katya pulled out Mozart's *Sonata Fantasia* in C minor. She played very well, although a little too precisely and drily. She sat upright and motionless without taking her eyes off the music, her lips tightly compressed, and only towards the end of the sonata her face started to glow, her hair loosened and a little lock fell over her dark brow.

Arkady was especially struck by the last part of the sonata, the part where the enchanting gaiety of the careless melody at its height is suddenly broken into by the pangs of such a sad and almost tragic suffering ... but the ideas inspired in him by the sounds of Mozart were not related to Katya. Looking at her, he merely thought, "Well, that young lady doesn't play too badly, and she's not bad looking, either."

When she had finished the sonata, Katya, without taking her hands from the keys, asked, "Is that enough?"

Arkady said that he would not venture to trouble her further, and began talking to her about

Mozart; he asked her whether she had chosen that sonata herself, or someone else had recommended it to her. But Katya answered him in monosyllables and withdrew into herself. When this happened, she did not come out again quickly; at such times her face took on an obstinate, almost stupid expression. She was not exactly shy, but she was diffident and rather overawed by her sister, who had educated her, but who never even suspected that such a feeling existed in Katya. Arkady was at length reduced to calling Fifi over to him and stroking her on the head with a benevolent smile in order to create the impression of being at his ease. Katya went on arranging her flowers.

Meanwhile Bazarov was losing and losing. Anna Sergeyevna played cards with masterly skill; Porfiri Platonich also knew how to hold his own. Bazarov lost a sum, which though trifling in itself, was none too pleasant for him. At supper Anna Sergeyevna again turned the conversation to botany.

"Let us go for a walk tomorrow morning," she said to him; "I want you to teach me the Latin names of several wild plants and their species."

"What's the good of the Latin names to you?" asked Bazarov.

"Order is needed for everything," she answered.

"What a wonderful woman Anna Sergeyevna is!" cried Arkady, when he was alone in their room with his friend.

"Yes," answered Bazarov, "a female with brains; and she's seen life too."

"In what sense do you mean that, Evgeny Vassilich?"

"In a good sense, in a good sense, my worthy Arkady Nikolayevich! I'm sure she also manages her estate very efficiently. But what is wonderful is not her, but her sister."

"What? That little dark creature?"

"Yes, the little dark creature – she's fresh, untouched and shy and silent, anything you want ... one could work on her and make something out of her – but the other – she's an experienced hand."

Arkady did not answer Bazarov, and each of them got into bed occupied with his own particular thoughts.

Anna Sergeyevna was also thinking about her guests that evening. She liked Bazarov for his absence of flattery and for his definite downright views. She found in him something new, which she had not met before, and she was curious. Anna Sergeyevna was a rather strange person. Having no prejudices at all, and no strong convictions either, she neither avoided things nor went out of her way to secure anything special. She was clear-sighted and she had many interests, but nothing completely satisfied her; indeed, she hardly desired any complete satisfaction. Her mind was at once inquiring and indifferent; though her doubts were never soothed by forgetfulness, they never grew powerful enough to agitate her disagreeably. Had she not been rich and independent, she would probably have thrown herself into the struggle and experienced passion ... But life ran easily for her, although she was sometimes bored, and she went on from day to day without hurrying and only rarely feeling disturbed. Rainbow-colored visions sometimes glowed before her eyes, but she breathed more peacefully when they faded away, and she did not hanker after them. Her imagination certainly overstepped the limits of conventional morality, but all the time her blood flowed as quietly as ever in her charmingly graceful, tranquil body. Sometimes, emerging from her fragrant bath, warm and languid, she would start musing on the emptiness of life, its sorrow, labor and vindictiveness ... her soul would be filled with sudden daring and burn with generous ardor; but then a draught would blow from a half-open window and Anna Sergeyevna would shrink back into herself with a plaintive, almost angry feeling, and there was only one thing she needed at that particular moment – to get away from that nasty draught.

Like all women who have not succeeded in loving, she wanted something without knowing what it was. Actually she wanted nothing, though it seemed to her that she wanted everything. She could hardly endure the late Odintsov (she married him for practical reasons though she might not have agreed to become his wife if she had not regarded him as a good-natured man), and she had conceived a hidden repugnance for all men, whom she could think of only as slovenly, clumsy, dull, feebly irritating creatures.

Once, somewhere abroad, she had met a handsome young Swede with a chivalrous expression and with honest eyes under an open brow; he made a strong impression on her, but that had not prevented her from returning to Russia.

"A strange man this doctor," she thought as she lay in her magnificent bed, on lace pillows under a light silk eiderdown. Anna Sergeyevna had inherited from her father some of his passion for luxury. She had been devoted to him, and he had idolized her, used to joke with her as though she were a friend and equal, confided his secrets to her and asked her advice. Her mother she scarcely remembered.

"This doctor is a strange man," she repeated to herself. She stretched, smiled, clasped her hands behind her head, ran her eyes over two pages of a stupid French novel, dropped the book – and fell asleep, pure and cold in her clean and fragrant linen.

The following morning Anna Sergeyevna went off botanizing with Bazarov immediately after breakfast and returned just before dinner; Arkady did not go out anywhere, but spent about an hour with Katya. He was not bored in her company. She offered of her own accord to play the Mozart sonata again; but when Madame Odintsov came back at last and he caught sight of her, he felt a sudden pain in his heart ... She walked through the garden with a rather tired step, her cheeks were burning and her eyes shone more brightly than usual under her round straw hat. She was twirling in her fingers the thin stalk of some wild flower, her light shawl had slipped down to her elbows, and the broad grey ribbons of her hat hung over her bosom. Bazarov walked behind her, self-confident and casual as ever, but Arkady disliked the expression of his face, although it was cheerful and even affectionate. Bazarov muttered "Good day" between his teeth and went straight to his room, and Madame Odintsov shook Arkady's hand absent-mindedly and also walked past him.

"Why good day?" thought Arkady. "As if we had not seen each other already today!"

Chapter 17

As we all know, time sometimes flies like a bird, and sometimes crawls like a worm, but people may be unusually happy when they do not even notice whether time has passed quickly or slowly; in this way Arkady and Bazarov spent a whole fortnight with Madame Odintsov. Such a result was achieved partly by the order and regularity which she had established in her house and mode of life. She adhered strictly to this order herself and obliged others to submit to it as well. Everything during the day was done at a fixed time. In the morning, at eight o'clock precisely, the whole party assembled for tea; from then till breakfast everyone did what he liked, the hostess herself was engaged with her bailiff (the estate was run on the rental system), her butler, and her head housekeeper. Before dinner the party met again for conversation or reading; the evening was devoted to walking, cards, or music; at half-past ten Anna Sergeyevna retired to her own room, gave her orders for the next day and went to bed. Bazarov did not care for this measured and rather formal regularity in daily life, like "gliding along rails" he called it; livened footmen and stately butlers offended his democratic sentiments. He declared that once you went so far you might as well dine in the English style – in tail coats and white ties. He once spoke out his views on the subject to Anna Sergeyevna. Her manner was such that people never hesitated to say what they thought in front of her. She heard him out, and then remarked, "From your point of view you are right – and perhaps in that way I am too much of a lady – but one must lead an orderly life in the country; otherwise one is overcome by boredom," – and she continued to go her own way. Bazarov grumbled, but both he and Arkady found life easy at Madame Odintsov's just because everything in the house ran so smoothly "on rails." Nevertheless some change had occurred in both the young men since the first days of their stay at Nikolskoe. Bazarov, whose company Anna Sergeyevna obviously enjoyed, though she rarely agreed with him, began to show quite unprecedented signs of unrest; he was easily irritated, spoke with reluctance, often looked angry, and could not sit still in one place, as if moved about by some irresistible desire; while Arkady, who had conclusively made up his mind that he was in love with Madame Odintsov, began to abandon himself to a quiet melancholy. This melancholy, however, did not prevent him from making friends with Katya; it even helped him to develop a more affectionate relationship with her. "She does not appreciate me!" he thought. "So be it...! but here is a kind person who does not repulse me," and his heart again knew the sweetness of generous emotions. Katya vaguely understood that he was seeking a kind of consolation in her company, and did not deny him or herself the innocent pleasure of a shy confidential friendship. They did not talk to each other in Anna

Sergeyevna's presence; Katya always shrank into herself under her sister's sharp eyes, while Arkady naturally could pay attention to nothing else when he was close to the object of his love; but he felt happy with Katya when he was alone with her. He knew that it was beyond his power to interest Madame Odintsov; he was shy and at a loss when he was left in her company, nor had she anything special to say to him; he was too young for her. On the other hand, with Katya Arkady felt quite at home; he treated her indulgently, encouraged her to talk about her own impressions of music, novels, verses and other trifles, without noticing or acknowledging that these trifles interested him also. Katya, for her part, did not interfere with his melancholy. Arkady felt at ease with Katya, and Madame Odintsov with Bazarov, so it usually happened that after the two couples had been together for a while, they went off on their separate ways, especially during walks. Katya adored nature, and so did Arkady, though he did not dare to admit it; Madame Odintsov, like Bazarov, was rather indifferent to natural beauties. The continued separation of the two friends produced its consequences; their relationship began to change. Bazarov gave up talking to Arkady about Madame Odintsov, he even stopped abusing her "aristocratic habits"; however, he continued to praise Katya, and advised Arkady only to restrain her sentimental tendencies, but his praises were hurried and perfunctory, his advice was dry, and in general he talked much less to Arkady than before

... he seemed to avoid him, he was ill at ease in his presence...

Arkady observed all this, but kept his observations to himself.

The real cause of all this "novelty" was the feeling inspired in Bazarov by Madame Odintsov, a feeling which at once tortured and maddened him, and which he would have promptly denied with contemptuous laughter and cynical abuse if anyone had even remotely hinted at the possibility of what was happening within him. Bazarov was very fond of women and of feminine beauty, but love in the ideal, or as he called it romantic, sense, he described as idiocy, unpardonable folly; he regarded chivalrous feelings as a kind of deformity or disease, and had more than once expressed his amazement that Toggenburg and all the minnesingers and troubadours had not been shut up in a lunatic asylum. "If a woman appeals to you," he used to say, "try to gain your end; and if you can't – well, just turn your back on her – there are lots more good fish in the sea." Madame Odintsov appealed to him; the rumors he had heard about her, the freedom and independence of her ideas, her obvious liking for him – all seemed to be in his favor; but he soon saw that with her he could not "gain his end," and as for turning his back on her, he found, to his own amazement, he had no strength to do so. His blood was on fire directly he thought about her; he could easily have mastered his blood, but something else was taking possession of him, something he had never allowed, at which he had always scoffed and at which his pride revolted. In his conversations with Anna Sergeyevna he expressed more strongly than ever his calm indifference to any kind of "romanticism"; but when he was alone he indignantly recognized romanticism in himself. Then he would go off into the forest, and stride about smashing the twigs which came in his way and cursing under his breath both her and himself; or he would go into the hayloft in the barn, and obstinately closing his eyes, force himself to sleep, in which, of course, he did not always succeed. Suddenly he would imagine those chaste hands twining themselves around his neck, those proud lips responding to his kisses, those intelligent eyes looking with tenderness – yes, with tenderness – into his, and his head went round, and he forgot himself for a moment, till indignation boiled up again within him. He caught himself indulging in all sorts of "shameful thoughts," as though a devil were mocking at him. It seemed to him sometimes that a change was also taking place in Madame Odintsov, that her face expressed something unusual, that perhaps ... but at that point he would stamp on the ground, grind his teeth or clench his fist.

Meanwhile he was not entirely mistaken. He had struck Madame Odintsov's imagination; he interested her; she thought a lot about him. In his absence she was not exactly bored, she did not wait for him with impatience, but when he appeared she immediately became livelier; she enjoyed being left alone with him and she enjoyed talking to him, even when he annoyed her or offended her taste and her refined habits. She seemed eager both to test him and to analyze herself.

One day, walking with her in the garden, he abruptly announced in a surly voice that he intended to leave very soon to go to his father's place ... She turned white, as if something had pricked her heart; she was surprised at the sudden pain she felt and pondered long afterwards on what it could mean. Bazarov had told her about his departure without any idea of trying out the effect of the news upon her; he never fabricated stories. That same morning he had seen his father's bailiff, Timofeich, who had looked after him as a child. This Timofeich, an experienced and astute little old man, with faded yellow hair, a weather-beaten red face and with tiny teardrops in his shrunken eyes, had appeared quite unexpectedly in front of Bazarov, in his short coat of thick grey-blue cloth, leather girdle and tarred boots.

"Hullo, old man, how are you?" exclaimed Bazarov.

"How do you do, Evgeny Vassilich?" began the little old man, smiling with joy, so that his whole face was immediately covered with wrinkles.

"What have you come here for? They sent you to find me, eh?"

"Fancy that, sir! How is it possible?" mumbled Timofeich (he remembered the strict injunctions he had received from his master before he left). "We were sent to town on the master's business and heard news of your honor, so we turned off on the way – well – to have a look at your honor ... as if we could think of disturbing you!"

"Now then, don't lie!" Bazarov cut him short. "It's no use your pretending this is on the road to the town."

Timofeich hesitated and said nothing.

"Is my father well?"

"Thank God, yes!"

"And my mother?"

"Arina Vlasyevna too, glory be to God."

"They're expecting me, I suppose."

The old man leaned his little head on one side.

"Oh, Evgeny Vassilich, how they wait for you! Believe me, it makes the heart ache to see them."

"All right, all right, don't rub it in. Tell them I'm coming soon."

"I obey," answered Timofeich with a sigh.

As he left the house he pulled his cap down with both hands over his head, then clambered into a dilapidated racing carriage, and went off at a trot, but not in the direction of the town.

On the evening of that day Madame Odintsov was sitting in one room with Bazarov while Arkady walked up and down the hall listening to Katya playing the piano. The princess had gone upstairs to her own room; she always loathed visitors, but she resented particularly the "new raving lunatics," as she called them. In the main rooms she only sulked, but she made up for that in her own room by bursting into such a torrent of abuse in front of her maid that the cap danced on her head, wig and all. Madame Odintsov knew all about this.

"How is it that you are proposing to leave us," she began; "what about your promises?"

Bazarov made a movement of surprise. "What promises?"

"Have you forgotten? You intended to give me some chemistry lessons."

"It can't be helped! My father expects me; I can't put it off any longer. Besides, you can read Pelouse et Frémy, *Notions Générales de Chimie;* it's a good book and clearly written. You will find in it all you need."

"But you remember you assured me that a book can't take the place of ... I forget how you put it, but you know what I mean ... don't you remember?"

"It can't be helped," repeated Bazarov.

"Why should you go?" said Madame Odintsov, dropping her voice.

He glanced at her. Her head had fallen on the back of the arm-chair and her arms, bare to the elbow, were folded over her bosom. She seemed paler in the light of the single lamp covered with a translucent paper shade. A broad white dress covered her completely in its soft folds; even the tips of her feet, also crossed, were hardly visible.

"And why should I stay?" answered Bazarov.

Madame Odintsov turned her head slightly. "You ask why. Have you not enjoyed staying here? Or do you think no one will miss you when you are gone?"

"I am sure of that."

Madame Odintsov was silent for a moment. "You are wrong in thinking so. But I don't believe you. You can't say that seriously." Bazarov continued to sit motionless. "Evgeny Vassilich, why don't you speak?"

"What am I to say to you? There is no point in missing people, and that applies to me even more than to most."

"Why so?"

"I'm a straightforward uninteresting person. I don't know how to talk."

"You are fishing for compliments, Evgeny Vassilich."

"That's not my custom. Don't you know yourself that the graceful side of life, which you value so highly, is beyond my reach?"

Madame Odintsov bit the corner of her handkerchief.

"You may think what you like, but I shall find it dull when you go away."

"Arkady will stay on," remarked Bazarov. Madame Odintsov slightly shrugged her shoulders.

"It will be dull for me," she repeated.

"Really? In any case you won't feel like that for long."

"What makes you suppose so?"

"Because you told me yourself that you are bored only when your orderly routine is disturbed. You have organized your life with such impeccable regularity that there can't be any place left in it for boredom or sadness ... for any painful emotions."

"And do you consider that I am so impeccable ... I mean, that I have organized my life so thoroughly...."

"I should think so! For example, in five minutes the clock will strike ten and I already know in advance that you will turn me out of the room."

"No, I won't turn you out, Evgeny Vassilich. You may stay. Open that window ... I feel half stifled."

Bazarov got up and pushed the window; it flew wide open with a crash ... he had not expected it to open so easily; also, his hands were trembling. The soft dark night looked into the room, with its nearly black sky, its faintly rustling trees, and the fresh fragrance of the pure open air.

"Draw the blind and sit down," said Madame Odintsov. "I want to have a talk with you before you go away. Tell me something about yourself; you never talk about yourself."

"I try to talk to you about useful subjects, Anna Sergeyevna."

"You are very modest ... but I should like to know something about you, about your family and your father, for whom you are forsaking us."

"Why is she talking like this?" thought Bazarov.

"All that is very uninteresting," he said aloud, "particularly for you. We are obscure people."

"You regard me as an aristocrat?"

Bazarov lifted his eyes and looked at Madame Odintsov.

"Yes," he said with exaggerated harshness.

She smiled. "I see you know me very little, though of course you maintain that all people are alike and that it is not worth while studying individuals. I will tell the story of my life sometime ... but first tell me yours."

"I know you very little," repeated Bazarov. "Perhaps you are right; perhaps really everyone is a riddle. You, for instance; you avoid society, you find it tedious – and you invited two students to stay with you. What makes you, with your beauty and your intelligence, live permanently in the country?"

"What? What did you say?" Madame Odintsov interposed eagerly, "with ... my beauty?"

Bazarov frowned. "Never mind about that," he muttered; "I wanted to say that I don't properly understand why you settled in the country!"

"You don't understand it ... yet you explain it to yourself somehow?"

"Yes ... I suppose that you prefer to remain in one place because you are self-indulgent, very fond of comfort and ease and very indifferent to everything else."

Madame Odintsov smiled again.

"You absolutely refuse to believe that I am capable of being carried away by anything?"

Bazarov glanced at her from under his brows.

"By curiosity – perhaps, but in no other way."

"Indeed? Well, now I understand why we have become such friends, you are just like me—"

"We have become friends...," Bazarov muttered in a hollow voice.

"Yes.... Why, I had forgotten that you want to go away."

Bazarov got up. The lamp burned dimly in the darkening, isolated fragrant room; the blind swayed from time to time and let in the stimulating freshness of the night and its mysterious whispers. Madame Odintsov did not stir, but a hidden excitement gradually took possession of her ... It communicated itself to Bazarov. He suddenly felt he was alone with a young and beautiful woman...

"Where are you going?" she said slowly. He made no answer and sank into a chair.

"And so you consider me a placid, pampered, self-indulgent creature," she continued in the same tone and without taking her eyes off the window. "But I know so much about myself that I am unhappy."

"You unhappy! What for? Surely you can't attach any importance to slanderous gossip!"

Madame Odintsov frowned. She was upset that he had understood her words in that way.

"Such gossip does not even amuse me, Evgeny Vassilich, and I am too proud to allow it to disturb me. I am unhappy because ... I have no desires, no love of life. You look at me suspiciously; you think those are the words of an aristocrat who sits in lace on a velvet chair. I don't deny for a moment that I like what you call comfort, and at the same time I have little desire to live. Reconcile that contradiction as best you can. Of course it is all sheer romanticism to you."

Bazarov shook his head; "You are healthy, independent and rich; what more is left? What do you want?"

"What do I want," repeated Madame Odintsov and sighed. "I am very tired, I am old, I feel as if I had lived a very long time. Yes, I am old—" she added, softly drawing the ends of her shawl over her bare arms. Her eyes met Bazarov's and she blushed slightly. "So many memories are behind me; life in Petersburg, wealth, then poverty, then my father's death, marriage, then traveling abroad, as was inevitable ... so many memories and so little worth remembering, and in front of me – a long, long road without a goal ... I have not even the desire to go on."

"Are you so disappointed?" asked Bazarov.

"No," answered Madame Odintsov, speaking with deliberation, "but I am dissatisfied. I think if I were strongly attached to something...."

"You want to fall in love," Bazarov interrupted her, "but you can't love. That is your unhappiness."

Madame Odintsov started looking at the shawl over her sleeve.

"Am I incapable of love?" she murmured.

"Hardly! But I was wrong in calling it unhappiness. On the contrary, a person should rather be pitied when that happens to him."

"When what happens to him?"

"Falling in love."

"And how do you know that?"

"I have heard it," answered Bazarov angrily. "You are flirting," he thought. "You're bored and are playing with me for want of anything better to do, while I...." Truly his heart was torn.

"Besides, you may be expecting too much," he said, leaning forward with his whole body and playing with the fringe of his chair.

"Perhaps. I want everything or nothing. A life for a life, taking one and giving up another without hesitation and beyond recall. Or else better have nothing!"

"Well," observed Bazarov, "those are fair terms, and I'm surprised that so far you ... haven't found what you want."

"And do you think it would be easy to give oneself up entirely to anything?"

"Not easy, if you start reflecting, waiting, estimating your value, appraising yourself, I mean; but to give oneself unreasoningly is very easy."

"How can one help valuing oneself? If I have no value, then who needs my devotion?"

"That is not my affair; it is for another person to investigate my value. The main thing is to know how to devote oneself."

Madame Odintsov leaned forward from the back of her chair.

"You speak as if you had experienced it all yourself," she said. "It happened to come up in the course of our conversation; but all that, as you know, is not in my line."

"But could you devote yourself unreservedly?"

"I don't know. I don't want to boast."

Madame Odintsov said nothing and Bazarov remained silent. The sounds of the piano floated up to them from the drawing room.

"How is it that Katya is playing so late?" observed Madame Odintsov.

Bazarov got up.

"Yes, it really is late now, time for you to go to bed."

"Wait a little, why should you hurry? ... I want to say one word to you."

"What is it?"

"Wait a little," whispered Madame Odintsov. Her eyes rested on Bazarov; it seemed as if she was examining him attentively.

He walked across the room, then suddenly came up to her, hurriedly said "Good-by," squeezed her hand so that she almost screamed and went out. She raised her compressed fingers to her lips, breathed on them, then rose impulsively from her arm-chair and moved rapidly towards the door, as if she wanted to bring Bazarov back ... A maid entered the room carrying a decanter on a silver tray. Madame Odintsov stood still, told the maid she could go, and sat down again deep in thought. Her hair slipped loose and fell in a dark coil over her shoulders. The lamp went on burning for a long time in her room while she still sat there motionless, only from time to time rubbing her hands which were bitten by the cold night air.

Bazarov returned to his bedroom two hours later, his boots wet with dew, looking disheveled and gloomy. He found Arkady sitting at the writing desk with a book in his hands, his coat buttoned up to the neck.

"Not in bed yet?" he exclaimed with what sounded like annoyance.

"You were sitting a long time with Anna Sergeyevna this evening," said Arkady without answering his question.

"Yes, I sat with her all the time you were playing the piano with Katerina Sergeyevna."

"I was not playing...." began Arkady and stopped. He felt that tears were rising in his eyes and he did not want to cry in front of his sarcastic friend.

Chapter 18

The next day when Madame Odintsov came down to tea, Bazarov sat for a long time bending over his cup, then suddenly glanced up at her ... she turned towards him as if he had touched her, and he fancied that her face was paler since the night before. She soon went off to her own room and did not reappear till breakfast. It had rained since early morning, so that there was no question of going for walks. The whole party assembled in the drawing room. Arkady took up the last number of a journal and began to read. The princess, as usual, first tried to express angry amazement by her facial expression, as though he were doing something indecent, then glared angrily at him, but he paid no attention to her.

"Evgeny Vassilich," said Anna Sergeyevna, "let us go to my room. I want to ask you ... you mentioned a textbook yesterday...."

She got up and went to the door. The princess looked round as if she wanted to say, "Look at me; see how shocked I am!" and again stared at Arkady, but he merely raised his head, and exchanging glances with Katya, near whom he was sitting, he went on reading.

Madame Odintsov walked quickly into her study. Bazarov followed her without raising his eyes, and only listening to the delicate swish and rustle of her silk dress gliding in front of him. Madame Odintsov sat down in the same arm-chair in which she had sat the evening before, and Bazarov also sat down in his former place.

"Well, what is that book called?" she began after a short silence.

"Pelouse et Fré, *Notions Générales...,*" answered Bazarov. "However, I might recommend to you also Ganot, *Traité élémentaire de Physique Expérimentale.* In that book the illustrations are clearer, and as a complete text-book–"

Madame Odintsov held out her hand.

"Evgeny Vassilich, excuse me, but I didn't invite you here to discuss textbooks. I wanted to go on with our conversation of last night. You went away so suddenly ... It won't bore you?"

"I am at your service, Anna Sergeyevna. But what were we talking about last night?"

Madame Odintsov cast a sidelong glance at Bazarov.

"We were talking about happiness, I believe. I told you about myself. By the way, I just mentioned the word 'happiness.' Tell me, why is it that even when we are enjoying, for instance, music, a beautiful evening, or a conversation with agreeable people, it all seems to be rather a hint of immeasurable happiness existing somewhere apart, rather than genuine happiness, such, I mean, as we ourselves can really possess? Why is it? Or perhaps you never experience that kind of feeling?"

"You know the saying, 'Happiness is where we are not,'" replied Bazarov. "Besides, you told me yesterday that you are discontented. But it is as you say, no such ideas ever enter my head."

"Perhaps they seem ridiculous to you?"

"No, they just don't enter my head."

"Really. Do you know, I should very much like to know what you do think about?"

"How? I don't understand you."

"Listen, I have long wanted to have a frank talk with you. There is no need to tell you – for you know it yourself – that you are not an ordinary person; you are still young – your whole life lies before you. For what are you preparing yourself? What future awaits you? I mean to say, what purpose are you aiming at, in what direction are you moving, what is in your heart? In short, who and what are you?"

"You surprise me, Anna Sergeyevna. You know, that I am studying natural science and who I...."

"Yes, who are you?"

"I have already told you that I am going to be a district doctor."

Anna Sergeyevna made an impatient movement.

"What do you say that for? You don't believe it yourself. Arkady might answer me in that way, but not you."

"How does Arkady come in?"

"Stop! Is it possible you could content yourself with such a humble career, and aren't you always declaring that medicine doesn't exist for you? You – with your ambition – a district doctor! You answer me like that in order to put me off because you have no confidence in me. But you know, Evgeny Vassilich, I should be able to understand you; I also have been poor and ambitious, like you; perhaps I went through the same trials as you."

"That's all very well, Anna Sergeyevna, but you must excuse me ... I am not in the habit of talking freely about myself in general, and there is such a gulf between you and me...."

"In what way, a gulf? Do you mean to tell me again that I am an aristocrat? Enough of that, Evgeny Vassilich; I thought I had convinced you...."

"And apart from all that," broke in Bazarov, "how can we want to talk and think about the future, which for the most part doesn't depend on ourselves? If an opportunity turns up of doing something – so much the better, and if it doesn't turn up – at least one can be glad that one didn't idly gossip about it beforehand."

"You call a friendly conversation gossip! Or perhaps you consider me as a woman unworthy of your confidence? I know you despise us all!"

"I don't despise you, Anna Sergeyevna, and you know that."

"No, I don't know anything ... but let us suppose so. I understand your disinclination to talk about your future career, but as to what is taking place within you now...."

"Taking place!" repeated Bazarov. "As if I were some kind of government or society! In any case, it is completely uninteresting, and besides, can a person always speak out loud of everything which 'takes place' within him!"

"But I don't see why you shouldn't speak freely, about everything you have in your heart."

"Can *you*?" asked Bazarov.

"I can," answered Anna Sergeyevna, after a moment's hesitation.

Bazarov bowed his head. "You are luckier than I."

"As you like," she continued, "but still something tells me that we did not get to know each other for nothing, that we shall become good friends. I am sure that your – how shall I say – your constraint, your reserve, will disappear eventually."

"So you have noticed in me reserve ... and, how did you put it – constraint?"

"Yes."

Bazarov got up and went to the window.

"And would you like to know the reason for this reserve, would you like to know what is happening within me?"

"Yes," repeated Madame Odintsov, with a sort of dread which she did not quite understand.

"And you will not be angry?"

"No."

"No?" Bazarov was standing with his back to her. "Let me tell you then that I love you like a fool, like a madman ... There, you've got that out of me."

Madame Odintsov raised both her hands in front of her, while Bazarov pressed his forehead against the windowpane. He was breathing hard; his whole body trembled visibly. But it was not the trembling of youthful timidity, not the sweet awe of the first declaration that possessed him: it was passion beating within him, a powerful heavy passion not unlike fury and perhaps akin to it ... Madame Odintsov began to feel both frightened and sorry for him.

"Evgeny Vassilich...," she murmured, and her voice rang with unconscious tenderness.

He quickly turned round, threw a devouring look at her – and seizing both her hands, he suddenly pressed her to him.

She did not free herself at once from his embrace, but a moment later she was standing far away in a corner and looking from there at Bazarov. He rushed towards her...

"You misunderstood me," she whispered in hurried alarm. It seemed that if he had made one more step she would have screamed ... Bazarov bit his lips and went out.

Half an hour later a maid gave Anna Sergeyevna a note from Bazarov; it consisted merely of one line: "Am I to leave today, or can I stop till tomorrow?"

"Why should you leave? I did not understand you – you did not understand me," Anna Sergeyevna answered, but to herself she thought "I did not understand myself either."

She did not show herself till dinnertime, and kept walking up and down her room, with her arms behind her back, sometimes stopping in front of the window or the mirror, and sometimes slowly rubbing her handkerchief over her neck, on which she still seemed to feel a burning spot. She asked herself what had impelled her to get that out of him, as Bazarov had expressed it, to secure his confidence, and whether she had really suspected nothing ... "I am to blame," she concluded aloud, "but I could not have foreseen this." She became pensive and blushed when she recalled Bazarov's almost animal face when he had rushed at her...

"Or?" she suddenly uttered aloud, stopped short and shook her curls ... she caught sight of herself in the mirror; her tossed-back head, with a mysterious smile on the half-closed, half-open eyes and lips, told her, it seemed, in a flash something at which she herself felt confused...

"No," she decided at last. "God alone knows what it would lead to; he couldn't be trifled with; after all, peace is better than anything else in the world."

Her own peace of mind was not deeply disturbed; but she felt sad and once even burst into tears, without knowing why – but not on account of the insult she had just experienced. She did not feel insulted; she was more inclined to feel guilty. Under the influence of various confused impulses, the consciousness that life was passing her by, the craving for novelty, she had forced herself to move on to a certain point, forced herself also to look beyond it – and there she had seen not even an abyss, but only sheer emptiness ... or something hideous.

Chapter 19

In spite of her masterly self-control and superiority to every kind of prejudice, Madame Odintsov felt awkward when she entered the dining room for dinner. However, the meal went off quite satisfactorily. Porfiri Platonich turned up and told various anecdotes; he had just returned from the town. Among other things, he announced that the governor had ordered his secretaries on special commissions to wear spurs, in case he might want to send them off somewhere on horseback, at greater speed. Arkady talked in an undertone to Katya, and attended diplomatically to the princess. Bazarov maintained a grim and obstinate silence. Madame Odintsov glanced at him twice, not furtively, but straight in his face, which looked stern and choleric, with downcast eyes and a contemptuous determination stamped on every feature, and she thought: "No ... no ... no." After dinner, she went with the whole company into the garden, and seeing that Bazarov wanted to speak to her, she walked a few steps to one side and stopped. He approached her, but even then he did not raise his eyes and said in a husky voice: "I have to apologize to you, Anna Sergeyevna. You must be furious with me."

"No, I'm not angry with you, Evgeny Vassilich, but I'm upset."

"So much the worse. In any case I've been punished enough. I find myself, I'm sure you will agree, in a very stupid position. You wrote to me, 'Why go away?' But I can't stay and I don't want to. Tomorrow I shall no longer be here."

"Evgeny Vassilich, why are you...."

"Why am I going away?"

"No, I didn't mean that."

"The past won't return, Anna Sergeyevna, but sooner or later this was bound to happen. Therefore I must go. I can imagine only one condition which would have enabled me to stay: but that condition will never be. For surely – excuse my impudence – you don't love me and never will love me?"

Bazarov's eyes glittered for a moment from under his dark brows.

Anna Sergeyevna did not answer him.

"I'm afraid of this man," was the thought that flashed through her mind.

"Farewell then," muttered Bazarov, as if he guessed her thought, and he turned back to the house.

Anna Sergeyevna followed him slowly, and calling Katya to her, she took her arm. She kept Katya by her side till the evening. She did not play cards and kept on laughing, which was not at all in keeping with her pale and worried face. Arkady was perplexed, and looked at her, as young people do, constantly wondering: "What can it mean?" Bazarov shut himself up in his room and only reappeared at teatime. Anna Sergeyevna wanted to say a kind word to him, but she could not bring herself to address him...

An unexpected incident rescued her from her embarrassment: the butler announced the arrival of Sitnikov.

Words can hardly describe the strange figure cut by the young champion of progress as he fluttered into the room. He had decided with his characteristic impudence to go to the country to visit a woman whom he hardly knew, who had never invited him, but with whom, as he had ascertained, such talented people and intimate friends of his were staying; nevertheless, he was trembling to the marrow of his bones with fright, and instead of bringing out the excuses and compliments which he had learned by heart beforehand, he muttered something idiotic about Evdoksya Kukshina having sent him to inquire after Anna Sergeyevna's health and that Arkady Nikolayevich had always spoken to him in terms of the highest praise ... At this point he faltered and lost his presence of mind so completely that he sat down on his hat. However, since no one turned him out, and Anna Sergeyevna even introduced him to her aunt and sister, he soon recovered himself and began to chatter to his heart's content. The introduction of something commonplace is often useful in life; it relieves an overstrained tension, and sobers down self-confident or self-sacrificing feelings by recalling how closely it is related to them. With Sitnikov's appearance everything became somehow duller, more trivial – and easier: they all even ate supper with a better appetite, and went to bed half an hour earlier than usual.

"I can now repeat to you," said Arkady, as he lay down in bed, to Bazarov, who was also undressing, "what you once said to me: 'Why are you so melancholy? It looks as though you were fulfilling some sacred duty.'"

For some time past a tone of artificially free-and-easy banter had sprung up between the two young men, always a sure sign of secret dissatisfaction or of unexpressed suspicion.

"I'm going to my father's place tomorrow," said Bazarov.

Arkady raised himself and leaned on his elbow. He felt both surprised and somehow pleased. "Ah," he remarked, "and is that why you are sad?"

Bazarov yawned. "If you know too much, you grow old."

"And what about Anna Sergeyevna?"

"What about her?"

"I mean, will she let you go?"

"I'm not in her employment."

Arkady became thoughtful while Bazarov lay down and turned his face to the wall. Some minutes passed in silence.

"Evgeny!" suddenly exclaimed Arkady.

"Well?"

"I shall also leave tomorrow."

Bazarov made no answer.

"Only I shall go home," continued Arkady. "We will go together as far as Khokhlovsky, and there you can get horses at Fedot's. I should have been delighted to meet your people, but I'm afraid I should only get in their way and yours. Of course you're coming back to stay with us?"

"I've left all my things with you," said Bazarov, without turning round.

"Why doesn't he ask me why I'm going away? – and just as suddenly as he is?" thought Arkady. "As a matter of fact, why am I going, and why is he?" he went on reflecting. He could find no satisfactory answer to his own question, though his heart was filled with some bitter feeling. He felt he would find it hard to part from this life to which he had grown so accustomed; but for him to stay on alone would also be queer. "Something has happened between them," he reasoned to himself; "what's the good of my hanging around here after he has gone? Obviously I should bore her stiff, and lose even the little that remains for me." He began to conjure up a picture of Anna Sergeyevna; then other features gradually eclipsed the lovely image of the young widow.

"I'm sorry about Katya too," Arkady whispered to his pillow, on which a tear had already fallen ... Suddenly he shook back his hair and said aloud: "What the devil brought that idiotic Sitnikov here?"

Bazarov started to move about in his bed, and then made the following answer: "I see you're still stupid, my boy. Sitnikovs are indispensable to us. For me, don't you understand – I need such blockheads. In fact, it's not for the gods to bake bricks..."

"Oho!" thought Arkady, and only then he saw in a flash the whole fathomless depth of Bazarov's conceit. "So you and I are gods, in that case? At least, you're a god, but I suppose I'm one of the blockheads."

"Yes," repeated Bazarov gloomily. "You're still stupid."

Madame Odintsov expressed no particular surprise when Arkady told her the next day that he was going with Bazarov; she seemed tired and preoccupied. Katya looked at him with silent gravity. The princess went so far as to cross herself under her shawl, so that he could not help noticing it; but Sitnikov, on the other hand, was most disconcerted. He had just appeared for breakfast in a smart new costume, not this time in the Slavophil fashion; the previous evening he had astonished the man appointed to look after him by the quantity of linen he had brought, and now all of a sudden his comrades were deserting him! He took a few quick steps, darted round like a hunted hare on the edge of a wood, and abruptly, almost with terror, almost with a wail, he announced that he also proposed to leave. Madame Odintsov made no attempt to detain him.

"My carriage is very comfortable," added the unlucky young man, turning to Arkady; "I can take you, while Evgeny Vassilich takes your tarantass, so that will be even more convenient."

"But really, it's quite off your road, and it's a long way to where I live."

"Never mind, that's nothing; I've plenty of time, besides I have business in that direction."

"Selling vodka?" asked Arkady, rather too contemptuously. But Sitnikov was already reduced to such despair that he did not even laugh as he usually did. "I assure you, my carriage is extremely comfortable," he muttered, "and there will be room for everyone."

"Don't upset Monsieur Sitnikov by refusing...," murmured Anna Sergeyevna.

Arkady glanced at her and bowed his head significantly.

The visitors left after breakfast. As she said good-by to Bazarov, Madame Odintsov held out her hand to him, and said, "We shall meet again, shan't we?"

"As you command," answered Bazarov.

"In that case, we shall."

Arkady was the first to go out into the porch; he climbed into Sitnikov's carriage. The butler tucked him in respectfully, but Arkady would gladly have struck him or burst into tears. Bazarov seated himself in the tarantass. When they reached Khokhlovsky, Arkady waited till Fedot, the keeper of the posting station, had harnessed the horses, then going up to the tarantass, he said with his old smile to Bazarov, "Evgeny, take me with you, I want to come to your place."

"Get in," muttered Bazarov between his teeth.

Sitnikov, who had been walking up and down by the wheels of his carriage, whistling boldly, could only open his mouth and gape when he heard these words; while Arkady coolly pulled his luggage out of the carriage, took his seat beside Bazarov, and, bowing politely to his former traveling companion, shouted, "Drive off!" The tarantass rolled away and was soon out of sight ... Sitnikov, utterly confused, looked at his coachman, but he was flicking his whip round the tail of the off-side horse. Finally Sitnikov jumped into his carriage – and yelling at two passing peasants, "Put on your caps, fools!" he drove to the town, where he arrived very late, and where the next day, at Madame Kukshin's he spoke severely about two "disgustingly stuck-up and ignorant fellows."

Sitting in the tarantass alongside Bazarov, Arkady pressed his friend's hand warmly, and for a long time he said nothing. It seemed as though Bazarov appreciated both Arkady's action and his silence. He had not slept at all the previous night, neither had he smoked, and for several days he had scarcely eaten anything. His thin profile stood out darkly and sharply from under his cap, which was pulled down over his eyebrows.

"Well, brother," he said at last, "give me a cigar ... but look, I say, is my tongue yellow?"

"It's yellow," answered Arkady.

"Hm – yes ... and the cigar has no taste. The machine is out of gear."

"You have certainly changed lately," observed Arkady.

"That's nothing; we shall soon recover. One thing bothers me – my mother is so softhearted; if your tummy doesn't grow round as a barrel and you don't eat ten times a day, she's in despair. My father's all right, he's been everywhere and known all the ups and downs. No, I can't smoke," he added, and flung the cigar away into the dusty road.

"Do you think it's another sixteen miles to your place?" asked Arkady.

"Yes, but ask this wise man." He pointed to the peasant sitting on the box, a laborer of Fedot's.

But the wise man only answered: "Who's to know? miles aren't measured hereabouts," and went on swearing under his breath at the shaft horse for "kicking with her headpiece," by which he meant, jerking her head.

"Yes, yes," began Bazarov, "it's a lesson for you, my young friend, an instructive example. The devil knows what rubbish it is. Every man hangs by a thread, any minute the abyss may open under his feet, and yet he must go and invent for himself all kinds of troubles and spoil his life."

"What are you hinting at?" asked Arkady.

"I'm not hinting at anything; I'm saying plainly that we both behaved like fools. What's the use of talking about it? But I've noticed in hospital work, the man who's angry with his illness – he's sure to get over it."

"I don't quite understand you," remarked Arkady, "it seems you have nothing to complain about."

"Well, if you don't quite understand me, I'll tell you this; to my mind it's better to break stones on the road than to let a woman get the mastery of even the end of one's little finger. That's all...," Bazarov was about to utter his favorite word "romanticism," but checked himself and said "rubbish." "You won't believe me now, but I'll tell you; you and I fell into feminine society and very nice we found it; but we throw off that sort of society – it's like taking a dip in cold water on a hot day. A man has no time for these trifles. A man must be untamed, says an old Spanish proverb. Now you, my wise friend," he added, addressing the peasant on the box. "I suppose you have a wife?"

The peasant turned his dull bleary-eyed face towards the two young friends.

"A wife? Yes. How could it be otherwise?"

"Do you beat her?"

"My wife? Anything may happen. We don't beat her without a reason."

"That's fine. Well, and does she beat you?"

The peasant tugged at the reins. "What things you say, sir. You like a joke." He was obviously offended.

"You hear, Arkady Nikolayevich. But we've been properly beaten – that's what comes of being educated people."

Arkady gave a forced laugh, while Bazarov turned away and did not open his mouth again for the rest of the journey.

Those sixteen miles seemed to Arkady quite like double the distance. But at last on the slope of some rising ground the little village where Bazarov's parents lived came into sight. Close to it, in a young birch copse, stood a small house with a thatched roof. Two peasants with their hats on stood near the first hut swearing at each other. "You're a great swine," said one, "you're worse than a little sucking pig." "And your wife's a witch," retorted the other.

"By their unconstrained behavior," remarked Bazarov to Arkady, "and by the playfulness of their phraseology, you can guess that my father's peasants are not overmuch oppressed. But there he is himself coming out on the steps of the house. He must have heard the bells; it's him all right, I recognize his figure; ay! ay! only how grey he's grown, poor old chap!"

Chapter 20

Bazarov leaned out of the tarantass, while Arkady stretched out his head from behind his companion's back and saw standing on the steps of the little house a tall thinnish man with ruffled hair and a sharp aquiline nose, dressed in an old military coat, not buttoned up. He stood with his legs wide apart, smoking a long pipe and screwing up his eyes to keep the sun out of them.

The horses stopped.

"Arrived at last!" exclaimed Bazarov's father, still continuing to smoke, though the pipe was fairly jumping up and down between his fingers. "Come, get out, get out, let me hug you."

He began embracing his son ... "Enyusha, Enyusha," resounded a woman's quavering voice. The door flew open and on the threshold appeared a plump little old woman in a white cap and short colored jacket. She cried, staggered, and would probably have fallen if Bazarov had not supported her. Her plump little hands were instantly twined round his neck, her head was pressed to his breast, and there followed a complete hush, only interrupted by the sound of her broken sobs.

Old Bazarov breathed hard and screwed up his eyes more than before.

"There, that's enough, enough, Arisha! leave off!" he said, exchanging a look with Arkady, who remained standing motionless by the tarantass, while even the peasant on the box turned his head away. "That's quite unnecessary! Please leave off."

"Ah, Vassily Ivanich," faltered the old woman, "for what ages, my dear one, my darling, Enyushenka...," and without unclasping her hands, she drew back her wrinkled face, wet with tears, and overwhelmed with tenderness, and looked at him with blissful and somehow comic eyes and then again fell on his neck.

"Well, yes of course, that's all in the nature of things," remarked Vassily Ivanich. "Only we had better come indoors. Here's a visitor arrived with Evgeny. You must excuse this," he added, turning to Arkady and slightly scraping the ground with his foot: "You understand, a woman's weakness, and well, a mother's heart."

His own lips and eyebrows were quivering and his chin shook – but obviously he was trying to master his feelings and to appear almost indifferent. Arkady bowed.

"Let's go in, mother, really," said Bazarov, and he led the enfeebled old woman into the house. He put her in a comfortable arm-chair, once more hurriedly embraced his father, and introduced Arkady to him.

"Heartily glad to make your acquaintance," said Vassily Ivanich, "but you mustn't expect anything grand: we live very simply here, like military people. Arina Vlasyevna, pray calm yourself; what faintheartedness! Our guest will think ill of you."

"My good sir," said the old woman through her tears, "I haven't the honor of knowing your name and your father's."

"Arkady Nikolayevich," interposed Vassily Ivanich solemnly, in a low voice.

"Excuse a foolish old woman like me." She blew her nose, and bending her head from left to right, she carefully wiped one eye after the other. "You must excuse me. I really thought I should die, that I should not live to see again my darling–"

"Well and here we have lived to see him again, madam," put in Vassily Ivanovich. "Tanyushka," he said, turning to a bare-legged little girl of thirteen in a bright red cotton dress, who was shyly peeping in at the door, "bring your mistress a glass of water – on a tray, do you hear? – and you, gentlemen," he added with a kind of old-fashioned playfulness – "allow me to invite you into the study of a retired veteran."

"Just once more let me embrace you, Enyushka," groaned Arina Vlasyevna. Bazarov bent down to her. "Gracious, how handsome you've grown!"

"Well, I don't know about being handsome," remarked Vassily Ivanovich. "But he's a man, as the saying goes – *ommfay*. And now I hope, Arina Vlasyevna, having satisfied your maternal heart, you will turn your thoughts to satisfying the appetites of our dear guests, because, as you know, even nightingales can't be fed on fairy tales."

The old lady rose from her chair. "This very minute, Vassily Ivanovich, the table shall be laid. I will myself run to the kitchen and order the samovar to be brought in; everything will be ready, everything. Why, for three whole years I have not seen him, have not been able to give him food or drink – is that nothing?"

"Well, you see to things, little hostess, bustle about, don't put us to shame; and you, gentlemen, I beg you to follow me. Here is Timofeich come to pay his respects to you, Evgeny. And the old dog, I dare say he too is delighted. Ay, aren't you delighted, old dog? Be so good as to follow me."

And Vassily Ivanovich went bustling ahead, shuffling and flapping with his down-at-heel slippers.

His whole house consisted of six tiny rooms. One of these – the one into which he led our friends – was called the study. A thick-legged table, littered with papers blackened by an ancient accumulation of dust as if they had been smoked, occupied the whole space between the two windows; on the walls hung Turkish firearms, whips, a saber, two maps, some anatomical diagrams, a portrait of Hufeland, a monogram woven out of hair in a blackened frame, and a diploma under glass; a leather sofa, torn and worn hollow in places, stood between two huge cupboards of Karelian birchwood; on the shelves, books, little boxes, stuffed birds, jars and phials were crowded together in confusion; in one corner lay a broken electric battery.

"I warned you, my dear guest," began Vassily Ivanovich, "that we live, so to speak, bivouacking..."

"Now stop that, what are you apologizing for?" Bazarov interrupted. "Kirsanov knows very well that we're not Croesuses and that you don't live in a palace. Where are we going to put him, that's the question?"

"To be sure, Evgeny, there's an excellent room in the little wing; he will be very comfortable there."

"So you've had a wing built on?"

"Of course, where the bathhouse is," put in Timofeich. "That is next to the bathroom," Vassily Ivanovich added hurriedly. "It's summer now ... I will run over there at once and arrange things; and you, Timofeich, bring in their luggage meanwhile. Of course I hand over my study to you, Evgeny. Suum cuique."

"There you have him! A most comical old chap and very good-natured," remarked Bazarov, as soon as Vassily Ivanovich had gone. "Just as queer a fish as yours, only in a different way. He chatters too much."

"And your mother seems a wonderful woman," remarked Arkady.

"Yes, there's no humbug about her. You just see what a dinner she'll give us."

"They weren't expecting you today, sir, they've not brought any beef," observed Timofeich, who was just dragging in Bazarov's trunk.

"We shall manage all right even without beef; you can't squeeze water from a stone. Poverty, they say, is no crime."

"How many serfs has your father?" asked Arkady suddenly. "The property is not his, but mother's; there are fifteen serfs, if I remember."

"Twenty-two in all," added Timofeich in a dissatisfied tone. The shuffling of slippers was heard and Vassily Ivanovich reappeared. "In a few minutes your room will be ready to receive you," he exclaimed triumphantly. "Arkady – Nikolaich? I think that's how I should call you. And here is your servant," he added, indicating a boy with close-cropped hair, who had come in with him, wearing a long blue caftan with holes in the elbows and a pair of boots which did not belong to him. "His name is Fedka, I repeat again, though my son has forbidden it, you must not expect anything grand. But this fellow knows how to fill a pipe. You smoke, of course?"

"I prefer to smoke cigars," answered Arkady.

"And you're quite right there. I like cigars myself, but in these remote parts it is extremely difficult to get them."

"Enough crying poverty," interrupted Bazarov. "You had better sit down on the sofa here and let us have a look at you."

Vassily Ivanovich laughed and sat down. His face was very much like his son's, only his brow was lower and narrower, his mouth rather wider, and he never stopped making restless movements, shrugged his shoulders as though his coat cut him under the armpits, blinked, cleared his throat and gesticulated with his fingers, whereas his son's most striking characteristic was the nonchalant immobility of his manner.

"Crying poverty," repeated Vassily Ivanovich. "You must suppose, Evgeny, that I want our guest, so to speak, to take pity on us, by making out that we live in such a wilderness. On the contrary I maintain that for a thinking man there is no such thing as a wilderness. At least I try, as far as possible, not to grow rusty, so to speak, not to fall behind the times."

Vassily Ivanovich drew out of his pocket a new yellow silk handkerchief, which he had found time to snatch up when he ran over to Arkady's room, and flourishing it in the air, he went on: "I am not speaking now of the fact that I, for instance, at the cost of quite considerable sacrifices to myself, have put my peasants on the rent system and given up my land to them in return for half the proceeds. I considered it my duty; common sense alone demands that it should be done, though other landowners don't even think about doing it. But I speak now of the sciences, of education."

"Yes, I see you have here the *Friend of Health* for 1855," remarked Bazarov.

"That was sent me by an old comrade as a friendly gesture," Vassily Ivanovich hastily announced; "but we have, for instance, some idea even of phrenology," he added, addressing himself principally to Arkady, and pointing out a small plaster head on the cupboard, divided into numbered squares; "even Schenlein is not unknown to us – and Rademacher."

"Do people still believe in Rademacher in this province?" inquired Bazarov.

Vassily Ivanovich cleared his throat. "In this province ... of course gentlemen, you know better; how could we keep pace with you? You are here to take our places. Even in my time, there was a so-called *humouralist* Hoffman, and a certain Brown with his *vitalism* – they seemed very ridiculous to us, but they, too, had great reputations at one time. Someone new has taken Rademacher's place with you; you bow down to him, but in another twenty years it will probably be his turn to be laughed at."

"For your consolation I can tell you," said Bazarov, "that we nowadays laugh at medicine altogether and bow down to nobody."

"How do you mean? Surely you want to be a doctor."

"Yes, but the one doesn't prevent the other."

Vassily Ivanovich poked his middle finger into his pipe, where a little smoldering ash was left. "Well, perhaps, perhaps – I'm not going to dispute. What am I? A retired army doctor, valla too; and now farming has fallen to my lot. I served in your grandfather's brigade," he addressed himself to Arkady again. "Yes, yes, I have seen many sights in my time. And I mixed with every kind of society. I myself, the man you see before you, have felt the pulse of Prince Wittgenstein and of Zhukovsky! They were in the southern army, the fourteenth, you understand" (and here Vassily Ivanovich pursed his lips significantly). "I knew them all inside out. Well, well, but my work was only on one side; stick to your lancet and be content! Your grandfather was a very honorable man and a real soldier."

"Confess, he was a regular blockhead," remarked Bazarov lazily.

"Ah, Evgeny, how can you use such an expression? Do consider ... of course General Kirsanov was not one of those..."

"Well, drop him," interrupted Bazarov. "As I was driving along I was pleased to see your birch plantation; it has sprung up admirably."

Vassily Ivanovich brightened. "And you must see the little garden I've got now. I planted every tree myself. I have fruit, raspberries and all kinds of medicinal herbs. However much you young gentlemen may know, old Paracelsus spoke the sacred truth; in herbis, verbis et lapidibus ... I've retired from practice, as you know, but at least twice a week something happens to bring me back to my old work. They come for advice – I can't drive them away – and sometimes the poor people need help. Indeed there are no doctors here at all. One of the neighbors here, a retired major, just imagine it, he doctors the people too. I ask the question: 'Has he studied medicine?' They answer: 'No, he hasn't studied, he does it more from philanthropy' ... ha! ha! from philanthropy! What do you think of that? Ha! ha!"

"Fedka! fill me a pipe!" said Bazarov sternly.

"And there's another doctor here who had just visited a patient," continued Vassily Ivanovich in a kind of desperation, "but the patient had already gone *ad patres;* the servant wouldn't let the doctor in, and tells him: 'You're no longer needed.' He never expected this, got confused and asked: 'Well, did your master hiccup before he died?' 'Yes.' 'Did he hiccup much?' 'Yes.' 'Ah, well, that's all right,' and off he went again. Ha! ha! ha!"

The old man laughed alone. Arkady managed to show a smile on his face. Bazarov merely stretched himself. The conversation continued in this way for about an hour. Arkady found time to go to his room which turned out to be the anteroom to the bathroom, but it was very cosy and clean. At last Tanyushka came in and announced that dinner was ready.

Vassily Ivanovich was the first to get up. "Come, gentlemen, you must pardon me generously if I have bored you. Maybe my good wife will give you better satisfaction."

The dinner, though hastily prepared, was very good and even abundant; only the wine was not quite up to the mark; it was sherry, almost black, bought by Timofeich in the town from a well-known merchant, and it had a flavor of copper or resin; the flies also were a nuisance. On ordinary days a serf boy used to keep driving them away with a big green branch, but on this occasion Vassily Ivanovich had sent him away for fear of adverse criticism from the younger generation. Arina Vlasyevna had changed her dress, and was wearing a high cap with silk ribbons and a pale blue flowered shawl. She started crying again as soon as she caught sight of her Enyusha, but her husband did not need to admonish her; she herself made haste to dry her tears in order not to spoil her shawl. Only the young men ate; the host and hostess had both dined long ago. Fedka waited at table, obviously encumbered by his unfamiliar boots; he was helped by a woman with a masculine cast of face and one eye, called Anfisushka; she fulfilled the duties of housekeeper, poultry woman and laundress. Vassily Ivanovich walked up and down throughout the dinner, and with a perfectly contented and even blissful face talked about the grave anxieties he had felt about Napoleon's policy and the complications of the Italian question. Arina Vlasyevna took no notice of Arkady and did not press him to eat; leaning her round face on her little fist, her full cherry-colored lips and the little moles on her cheeks and over her eyebrows adding to her extremely kind, good-natured expression, she did not take her eyes off her son and constantly sighed; she was dying to know for how long he would stay, but she was afraid to ask him. "What if he stays for two days?" she thought, and her heart sank. After the roast Vassily Ivanovich disappeared for a moment and returned with an opened half-bottle of champagne.

"Here," he exclaimed, "though we do live in the wilds, we have something to make merry with on festive occasions!" He poured out three full glasses and a little wineglass, proposed the health of "our invaluable guests," and at once tossed off his glass in military fashion and made Arina Vlasyevna drink her wineglass to the last drop. When the time came for the sweet preserves, Arkady, who could not bear anything sweet, thought it his duty, however, to taste four different kinds which had been freshly made – all the more since Bazarov flatly refused them and began at once to smoke a cigar. Afterwards tea was served with cream, butter and rolls; then Vassily Ivanovich took them all out into the garden to admire the beauty of the evening. As they passed a garden seat he whispered to Arkady, "This is the spot where I love to meditate as I watch the sunset; it suits a recluse like me. And there, a little farther off, I have planted some of the trees beloved by Horace."

"What trees?" asked Bazarov, overhearing, "Oh ... acacias."

Bazarov began to yawn.

"I suppose it is time our travelers were in the embrace of Morpheus," observed Vassily Ivanovich.

"In other words, it's time for bed," Bazarov interposed. "That's a correct judgment; it certainly is high time!"

Saying good night to his mother, he kissed her on the forehead while she embraced him and secretly behind his back she gave him her blessing three times. Vassily Ivanovich showed Arkady to his room and wished him "as refreshing repose as I also enjoyed at your happy years." In fact Arkady slept extremely well in his bathhouse; it smelt of mint, and two crickets behind the stove rivaled each other in their prolonged drowsy chirping. Vassily Ivanovich went from Arkady's room to his own study and, settling down on the sofa at his son's feet, was looking forward to having a chat with him; but Bazarov sent him away at once, saying he felt sleepy, but he did not fall asleep till morning. With wide-open eyes he stared angrily into the darkness; memories of childhood had no power over him, and besides he had not yet been able to rid himself of the impression of his recent bitter experiences. Arina Vlasyevna first prayed to her heart's content, then she had a long, long conversation with Anfisushka, who stood rooted to the spot in front of her mistress, and fixing her solitary eye upon her, communicated in a mysterious whisper all her observations and conjectures about Evgeny Vassilevich. The old lady's head was giddy with happiness, wine and tobacco smoke; her husband tried to talk to her – but with a wave of the hand he gave it up.

Arina Vlasyevna was a genuine Russian lady of olden times; she ought to have lived two centuries before, in the ancient Moscow days. She was very devout and emotional; she believed in fortunetelling, charms, dreams and omens of every conceivable kind; she believed in the prophecies of crazy people, in house spirits, in wood spirits, in unlucky meetings, in the evil eye, in popular remedies; she ate specially prepared salt on Holy Thursday and believed that the end of the world was close at hand; she believed that if on Easter Sunday the candles did not go out at Vespers, then there would be a good crop of buckwheat, and that a mushroom will not grow after a human eye has seen it; she believed that the devil likes to be where there is water, and that every Jew has a blood-stained spot on his breast; she was afraid of mice, of snakes, of frogs, of sparrows, of leeches, of thunder, of cold water, of draughts, of horses, of goats, of red-haired people and of black cats; she regarded crickets and dogs as unclean animals; she never ate veal, pigeons, crayfish, cheese, asparagus, Jerusalem artichokes, hares, or watermelons because a cut watermelon suggested the head of John the Baptist; she could not speak of oysters without a shudder; she enjoyed eating – but strictly observed fasts; she slept ten hours out of the twenty-four – and never went to bed at all if Vassily Ivanovich had so much as a headache; she had never read a single book except *Alexis or the Cottage in the Forest;* she wrote one or at most two letters in a year, but she was an expert housewife, knew all about preserving and jam making, though she touched nothing with her own hands and was usually reluctant to move from her place. Arina Vlasyevna was very kindhearted and in her own way far from stupid. She knew that the world is divided into masters whose duty it is to command, and simple people whose duty it is to serve – and so she felt no disgust for servile behavior or bowing to the ground; but she treated affectionately and gently those in subjection to her, never let a single beggar go away empty-handed, and never spoke ill of anyone, though she was fond of gossip. In her youth she had been very pretty, had played the clavichord and spoken a little French; but in the course of many years of wandering with her husband, whom she had married against her will, she had grown stout and forgotten both music and French. Her son she loved and feared unutterably; she had handed over the management of her little estate to Vassily Ivanovich – and she no longer took any part in it; she would groan, wave her handkerchief and raise her eyebrows higher and higher in horror directly her old husband began to discuss impending land reforms and his own plans. She was apprehensive, always expecting some great calamity, and would weep at once whenever she remembered anything sad ... Nowadays such women have almost ceased to exist. God knows whether this should be a cause for rejoicing!

Chapter 21

On getting up, Arkady opened the window, and the first object which met his eyes was Vassily Ivanovich. In a Turkish dressing gown tied round the waist with a pocket handkerchief, the old man was zealously digging his kitchen garden. He noticed his young visitor and leaning on his spade he called out, "Good health to you! How did you sleep?"

"Splendidly," answered Arkady.

"And here I am, as you see, like some Cincinnatus, preparing a bed for late turnips. The time has come now – and thank God for it! – when everyone should secure his sustenance by the work of his own hands: it is useless to rely on others; one must labor oneself. So it turns out that Jean Jacques Rousseau is right. Half an hour ago, my dear young sir, you could have seen me in an entirely different position. One peasant woman, who complained of looseness – that's how they express it, but in our language, dysentery – I – how shall I express it? I injected her with opium; and for another I extracted a tooth. I offered her an anesthetic, but she refused. I do all that gratis – *anamatyer.* However, I'm used to it; you see I'm a plebeian, homo nous – not one of the old stock, not like my wife ... But wouldn't you like to come over here in the shade and breathe the morning freshness before having tea?"

Arkady went out to him.

"Welcome once more!" said Vassily Ivanovich, raising his hand in a military salute to the greasy skullcap which covered his head. "You, I know, are accustomed to luxury and pleasures, but even the great ones of this world do not disdain to spend a brief time under a cottage roof."

"Gracious heavens," protested Arkady, "as if I were a great one of this world! And I'm not accustomed to luxury either."

"Pardon me, pardon me," replied Vassily Ivanovich with an amiable grimace. "Though I am a back number now, I also have knocked about the world – I know a bird by its flight. I am something of a psychologist in my way, and a physiognomist. If I had not, I venture to say, been granted that gift, I should have come to grief long ago; a little man like me would have been blotted out. I must tell you without flattery, the friendship I observe between you and my son sincerely delights me. I have just seen him; he got up very early as he habitually does – you probably know that – and ran off for a ramble in the neighborhood. Permit me to be so inquisitive – have you known my Evgeny long?"

"Since last winter."

"Indeed. And permit me to question you further – but why shouldn't we sit down? Permit me as a father to ask you frankly: what is your opinion of my Evgeny?"

"Your son is one of the most remarkable men I have ever met," answered Arkady emphatically.

Vassily Ivanovich's eyes suddenly opened wide, and a slight flush suffused his cheeks. The spade dropped from his hand.

"And so you expect...," he began.

"I'm convinced," interrupted Arkady, "that your son has a great future before him, that he will do honor to your name. I've felt sure of that ever since I met him."

"How – how did it happen?" articulated Vassily Ivanovich with some effort. An enthusiastic smile parted his broad lips and would not leave them.

"Would you like me to tell you how we met?"

"Yes ... and all about it–"

Arkady began his story and spoke of Bazarov with even greater warmth, even greater enthusiasm than he had done on that evening when he danced a mazurka with Madame Odintsov.

Vassily Ivanovich listened and listened, blew his nose, rolled his handkerchief up into a ball with both hands, cleared his throat, ruffled up his hair – and at length could contain himself no longer; he bent down to Arkady and kissed him on the shoulder. "You have made me perfectly happy," he said, without ceasing to smile. "I ought to tell you, I ... idolize my son; I won't even speak of my old wife – naturally, a mother – but I dare not show my feelings in front of him, because he disapproves of that. He is opposed to every demonstration of emotion; many people even find fault with him for such strength of character, and take it for a sign of pride or lack of feeling; but people like him ought not to be judged by any ordinary standards, ought they? Look at this, for example; others in his place would have been a constant drag on their parents; but he – would you believe it? – from the day he was born he has never taken a farthing more than he could help, that's God's truth."

"He is a disinterested, honest man," remarked Arkady.

"Exactly so, disinterested. And I not only idolize him, Arkady Nikolaich, I am proud of him, and the height of my only ambition is that some day there will be the following words in his biography:

> "'The son of an ordinary army doctor, who was able, however, to recognize his talent early and spared no pains for his education...'"

The old man's voice broke.

Arkady pressed his hand.

"What do you think?" inquired Vassily Ivanovich after a short silence, "surely he will not attain in the sphere of medicine the celebrity which you prophesy for him?"

"Of course, not in medicine, though even there he will be one of the leading scientific men."

"In what then, Arkady Nikolaich?"

"It would be hard to say now, but he will be famous."

"He will be famous," repeated the old man, and he relapsed into thought.

"Arina Vlasyevna sent me to call you in to tea," announced Anfisushka, passing by with a huge dish of ripe raspberries.

Vassily Ivanovich started. "And will the cream be cooled for the raspberries?"

"Yes."

"Be sure it is cold! Don't stand on ceremony. Arkady Nikolaich – take some more. How is it Evgeny doesn't come back?"

"I'm here," called Bazarov's voice from inside Arkady's room.

Vassily Ivanovich turned round quickly.

"Aha, you wanted to pay a visit to your friend; but you were too late, amice, and we have already had a long conversation. Now we must go in to tea; mother has sent for us. By the way, I want to have a talk with you."

"What about?"

"There's a peasant here; he's suffering from icterus..."

"You mean jaundice?"

"Yes, a chronic and very obstinate case of icterus. I have prescribed him centaury and St. John's wort, told him to eat carrots, given him soda; but all those are palliative measures; we need some more radical treatment. Although you laugh at medicine, I'm sure you can give me some practical advice. But we will talk about that later. Now let us go and drink tea."

Vassily Ivanovich jumped up briskly from the garden seat and hummed the air from *Robert le Diable.*

> "The law, the law we set ourselves,
>   To live, to live, for pleasure."

"Astonishing vitality," observed Bazarov, moving away from the window.

Midday arrived. The sun was burning from under a thin veil of unbroken whitish clouds. All was still; only the cocks in the village broke the silence by their vigorous crowing, which produced in everyone who heard it a strange sense of drowsiness and tedium; and from somewhere high up in a treetop sounded the plaintive and persistent chirp of a young hawk. Arkady and Bazarov lay in the shade of a small haystack, and put under themselves two armfuls of rustling dry but still green and fragrant grass.

"That poplar tree," began Bazarov, "reminds me of my childhood; it grows on the edge of the pit where the brick shed used to be, and in those days I firmly believed that the poplar and the pit possessed the peculiar power of a talisman; I never felt dull when I was near them. I did not understand then that I was not dull just because I was a child. Well, now I'm grown up, the talisman no longer works."

"How long did you live here altogether?" asked Arkady.

"Two years on end; after that we traveled about. We led a roving life, chiefly wandering from town to town."

"And has this house been standing long?"

"Yes. My grandfather built it, my mother's father."

"Who was he, your grandfather?"

"The devil knows – some kind of second-major. He served under Suvorov and always told stories about marching across the Alps – inventions probably."

"You have a portrait of Suvorov hanging in the drawing room. I like such little houses as yours, old-fashioned and warm; and they always have a special kind of scent about them."

"A smell of lamp oil and clover," remarked Bazarov, yawning. "And the flies in these dear little houses ... fugh!"

"Tell me," began Arkady after a short pause, "were they strict with you as a child?"

"You see what my parents are like. They're not a severe sort."

"Are you fond of them, Evgeny?"

"I am, Arkady."

"How they adore you!"

Bazarov was silent for a while. "Do you know what I'm thinking about?" he said at last, clasping his hands behind his head.

"No. What is it?"

"I'm thinking how happy life is for my parents! My father at the age of sixty can fuss around, chat about 'palliative measures,' heal people; he plays the magnanimous master with the peasants – has a gay time in fact; and my mother is happy too; her day is so crammed with all sorts of jobs, with sighs and groans, that she hasn't a moment to think about herself; while I..."

"While you?"

"While I think; here I lie under a haystack ... The tiny narrow space I occupy is so minutely small in comparison with the rest of space where I am not and which has nothing to do with me; and the portion of time in which it is my lot to live is so insignificant beside the eternity where I have not been and will not be ... And in this atom, in this mathematical point, the blood circulates, the brain works and wants something ... how disgusting! how petty!"

"Allow me to point out that what you say applies generally to everyone."

"You're right," interrupted Bazarov. "I wanted to say that they, my parents I mean, are occupied and don't worry about their own nothingness; it doesn't sicken them ... while I ... I feel nothing but boredom and anger."

"Anger? Why anger?"

"Why? How can you ask why? Have you forgotten?"

"I remember everything, but still I can't agree that you have any right to be angry. You're unhappy, I realize, but..."

"Ugh! I can see, Arkady Nikolaich, that you regard love like all modern young men; cluck, cluck, cluck, you call to the hen, and the moment the hen comes near, off you run! I'm not like that. But enough of it all. It's a shame to talk about what can't be helped." He turned over on his side. "Ah, there goes a brave ant dragging along a half-dead fly. Take her away, brother, take her! Don't pay any attention to her resistance; take full advantage of your animal privilege to be without pity – not like us self-destructive creatures!"

"What are you talking about, Evgeny? When did you destroy yourself?"

Bazarov raised his head.

"That's the only thing I'm proud of. I have not crushed myself, so a little woman can't crush me. Amen! It's all over. You won't hear another word from me about it."

Both friends lay for a time in silence.

"Yes," began Bazarov, "man is a strange animal. When one gets a side view from a distance of the dumb life our 'fathers' lead here, one thinks: what could be better? You eat and drink and know you are acting in the most righteous and sensible way. If not, you're devoured by the tedium of it. One wants to have dealings with people even if it's only to abuse them."

"One ought to arrange one's life so that every moment of it becomes significant," remarked Arkady thoughtfully.

"I dare say. The significant may be deceptive but sweet, though it's even quite possible to put up with the insignificant ... But petty squabbles, petty squabbles ... that's a misery."

"Petty squabbles don't exist for the man who refuses to recognize them as such."

"Hm ... what you have said is a commonplace turned upside-down."

"What? What do you mean by that phrase?"

"I'll explain; to say for instance that education is beneficial, that's a commonplace, but to say that education is harmful is a commonplace turned upside-down. It sounds more stylish, but fundamentally it's one and the same thing!"

"But where is the truth – on which side?"

"Where? I answer you like an echo; where?"

"You're in a melancholy mood today, Evgeny."

"Really? The sun must have melted my brain and I ought not to have eaten so many raspberries either."

"In that case it wouldn't be a bad plan to doze a bit," remarked Arkady.

"Certainly. Only don't look at me; everyone has a stupid face when he's asleep."

"But isn't it all the same to you what people think of you?"

"I don't quite know how to answer you. A real man ought not to worry about such things; a real man is not meant to be thought about, but is someone who must be either obeyed or hated."

"It's odd! I don't hate anyone," observed Arkady after a pause.

"And I hate so many. You're a tenderhearted listless creature; how could you hate anyone...? You're timid, you haven't much self-reliance."

"And you," interrupted Arkady, "do you rely on yourself? Have you a high opinion of yourself?"

Bazarov paused. "When I meet a man who can hold his own beside me," he said with slow deliberation, "then I'll change my opinion of myself. Hatred! You said, for instance, today as we passed the cottage of our bailiff Philip – the one that's so neat and clean – well, you said, Russia will achieve perfection when the poorest peasant has a house like that, and every one of us ought to help to bring it about ... And I felt such a hatred for this poorest peasant, this Philip or Sidor, for whom I have to be ready to sacrifice my skin and who won't even thank me for it – and why should he thank me? Well, suppose he lives in a clean house, while weeds grow out of me – so, what next?"

"That's enough, Evgeny ... listening to you today one would be driven to agree with those who reproach us for absence of principles."

"You talk like your uncle. Principles don't exist in general – you haven't yet managed to understand even that much! – but there are sensations. Everything depends on them."

"How is that?"

"Well, take me for instance; I adopt a negative attitude by virtue of my sensations; I like to deny, my brain is made like that – and there's nothing more to it. Why does chemistry appeal to me? Why do you like apples? – also by virtue of our sensations. It's all the same thing. People will never penetrate deeper than that. Not everyone would tell you so, and another time I shouldn't tell you so myself."

"What, and is honesty also – a sensation?"

"I should think so."

"Evgeny...!" began Arkady in a dejected tone.

"Well? What? That's not to your taste?" broke in Bazarov. "No, brother. If you've made up your mind to mow down everything – don't spare your own legs...! But we've philosophized enough. 'Nature heaps up the silence of sleep,' said Pushkin."

"He never said anything of the kind," retorted Arkady.

"Well, if he didn't, he might have and ought to have said it as a poet. By the way, he must have served in the army."

"Pushkin was never in the army!"

"Why, on every page of his one reads, to arms! to arms! for Russia's honor!"

"What legends you invent! Really, it's positive slander."

"Slander? There's a weighty matter. He's found a solemn word to frighten me with. Whatever slander you may utter against a man, you may be sure he deserves twenty times worse than that in reality."

"We had better go to sleep," said Arkady with vexation.

"With the greatest of pleasure," answered Bazarov.

But neither of them slept. Some kind of almost hostile feeling had taken hold of both young men. Five minutes later, they opened their eyes and glanced at each other in silence.

"Look," said Arkady suddenly, "a dry maple leaf has broken off and is falling to the ground; its movements are exactly like a butterfly's flight. Isn't it strange? Such a gloomy dead thing so like the most care-free and lively one."

"Oh, my friend Arkady Nikolaich," exclaimed Bazarov, "one thing I implore of you; no beautiful talk."

"I talk as I best know how to ... yes, really this is sheer despotism. A thought came into my head; why shouldn't I express it?"

"All right, and why shouldn't I express my thoughts? I think that sort of beautiful talk is positively indecent."

"And what is decent? Abuse?"

"Ah, so I see clearly you intend to follow in your uncle's footsteps. How pleased that idiot would be if he could hear you now!"

"What did you call Pavel Petrovich?"

"I called him, as he deserves to be called, an idiot."

"Really, this is unbearable," cried Arkady.

"Aha! family feeling spoke out," remarked Bazarov coolly. "I've noticed how obstinately it clings to people. A man is ready to give up everything and break with every prejudice; but to admit, for instance, that his brother who steals other people's handkerchiefs is a thief – that's beyond his power. And as a matter of fact – to think – my brother, mine – and no genius – that's more than one can swallow!"

"A simple sense of justice spoke in me and no family feeling at all," retorted Arkady vehemently. "But since you don't understand such a feeling, as it's not among your sensations, you're in no position to judge it!"

"In other words, Arkady Kirsanov is too exalted for my understanding. I bow down to him and say no more."

"That's enough, Evgeny; we shall end by quarreling."

"Ah, Arkady, do me a favor, let's quarrel properly for once, to the bitter end, to the point of destruction."

"But then perhaps we should end by..."

"By fighting?" broke in Bazarov. "Well? Here in the hay, in such idyllic surroundings, far from the world and from human eyes, it wouldn't matter. But you'd be no match for me. I'd have you by the throat at once..."

Barazov stretched out his long tough fingers.

Arkady turned round and prepared, as if joking, to resist ... But his friend's face struck him as so sinister – he saw such a grim threat in the crooked smile which twisted his lips, in his glaring eyes, that he felt instinctively taken aback...

"So that is where you have got to," said the voice of Vassily Ivanovich at this moment, and the old army doctor appeared before the young men dressed in a homemade linen jacket, with a straw hat, also homemade, on his head. "I've been looking for you everywhere ... But you've picked out a splendid place and you're perfectly employed. Lying on the earth and gazing up to heaven – do you know there's a special significance in that?"

"I gaze up to heaven only when I want to sneeze," growled Bazarov, and turning to Arkady, he added in an undertone: "A pity he interrupted us."

"Well, that's enough," whispered Arkady, and secretly squeezed his friend's hand. But no friendship can withstand such shocks for long.

"I look at you, my youthful friends," said Vassily Ivanovich meanwhile, shaking his head and leaning his folded arms on a skillfully bent stick which he himself had carved with a Turk's figure for a knob. "I look, and I can't refrain from admiration. You have so much strength, such youthful bloom, abilities and talents! Truly ... A Castor and Pollux."

"Get along with you – shooting off into mythology!" said Bazarov. "You can see he was a Latin scholar in his day. Why, I seem to remember, you won the silver medal for Latin composition, didn't you?"

"The Dioscuri, the Dioscuri!" repeated Vassily Ivanovich.

"Come, stop that, father; don't go sentimental."

"Just once in an age, surely it's permissible," murmured the old man. "Anyhow, I have not been searching for you, gentlemen, in order to pay you compliments, but in order to tell you, in the first place, that we shall soon be dining; and secondly, I wanted to warn you, Evgeny ... you are a sensible man, you know the world and you know what women are, and therefore you will excuse ... your mother wanted a service held for you in thanksgiving, for your arrival. Don't imagine that I'm asking you to attend that service – it's already over; but Father Alexei..."

"The parson?"

"Well, yes, the priest; he is – to dine with us ... I did not expect this and was not even in favor of it – but somehow it turned out like that – he misunderstood me – and, well, Arina Vlasyevna – besides, he's a worthy and reasonable man."

"I suppose he won't eat my share at dinner?" inquired Bazarov.

Vassily Ivanovich laughed. "The things you say!"

"Well, I ask nothing more. I'm ready to sit down at table with anyone."

Vassily Ivanovich set his hat straight.

"I was sure in advance," he said, "that you were above all such prejudices. Here am I, an old man of sixty-two, and even I have none." (Vassily Ivanovich dared not confess that he had himself wanted the thanksgiving service – he was no less devout than his wife.) "And Father Alexei very much wanted to make your acquaintance. You will like him, you'll see. He doesn't mind playing cards even, and he sometimes – but this is between ourselves – goes so far as to smoke a pipe."

"Fancy that. We'll have a round of whist after dinner and I'll beat him."

"Ha! ha! ha! we shall see; that's an open question."

"Well, won't it remind you of old times?" said Bazarov with a peculiar emphasis.

Vassily Ivanovich's bronzed cheeks blushed with confusion. "For shame, Evgeny, ... Let bygones be bygones. Well, I'm ready to confess before this gentleman, I had that very passion in my youth – and how I paid for it too...! But how hot it is. May I sit down with you? I hope I shan't be in your way."

"Not in the least," answered Arkady.

Vassily Ivanovich lowered himself, sighing, into the hay. "Your present quarters, my dear sirs," he began, "remind me of my military bivouacking existence, the halts of the field hospital somewhere like this under a haystack – and even for that we thanked God." He sighed. "What a lot I've experienced in my time. For instance, if you allow me, I will tell you a curious episode about the plague in Bessarabia."

"For which you won the Vladimir cross?" interposed Bazarov. "We know – we know ... By the way, why aren't you wearing it?"

"Why, I told you that I have no prejudices," muttered Vassily Ivanovich (only the evening before he had had the red ribbon unpicked from his coat) and he started to tell his story about the plague. "Why, he has fallen asleep," he whispered suddenly to Arkady, pointing to Evgeny, and winked good-naturedly. "Evgeny, get up!" he added loudly. "Let's go in to dinner."

Father Alexei, a handsome stout man with thick, carefully combed hair, with an embroidered belt round his mauve silk cassock, appeared to be a very skillful and adaptable person. He made haste to be the first to offer his hand to Arkady and Bazarov, as though realizing in advance that they did not want his blessing, and in general he behaved without constraint. He neither betrayed his own opinions nor provoked the other members of the company; he made an appropriate joke about seminary Latin and stood up in defense of his bishop; he drank two glasses of wine and refused a third; he accepted a cigar from Arkady, but did not smoke it on the spot, saying he would take it home with him. Only he had a somewhat unpleasant habit of raising his hand from time to time, slowly and carefully, to catch the flies on his face, and sometimes managing to squash them. He took his seat at the green card table with a measured expression of satisfaction, and ended by winning from Bazarov two and a half rubles in notes (they had no idea of how to reckon in silver in Arina Vlasyevna's house). She sat, as before, close to her son – she did not play cards – and as before she leaned her cheek on her little clenched hand; she got up only to order some fresh sweetmeat to be served. She was afraid to caress Bazarov, and he gave her no encouragement, for he did nothing to invite her caresses; and besides, Vassily Ivanovich had advised her not to "disturb" him too much. "Young men are not fond of that sort of thing," he explained to her. (There is no need to say what dinner was like that day; Timofeich in person had galloped off at dawn to procure some special Circassian beef; the bailiff had gone off in another direction for turbot, perch and crayfish; for mushrooms alone the peasant woman had been paid forty-two kopeks in copper); but Arina Vlasyevna's eyes, looking steadfastly at Bazarov, expressed not devotion and tenderness alone, for sorrow was visible in them also, mingled with curiosity and fear, and with a trace of humble reproachfulness.

Bazarov, however, was in no state of mind to analyze the exact expression of his mother's eyes; he seldom turned to her and then only with some short question. Once he asked her for her hand "for luck"; she quietly placed her soft little hand on his rough broad palm.

"Well," she asked after waiting for a time, "did it help?"

"Worse luck than before," he answered with a careless smile. "He plays too rashly," pronounced Father Alexei, as it were compassionately, and stroked his handsome beard.

"That was Napoleon's principle, good Father, Napoleon's," interposed Vassily Ivanovich, leading with an ace.

"But it brought him to the isle of St. Helena," observed Father Alexei, and trumped his ace.

"Wouldn't you like some black-currant tea, Enyushka?" asked Arina Vlasyevna.

Bazarov merely shrugged his shoulders.

"No!" he said to Arkady the following day, "I go away from here tomorrow. I'm bored; I want to work but I can't here. I will come again to your place; I left all my apparatus there. In your house at least one can shut oneself up, but here my father keeps on repeating to me, 'My study is at your disposal – nobody shall interfere with you,' and all the time he himself is hardly two steps away. And I'm ashamed somehow to shut myself away from him. It's the same thing with my mother. I hear how she sighs on the other side of the wall, and then if one goes in to see her – one has nothing to say."

"She will be most upset," said Arkady, "and so will he."

"I shall come back to them."

"When?"

"Well, when I'm on my way to Petersburg."

"I feel particularly sorry for your mother."

"How's that? Has she won your heart with her raspberries?"

Arkady lowered his eyes.

"You don't understand your mother, Evgeny. She's not only a very good woman, she's really very wise. This morning she talked to me for half an hour, and so interestingly, so much to the point."

"I suppose she was expatiating about me the whole time."

"We didn't talk about you only."

"Maybe as an outsider you see more. If a woman can keep up a conversation for half an hour, it's already a good sign. But I'm going away, all the same."

"It won't be easy for you to break the news to them. They are making plans for us a fortnight ahead."

"No; it won't be easy. Some devil drove me to tease my father today; he had one of his rent-paying peasants flogged the other day and quite rightly too – yes, yes, don't look at me in such horror – he did right because that peasant is a frightful thief and drunkard; only my father had no idea that I, as they say, became aware of the facts. He was very much embarrassed, and now I shall have to upset him as well ... Never mind! He'll get over it."

Bazarov said, "Never mind," but the whole day passed before he could bring himself to tell Vassily Ivanovich about his decision. At last when he was just saying good night to him in the study, he remarked with a strained yawn: "Oh yes ... I almost forgot to tell you – will you send to Fedot's for our horses tomorrow?"

Vassily Ivanovich was dumbfounded.

"Is Mr. Kirsanov leaving us then?"

"Yes, and I'm going with him."

Vassily Ivanovich almost reeled over. "You are going away?"

"Yes ... I must. Make the arrangements about the horses, please."

"Very good ... to the posting station ... very good – only – only – why is it?"

"I must go to stay with him for a short time. Afterwards I will come back here again."

"Ah! for a short time ... very good."

Vassily Ivanovich took out his handkerchief and as he blew his nose bent himself almost double to the ground. "All right, it will – all be done. I had thought you were going to stay with us ... a little longer. Three days ... after three years... that's rather little, rather little, Evgeny."

"But I tell you I'm coming back soon. I have to go."

"You have to ... Well! Duty comes before everything else ... So you want the horses sent? All right. Of course Anna and I never expected this. She has just managed to get some flowers from a neighbor; she wanted to decorate your room." (Vassily Ivanovich did not even mention that every morning the moment it was light he consulted with Timofeich, and standing with his bare feet in slippers, pulling out with trembling fingers one crumpled ruble note after another, entrusted him with various purchases, particularly of good things to eat, and of red wine, which, as far as he could observe, the young men liked extremely.) "Liberty – is the main thing – that is my principle ... one has no right to interfere ... no..."

He suddenly fell silent and made for the door.

"We shall soon see each other again, father, really."

But Vassily Ivanovich did not turn round, he only waved his hand and went out. When he got back to the bedroom, he found his wife in bed and began to say his prayers in a whisper in order not to wake her up. She woke, however.

"Is that you, Vassily Ivanovich?" she asked.

"Yes, little mother."

"Have you come from Enyusha? Do you know, I'm afraid he may not be comfortable on that sofa. I told Anfisushka to put out for him your traveling mattress and the new pillows; I should have given him our feather bed, but I seem to remember he doesn't like sleeping soft."

"Never mind, little mother, don't you worry. He's all right. Lord have mercy on us sinners," he continued his prayer in a low voice. Vassily Ivanovich felt sorry for his old wife; he did not wish to tell her overnight what sorrow there was in store for her.

Bazarov and Arkady left on the following day. From early morning the house was filled with gloom; Anfisushka let the dishes slip out of her hand; even Fedka became bewildered and at length took off his boots. Vassily Ivanovich fussed more than ever; obviously he was trying to make the best of it, talked loudly and stamped his feet, but his face looked haggard and he continually avoided looking his son in the eyes. Arina Vlasyevna wept quietly; she would have broken down and lost all control of herself if her husband had not spent two whole hours exhorting her early that morning. When Bazarov, after repeated promises to come back within a month at the latest, tore himself at last from the embraces detaining him, and took his seat in the tarantass, when the horses started, the bell rang and the wheels were moving – and when it was no longer any use gazing after them, when the dust had settled down, and Timofeich, all bent and tottering as he walked, had crept back to his little room; when the old people were left alone in the house, which also seemed to have suddenly shrunk and grown decrepit – Vassily Ivanovich, who a few moments before had been heartily waving his handkerchief on the steps, sank into a chair and his head fell on his breast.

"He has abandoned us, cast us off!" he muttered. "Abandoned us, he only feels bored with us now. Alone, all alone, like a solitary finger," he repeated several times, stretching out his hand with the forefinger standing out from the others.

Then Arina Vlasyevna came up to him and leaning her grey head against his grey head, she said: "What can we do, Vasya? A son is a piece broken off. He's like a falcon that flies home and flies away again when it wants; but you and I are like mushrooms growing in the hollow of a tree, we sit side by side without moving from the same place. Only I will never change for you, and you will always be the same for me."

Vassily Ivanovich took his hands from his face and embraced his wife, his friend, more warmly than he had ever embraced her in his youth; she comforted him in his sorrow.

Chapter 22

In silence, only rarely exchanging a few words, our friends traveled as far as Fedot's.

Bazarov was not altogether pleased with himself, and Arkady was displeased with him. He also felt gripped by that melancholy without a cause, which only very young people experience. The coachman changed the horses and getting up on to the box, inquired: "To the right or to the left?"

Arkady shuddered. The road to the right led to the town, and from there home; the road to the left led to Madame Odintsov's place. He looked at Bazarov. "Evgeny," he asked, "to the left?"

Bazarov turned away.

"What folly is this?" he muttered.

"I know it is folly," answered Arkady. "But what harm does it do? It's not for the first time."

Bazarov pulled his cap down over his forehead. "As you like," he said at last.

"Turn to the left," shouted Arkady.

The tarantass rolled off in the direction of Nikolskoe. But having decided on committing the folly, the friends maintained an even more obstinate silence than before, and seemed positively bad tempered.

Already, by the manner in which the butler met them in the porch of Madame Odintsov's house, the friends could guess that they had acted injudiciously in giving way so suddenly to a passing caprice. They were obviously not expected. They sat for quite a long time in the drawing room with rather stupid faces. At length Madame Odintsov came in to them. She greeted them with her usual politeness, but showed surprise at their rapid return, and judging by the deliberation of her gestures and words, she was not over pleased about it. They hastened to explain that they had only called there on their way, and within four hours must continue their journey to the town. She confined herself to a mild exclamation, asked Arkady to convey her greetings to his father, and sent for her aunt. The princess appeared, looking half asleep, which gave her wrinkled old face an even more hostile expression. Katya was unwell and did not leave her room. Arkady suddenly realized that he was at least as anxious to see Katya as to see Anna Sergeyevna herself. The four hours passed in small talk about one thing or another; Anna Sergeyevna both listened and talked without smiling. It was only when they were already saying good-by that her former friendliness seemed somehow to light up again in her.

"I have an attack of spleen just now," she said, "but don't pay any attention to that, and come here again – I say that to both of you – before long."

Both Bazarov and Arkady responded with a silent bow, took their seats in the carriage, and without stopping again anywhere, drove straight home to Maryino, where they arrived safely on the evening of the following day. During the whole journey neither of them so much as mentioned the name of Madame Odintsov; Bazarov, in particular, hardly opened his mouth, and kept staring sideways at the road with a kind of embittered concentration.

At Maryino everyone was overjoyed to see them. The prolonged absence of his son had begun to make Nikolai Petrovich uneasy; he uttered a joyful exclamation and bounced up and down on the sofa, dangling his legs, when Fenichka ran in to him with sparkling eyes and announced the arrival of the "young gentlemen"; even Pavel Petrovich felt to some degree pleasantly excited, and smiled indulgently as he shook hands with the returned wanderers. Talk and questions followed quickly; Arkady talked most, especially at supper, which lasted till long after midnight. Nikolai Petrovich ordered up some bottles of porter which had just been brought from Moscow, and he himself made merry till his cheeks turned purple, laughing repeatedly with a rather childlike but nervous laughter. Even the servants were affected by the general gaiety. Dunyasha ran up and down like one possessed, slamming doors from time to time; while Pyotr at three o'clock in the morning was still trying to play a Cossack waltz on the guitar. The strings emitted their sweet and plaintive sounds in the motionless air, but except for some short preliminary flourishes the cultured valet's efforts failed to produce any tune; nature had granted him no more talent for music than it had for anything else.

But meanwhile things had not been going too well at Maryino, and poor Nikolai Petrovich was having a hard time. Every day difficulties arose on the farm – senseless, distressing difficulties. The troubles with the hired laborers had become intolerable. Some gave notice or asked for higher wages, while others walked off with wages they had received in advance; the horses fell sick; the harness was damaged as though it had been burnt; the work was carelessly done; a threshing machine ordered from Moscow turned out to be unusable because it was too heavy; another winnowing machine was ruined the very first time it was used; half the cattle sheds were burned down because a blind old woman on the farm went with a blazing firebrand in windy weather to fumigate her cow ... of course, the old woman maintained that the whole mishap was due to the master's plan of introducing new-fangled cheeses and dairy products. The bailiff suddenly turned lazy and began to grow fat as every Russian grows fat when he gets an easy living. When he caught sight of Nikolai Petrovich in the distance, he would try to demonstrate his zeal by throwing a stick at a passing pig, or by threatening some half-naked ragamuffin, but for the rest of the time he was generally asleep. The peasants who had been put on the rent system did not pay in time and stole wood from the forest; almost every night the watchmen caught peasants' horses in the farm meadows and sometimes removed them after a scrimmage. Nikolai Petrovich would fix a money fine for damages, but the matter usually ended by the horses being returned to their owners after they had been kept for a day or two on the master's forage. On top of all this the peasants began to quarrel among themselves; brothers asked for their property to be divided, their wives could not get on together in one house; suddenly a quarrel would flare up, they would all rise to their feet, as though at a given signal, would run to the porch of the estate office, and crawl in front of the master, often in a drunken state with battered faces, demanding justice and retribution; an uproar and clamor would ensue, the shrill screams of the women mingling with the curses of the men. The contending parties had to be examined, and one had to shout oneself hoarse, knowing in advance that it was in any case quite impossible to reach a just settlement. There were not enough hands for the harvest; a neighboring yeoman, in the most benevolent manner, contracted to supply him with reapers for a commission of two rubles per acre – and cheated him in the most shameless way; his peasant women demanded exorbitant prices, and meanwhile the corn got spoiled; the harvest was not in the common ownership, but at the same time the Council of Guardians issued threats and demanded immediate and full payment of interest due...

"It's beyond my power!" exclaimed Nikolai Petrovich several times in despair. "I can't flog them myself; to send for the police – is against my principles, but without the fear of punishment you can do absolutely nothing with them!"

"Du calme, du calme," Pavel Petrovich would remark on these occasions, but he hummed to himself, frowned and twisted his mustache.

Bazarov held himself aloof from all the "squabbles," and indeed as a guest it was not incumbent on him to meddle in other people's affairs. On the day after his arrival in Maryino he set to work on his frogs, his infusoria, and his chemical experiments, and spent all his time over them. Arkady, on the contrary, considered it his duty, if not to help his father, at least to create an impression of being ready to help him. He listened to him patiently and sometimes gave his advice, not that he expected it to be acted upon, but in order to show his concern. The details of agricultural management were not repugnant to him; he even indulged in pleasant dreams about agricultural work, but at this time his mind was preoccupied with other ideas. To his own surprise Arkady found he was thinking incessantly of Nikolskoe; formerly he would have just shrugged his shoulders if anyone had told him he could feel bored under the same roof as Bazarov – particularly in his own home – but now he was bored and longed to get away. He tried walking till he was tired out, but that did not help either. One day when talking to his father, he found out that Nikolai Petrovich possessed a number of quite interesting letters, written to his wife by Madame

Odintsov's mother, and Arkady gave him no peace until he had taken out the letters, for which Nikolai Petrovich was obliged to rummage in twenty different drawers and boxes. Having gained possession of these crumbling papers, Arkady somehow calmed down as if he had secured a clearer vision of the goal towards which he ought now to move. "'I say that to both of you,'" he kept on repeating to himself, "those were the words she added. I shall go there, I shall go, hang it all!" Then he recalled his last visit, the cold reception and his previous embarrassment, and shyness overwhelmed him. But the adventurous daring of youth, the secret desire to try his luck, to test his powers independently without anyone else's protection – prevailed at last. Before ten days had passed after his return to Maryino, on the pretext of going to study the organization of Sunday schools, he galloped off again to the town, and from there on to Nikolskoe.

Uninterruptedly urging the driver forward, he dashed on like a young officer riding into battle; he felt at once frightened and lighthearted and breathless with impatience. "The main thing is – I mustn't think," he kept on saying to himself. His driver happened to be a high-spirited fellow, who stopped in front of every inn and exclaimed, "A drink?" or "What about a drink?" but, to make up for that, after the drink he did not spare his horses. At length there came into sight the high roof of the familiar house ... "What shall I do?" suddenly flashed through Arkady's mind. "Anyhow, I can't turn back now!" The three horses sped gaily on;

the driver yelled and whistled at them. Already the little bridge was echoing under the wheels and the horses' hoofs, and the avenue of lopped pines was drawing nearer ... he caught a glimpse of a woman's pink dress moving among the dark green trees, and a young face peeped out from under the light fringe of a parasol ... he recognized Katya, and she recognized him. Arkady ordered the driver to stop the galloping horses, jumped out of the carriage and went up to her.

"It's you!" she murmured and slowly blushed all over; "let us go to my sister, she's here in the garden; she will be pleased to see you."

Katya led Arkady into the garden. His meeting with her struck him as a particularly happy omen; he was delighted to see her, as though she were someone close to his heart. Everything had happened so agreeably; no butler, no formal announcement. At a turn in the path he caught sight of Anna Sergeyevna. She was standing with her back to him; hearing his footsteps, she gently turned round.

Arkady would have felt embarrassed again, but the first words which she uttered immediately set him at ease. "Welcome, you runaway!" she said in her smooth caressing voice, and came forward to meet him, smiling and screwing up her eyes from the sun and breeze. "Where did you find him, Katya?"

"I have brought you something, Anna Sergeyevna," he began, "which you certainly don't expect..."

"You have brought yourself; that's better than anything else."

Chapter 23

Having seen Arkady off with ironical sympathy, and given him to understand that he was not in the least deceived about the real object of his journey, Bazarov shut himself up in solitude, and set to work with feverish intensity. He no longer argued with Pavel Petrovich, particularly since the latter assumed in his presence an oppressively aristocratic manner and expressed his opinions more by inarticulate sounds than by words. Only on one occasion Pavel Petrovich fell into a controversy with the nihilist over the then much discussed question about the rights of the nobles in the Baltic provinces, but he quickly stopped himself, remarking with a chilly politeness: "However, we cannot understand one another; I, at least, have not the honor of understanding you."

"I should think not!" exclaimed Bazarov. "A human being can understand everything – how the ether vibrates, and what's going on in the sun; but how another person can blow his nose differently from him, that he's incapable of understanding."

"What, is that a joke?" remarked Pavel Petrovich in a questioning tone and walked away.

However, he sometimes asked permission to be present at Bazarov's experiments and once even placed his perfumed face, washed with the finest soap, over the microscope, in order to see how a transparent protozoon swallowed a green speck and busily chewed it with two very adroit organs which were in its throat. Nikolai Petrovich visited Bazarov much oftener than his brother; he would have come every day "to learn," as he expressed it, if the worries of his farm had not kept him too busy. He did not interfere with the young research worker; he used to sit down in a corner of the room and watch attentively, occasionally permitting himself some discreet question. During dinner and supper he used to try to turn the conversation to physics, geology or chemistry, since all other subjects, even agriculture, to say nothing of politics, might lead, if not to collisions, at least to mutual dissatisfaction. Nikolai Petrovich guessed that his brother's dislike of Bazarov had not diminished. A minor incident, among many others, confirmed his surmise. Cholera began to break out in some places in the neighborhood, and even "carried off" two people from Maryino itself. One night Pavel Petrovich had a rather severe attack of illness. He was in pain till the morning, but he never asked for Bazarov's help; when he met him the next day, in reply to his question why he had not sent for him, he answered, still very pale, but perfectly brushed and shaved. "Surely I remember you said yourself you don't believe in medicine." So the days passed. Bazarov went on working obstinately and grimly ... and meanwhile there was in Nikolai Petrovich's house one person to whom, if he did not open his heart, he was at least glad to talk ... that person was Fenichka.

He used to meet her chiefly in the early morning, in the garden or the farmyard; he never went to see her in her room and she had only once come to his door to inquire – should she give Mitya his bath or not? She not only had confidence in him and was not afraid of him, she felt freer and more at ease with him than she did with Nikolai Petrovich himself. It is hard to say how this came about; perhaps because unconsciously she felt in Bazarov the absence of anything aristocratic, of all that superiority which at once attracts and overawes. In her eyes he was both an excellent doctor and a simple man. She attended to her baby in his presence without any embarrassment, and once when she was suddenly overcome by giddiness and headache she took a spoonful of medicine from his hands. When Nikolai Petrovich was there she kept Bazarov somehow at a distance; she did this not out of hypocrisy but from a definite sense of propriety. Of Pavel Petrovich she was more afraid than ever; for some time he had begun to watch her, and would suddenly appear, as if he had sprung out of the earth behind her back, in his English suit with an impassive vigilant face and with his hands in his pockets.

"It's like having cold water thrown over one," said Fenichka to Dunyasha, who sighed in response and thought of another "heartless" man. Bazarov, without the faintest suspicion of the fact, had become the "cruel tyrant" of her heart.

Fenichka liked Bazarov, and he liked her also. His face was even transformed when he talked to her; it took on an open kindly expression, and his habitual nonchalance was modified by a kind of jocular attentiveness. Fenichka was growing prettier every day. There is a period in the life of young women when they suddenly begin to expand and blossom like summer roses; such a time had come for Fenichka. Everything contributed to it, even the June heat which was then at its height. Dressed in a light white dress, she seemed herself whiter and more graceful; the sun had not tanned her skin; but the heat, from which she could not protect herself, spread a slight flush over her cheeks and ears and a gentle languor through her whole body, reflected in the dreamy expression of her charming eyes. She was almost unable to work and kept on sighing and complaining with a comic helplessness.

"You should go oftener to bathe," Nikolai Petrovich told her. He had arranged a large bathing place covered with an awning in the only one of his ponds which had not yet completely dried up.

"Oh, Nikolai Petrovich! But you die before you get to the pond and on the way back you die again. You see, there's no shade in the garden."

"That's true, there's no shade," said Nikolai Petrovich, wiping his forehead.

One day at seven o'clock in the morning, Bazarov was returning from a walk and encountered Fenichka in the lilac arbor, which had long ceased to flower but was still thick with green leaves. She was sitting on the bench and had as usual thrown a white kerchief over her head; beside her lay a whole heap of red and white roses still wet with dew. He said good morning to her.

"Oh, Evgeny Vassilich!" she said and lifted the edge of her kerchief a little in order to look at him, in doing which her arm was bared to the elbow.

"What are you doing here?" said Bazarov, sitting down beside her. "Are you making a bouquet?"

"Yes, for the table at lunch. Nikolai Petrovich likes it."

"But lunch is still a long way off. What a mass of flowers."

"I gathered them now, for it will be hot later on and one can't go out. Even now one can only just breathe. I feel quite weak from the heat. I'm quite afraid I may get ill."

"What an idea! Let me feel your pulse."

Bazarov took her hand, felt for the evenly throbbing pulse but did not even start to count its beats.

"You'll live a hundred years," he said, dropping her hand.

"Ah, God forbid!" she cried.

"But why? Don't you want a long life?"

"Well, but a hundred years! We had an old woman of eighty-five near us – and what a martyr she was! Dirty, deaf, bent, always coughing, she was only a burden to herself. What kind of a life is that?"

"So it's better to be young."

"Well, isn't it?"

"But why is it better? Tell me!"

"How can you ask why? Why, here am I, now I'm young, I can do everything – come and go and carry, and I don't need to ask anyone for anything ... What can be better?"

"But it's all the same to me, whether I'm young or old."

"How do you mean – all the same? It's impossible what you say."

"Well, judge for yourself, Fedosya Nikolayevna, what good is my youth to me? I live alone, a solitary man..."

"That always depends on you."

"It doesn't all depend on me! At least someone ought to take pity on me."

Fenichka looked sideways at Bazarov, but said nothing. "What's that book you have?" she said, after a short pause.

"That? It's a scientific book, a difficult one."

"Are you still studying? Don't you find it dull? I should think you must know everything already."

"Evidently not everything. You try to read a little of it."

"But I don't understand a word of it. Is it Russian?" asked Fenichka, taking the heavily bound book in both hands. "How thick it is!"

"Yes, it's Russian."

"All the same I shan't understand anything."

"Well and I don't want you to understand it. I want to look at you while you are reading. When you read the tip of your nose moves so nicely."

Fenichka, who had started to spell out in a low voice an article "On Creosote" she had chanced upon, laughed and threw down the book ... it slipped from the bench to the ground. "I like it too when you laugh," remarked Bazarov.

"Oh, stop!"

"I like it when you talk. It's like a little brook babbling."

Fenichka turned her head away.

"What a one you are!" she murmured, as she went on sorting out the flowers. "And how can you like listening to me? You have talked with such clever ladies."

"Ah, Fedosya Nikolayevna! Believe me, all the clever ladies in the world aren't worth your little elbow."

"There now, what will you invent next!" whispered Fenichka, clasping her hands together.

Bazarov picked up the book from the ground.

"That's a medical book. Why do you throw it away?"

"Medical?" repeated Fenichka, and turned round to him. "Do you know, ever since you gave me those drops – do you remember? – Mitya has slept so well. I really don't know how to thank you; you are so good, really."

"But actually you have to pay doctors," said Bazarov with a smile. "Doctors, you know yourself, are grasping people."

Fenichka raised her eyes which seemed still darker from the whitish reflection cast on the upper part of her face, and looked at Bazarov. She did not know whether he was joking or not.

"If you want, we shall be very glad ... I shall have to ask Nikolai Petrovich..."

"You think I want money?" interrupted Bazarov. "No, I don't want money from you."

"What then?" asked Fenichka.

"What?" repeated Bazarov. "Guess."

"As if I'm likely to guess."

"Well, I will tell you; I want – one of those roses." Fenichka laughed again and even threw up her hands – so amused she was by Bazarov's request. She laughed and at the same time she felt flattered. Bazarov was watching her intently. "By all means," she said at length, and bending over the bench she began to pick out some roses. "Which will you have – a red or a white one?"

"Red, and not too large."

She sat up again. "Here, take it," she said, but at once drew back her outstretched hand, and biting her lips, looked towards the entrance of the summerhouse and then listened.

"What is it?" asked Bazarov. "Nikolai Petrovich?"

"No – he has gone to the fields ... and I'm not afraid of him ... but Pavel Petrovich ... I fancied."

"What?"

"It seemed to me he was passing by. No ... it was no one. Take it." Fenichka gave Bazarov the rose.

"What makes you afraid of Pavel Petrovich?"

"He always frightens me. One talks – and he says nothing, but just looks knowing. Of course, you don't like him either. You remember you were always quarreling with him. I don't know what you quarreled about, but I can see you turning him this way and that..."

Fenichka showed with her hands how in her opinion Bazarov turned Pavel Petrovich round about.

Bazarov smiled. "And if he defeated me," he asked, "would you stand up for me?"

"How could I stand up for you? But no, one doesn't get the better of you."

"You think so? But I know a hand which, if it wanted to, could knock me down with one finger."

"What hand is that?"

"Why, don't you know really? Smell the wonderful scent of this rose you gave me."

Fenichka stretched her little neck forward and put her face close to the flower, ... The kerchief slipped from her hair on to her shoulders, disclosing a soft mass of black shining and slightly ruffled hair.

"Wait a moment; I want to smell it with you," said Bazarov; he bent down and kissed her vigorously on her parted lips.

She shuddered, pushed him back with both her hands on his breast, but pushed weakly, so that he was able to renew and prolong his kiss.

A dry cough made itself heard behind the lilac bushes. Fenichka instantly moved away to the other end of the bench. Pavel Petrovich showed himself in the entrance, bowed slightly, muttered in a tone of sorrowful anger, "You are here!" and walked away. Fenichka at once gathered up all her roses and went out of the summerhouse.

"That was wrong of you, Evgeny Vassilich," she whispered as she left; there was a tone of sincere reproach in her whisper.

Bazarov remembered another recent scene and he felt both ashamed and contemptuously annoyed. But he shook his head at once, ironically congratulated himself on his formal assumption of the rôle of a Don Juan, and went back to his own room.

Pavel Petrovich went out of the garden and made his way with slow steps to the wood. He stayed there quite a long time, and when he returned to lunch, Nikolai Petrovich inquired anxiously whether he felt unwell; his face had turned so dark.

"You know I sometimes suffer from bilious attacks," Pavel Petrovich answered calmly.

Chapter 24

Two hours later he knocked at Bazarov's door.

"I must apologize for hindering you in your scientific researches," he began, seating himself in a chair by the window and leaning with both hands on a handsome walking-stick with an ivory knob (he usually walked without a stick), "but I am obliged to ask you to spare me five minutes of your time ... no more."

"All my time is at your disposal," answered Bazarov, whose face quickly changed its expression the moment Pavel Petrovich crossed the threshold.

"Five minutes will be enough for me. I have come to put one question to you."

"A question? What about?"

"I will tell you if you will be good enough to listen to me. At the beginning of your stay in my brother's house, before I had renounced the pleasure of conversing with you, I had occasion to hear your opinion on many subjects; but as far as I can remember, neither between us, nor in my presence, was the subject of single combats or dueling discussed. Allow me to hear what are your views on that subject?"

Bazarov, who had stood up to meet Pavel Petrovich, sat down on the edge of the table and folded his arms.

"My view is," he said, "that from the theoretical point of view dueling is absurd; but from the practical point of view – well, that's quite another matter."

"So, you mean to say, if I understand you rightly, that whatever theoretical views you may hold about dueling, you would in practice not allow yourself to be insulted without demanding satisfaction?"

"You have guessed my meaning completely."

"Very good. I am very glad to hear that from you. Your words release me from a state of uncertainty."

"Of indecision, do you mean?"

"That is all the same; I express myself in order to be understood; I ... am not a seminary rat. Your words have saved me from a rather grievous necessity. I have made up my mind to fight you."

Bazarov opened his eyes wide.

"Me?"

"Undoubtedly you."

"And what for, may I ask?"

"I could explain the reason to you," began Pavel Petrovich, "but I prefer to keep silent about it. To my mind your presence here is superfluous. I find you intolerable, I despise you, and if that is not enough for you..."

Pavel Petrovich's eyes flashed ... Bazarov's too were glittering.

"Very good," he said. "Further explanations are unnecessary. You've taken it into your head to try out on me your chivalrous spirit. I could refuse you this pleasure – but it can't be helped!"

"I am sensible of my obligations to you," answered Pavel Petrovich, "and I may count then on your accepting my challenge, without compelling me to resort to violent measures?"

"That means, speaking without metaphor, to that stick?" Bazarov remarked coolly. "That is entirely correct. You have no need to insult me; indeed it would not be quite safe ... you can remain a gentleman ... I accept your challenge also like a gentleman."

"Excellent," observed Pavel Petrovich, and put his stick down in the corner. "We will say a few words now about the conditions of our duel; but I should first like to know whether you consider it necessary to resort to the formality of a trifling dispute which might serve as a pretext for my challenge?"

"No, it's better without formalities."

"I also think so. I suggest it is also inappropriate to dwell further on the real reason for our skirmish. We cannot endure one another. What more is necessary?"

"What more is necessary?" repeated Bazarov ironically. "As regards the conditions of the duel itself, since we shall have no seconds – for where could we get them?"

"Exactly, where could we get any?"

"I therefore have the honor to put the following proposals to you; we shall fight early tomorrow morning, at six, let us say, behind the plantation, with pistols, at a distance of ten paces..."

"At ten paces? That will do; we can still hate each other at that distance."

"We could make it eight," remarked Pavel Petrovich.

"We could; why not?"

"We fire twice, and to be prepared for everything, let each put a letter in his pocket, accepting responsibility for his own end."

"I don't quite agree with that," said Bazarov. "It smacks too much of a French novel, a bit unreal."

"Perhaps. You will agree, however, that it would be unpleasant to incur the suspicion of murder?"

"I agree. But there is a means of avoiding that painful accusation. We shall have no seconds, but we could have a witness."

"And who, may I ask?"

"Why, Pyotr."

"Which Pyotr?"

"Your brother's valet. He's a man standing at the height of contemporary culture, who would play his part in such an affair with all the necessary; repeated Vassily *comilfo*."

"I think you are joking, sir."

"Not in the least. If you think over my suggestion you will be convinced that it is full of common sense and simplicity. Murder will out – but I can undertake to prepare Pyotr in a suitable manner and bring him to the field of battle."

"You persist in joking," said Pavel Petrovich, getting up from his chair. "But after the courteous readiness you have shown, I have no right to claim ... so everything is arranged ... by the way, I suppose you have no pistols?"

"How should I have pistols, Pavel Petrovich? I'm not an army man."

"In that case, I offer you mine. You may rest assured that I have not shot with them for five years."

"That's a very consoling piece of news.–"

Pavel Petrovich picked up his stick ... "And now, my dear sir, it only remains for me to thank you and to leave you to your studies. I have the honor to take leave of you."

"Until we have the pleasure of meeting again, my dear sir," said Bazarov, conducting his visitor to the door.

Pavel Petrovich went out; Bazarov remained standing for a moment in front of the door, then suddenly exclaimed, "What the devil – How fine and how stupid! A pretty farce we've been acting; like trained dogs dancing on their hind legs. But it was out of the question to refuse; I really believe he would have struck me, and then..." (Bazarov turned pale at the very thought; all his pride stood up on end.) "I might have had to strangle him like a kitten." He went back to his microscope, but his heart was beating fast and the composure so essential for accurate observation had disappeared. "He saw us today," he thought, "but can it be that he would do all this on account of his brother? And how serious a matter is it – a kiss? There must be something else in it. Bah! Isn't he in love with her himself? Obviously he's in love – it's as clear as daylight. What a mess, just think ... it's a bad business!" he decided at last. "It's bad from whatever angle one looks at it. In the first place to risk a bullet through one's brain, and then in any case to go away from here; and what about Arkady ... and that good-natured creature Nikolai Petrovich? It's a bad business."

The day passed in a peculiar calm and dullness. Fenichka gave no sign of life at all; she sat in her little room like a mouse in its hole. Nikolai Petrovich had a careworn look. He had just heard that his wheat crop on which he had set high hopes had begun to show signs of blight, Pavel Petrovich overwhelmed everyone, even Prokovich, with his icy politeness. Bazarov began a letter to his father, but tore it up and threw it under the table. "If I die," he thought, "they will hear about it; but I shan't die; no, I shall struggle along in this world for a long time yet." He gave Pyotr an order to come to him on important business the next morning as soon as it was light. Pyotr imagined that Bazarov wanted to take him to Petersburg. Bazarov went to bed late, and all night long he was oppressed by disordered dreams ... Madame Odintsov kept on appearing in them; now she was his mother and she was followed by a kitten with black whiskers, and this kitten was really Fenichka; then Pavel Petrovich took the shape of a great forest, with which he had still to fight. Pyotr woke him at four o'clock; he dressed at once and went out with him.

It was a lovely fresh morning; tiny flecked clouds stood overhead like fleecy lambs in the clear blue sky; fine dewdrops lay on the leaves and grass, sparkling like silver on the spiders' webs; the damp dark earth seemed still to preserve the rosy traces of the dawn; the songs of larks poured down from all over the sky. Bazarov walked as far as the plantation, sat down in the shade at its edge and only then disclosed to Pyotr the nature of the service he expected from him. The cultured valet was mortally alarmed; but Bazarov quieted him down by the assurance that he would have nothing to do except to stand at a distance and look on, and that he would not incur any sort of responsibility. "And besides," he added, "only think what an important part you have to play." Pyotr threw up his hands, cast down his eyes, and leaned against a birch tree, looking green with terror.

The road from Maryino skirted the plantation; a light dust lay on it, untouched by wheel or foot since the previous day. Bazarov found himself staring along this road, picking and chewing a piece of grass, and he kept on repeating to himself: "What a piece of idiocy!" The morning chill made him shiver twice ... Pyotr looked at him dismally, but Bazarov only smiled; he was not frightened.

The tramp of horses' hoofs could be heard coming along the road ... A peasant came into sight from behind the trees. He was driving before him two horses hobbled together, and as he passed Bazarov he looked at him rather strangely, without removing his cap, which evidently disturbed Pyotr, as an unlucky omen.

"There's someone else up early too," thought Bazarov, "but he at least has got up for work while we..."

"It seems the gentleman is coming," whispered Pyotr suddenly.

Bazarov raised his head and caught sight of Pavel Petrovich. Dressed in a light checked coat and snow-white trousers, he was walking quickly along the road; under his arm he carried a box wrapped in green cloth.

"Excuse me, I think I have kept you waiting," he said, bowing first to Bazarov and then to Pyotr, whom he treated respectfully at that moment as representing some kind of second. "I did not want to wake up my man."

"It doesn't matter," said Bazarov. "We've only just arrived ourselves."

"Ah! so much the better!" Pavel Petrovich looked around. "There's no one in sight; no one to interfere with us ... we can proceed?"

"Let us proceed."

"You don't demand any more explanations, I suppose."

"No, I don't."

"Would you like to load?" inquired Pavel Petrovich, taking the pistols out of the box.

"No; you load, and I will measure out the paces. My legs are longer," added Bazarov with a smile. "One, two, three..."

"Evgeny Vassilich," stammered Pyotr with difficulty (he was trembling as if he had fever), "say what you like, but I am going farther off."

"Four, five ... all right, move away, my good fellow; you can even stand behind a tree and stop up your ears, only don't shut your eyes; and if anyone falls, run and pick him up. Six ... seven ... eight..." Bazarov stopped. "Is that enough?" he asked, turning to Pavel Petrovich, "or shall I add two paces more?"

"As you like," replied the latter, pressing the second bullet into the barrel.

"Well, we'll make two paces more," Bazarov drew a line on the ground with the toe of his boot. "There's the barrier. By the way, how many paces may each of us go back from the barrier? That's an important question too. It was not discussed yesterday."

"I suppose, ten," replied Pavel Petrovich, handing Bazarov both pistols. "Will you be so good as to choose?"

"I will be so good. But you must admit, Pavel Petrovich, that our duel is unusual to the point of absurdity. Only look at the face of our second."

"You are disposed to laugh at everything," answered Pavel Petrovich. "I don't deny the strangeness of our duel, but I think it is my duty to warn you that I intend to fight seriously. *A bon entendeur, salut!*"

"Oh! I don't doubt that we've made up our minds to do away with each other; but why not laugh and unite *utile dulci?* So you can talk to me in French and I'll reply in Latin."

"I intend to fight seriously," repeated Pavel Petrovich and he walked off to his place. Bazarov on his side counted off ten paces from the barrier and stood still.

"Are you ready?" asked Pavel Petrovich.

"Perfectly."

"We can approach each other."

Bazarov moved slowly forward and Pavel Petrovich walked towards him, his left hand thrust in his pocket, gradually raising the muzzle of his pistol ... "He's aiming straight at my nose," thought Bazarov, "and how carefully he screws up his eyes, the scoundrel! Not an agreeable sensation. I'd better look at his watch-chain." Something whizzed by sharply close to Bazarov's ear, and a shot rang out at that moment. "I heard it, so it must be all right," managed to flash through Bazarov's brain. He took one more step, and without taking aim, pressed the trigger.

Pavel Petrovich swayed slightly and clutched at his thigh. A thin stream of blood began to trickle down his white trousers.

Bazarov threw his pistol aside and went up to his antagonist. "Are you wounded?" he asked.

"You had the right to call me up to the barrier," said Pavel Petrovich. "This is a trifle. According to our agreement, each of us has the right to one more shot."

"Well, but excuse me, we'll leave that to another time," answered Bazarov, and caught hold of Pavel Petrovich, who was beginning to turn pale. "Now I'm no longer a duelist but a doctor, and first of all I must have a look at your wound. Pyotr! Come here, Pyotr! Where have you hidden yourself?"

"What nonsense ... I need help from nobody," said Pavel Petrovich jerkily, "and – we must – again..." He tried to pull at his mustache, but his hand failed him, his eyes grew dim, and he fainted.

"Here's a pretty pass. A fainting-fit! What next!" Bazarov exclaimed involuntarily as he laid Pavel Petrovich on the grass. "Let's see what is wrong." He pulled out a handkerchief, wiped away the blood, and began to feel around the wound ... "The bone's not touched," he muttered through his teeth, "the bullet didn't go deep; only one muscle *vastus externus* grazed. He'll be dancing about in three weeks. Fainting! Oh these nervous people! Fancy, what a delicate skin."

"Is he killed?" whispered the trembling voice of Pyotr behind his back.

Bazarov looked round.

"Go for some water quickly, my good fellow, and he'll outlive you and me yet."

But the perfect servant failed apparently to understand his words and did not move from the spot. Pavel Petrovich slowly opened his eyes. "He's dying," murmured Pyotr and started crossing himself. "You are right ... what an idiotic face!" remarked the wounded gentleman with a forced smile.

"Go and fetch the water, damn you!" shouted Bazarov.

"There's no need ... it was a momentary vertigo. Help me to sit up ... there, that's right ... I only need something to bind up this scratch, and I can reach home on foot, or else you can send for a droshky for me. The duel, if you agree, need not be renewed. You have behaved honorably ... today, today – take note."

"There's no need to recall the past," answered Bazarov, "and as regards the future, it's not worth breaking your head about that either, for I intend to move off from here immediately. Let me bind up your leg now; your wound – is not dangerous, but it's always better to stop the bleeding. But first I must bring this corpse to his senses."

Bazarov shook Pyotr by the collar and sent him off to fetch a droshky.

"Mind you don't frighten my brother," Pavel Petrovich said to him; "don't inform him on any account."

Pyotr dashed off, and while he was running for a droshky, the two antagonists sat on the ground in silence. Pavel Petrovich tried not to look at Bazarov; he did not want to be reconciled to him in any case; he felt ashamed of his own arrogance, of his failure; he was ashamed of the whole affair he had arranged even though he realized it could not have ended more auspiciously. "At least he won't go on hanging around here," he consoled himself by thinking: "one should be thankful even for that." The prolonged silence was oppressive and awkward. Both of them felt ill at ease; each was conscious that the other understood him. For friends such a feeling is agreeable, but for those who are not friends it is most unpleasant, especially when it is impossible either to come to an understanding or to separate.

"Haven't I bound up your leg too tight?" asked Bazarov at last.

"No, not at all, it's excellent," answered Pavel Petrovich, and added after a pause, "we can't deceive my brother, he will have to be told that we quarreled about politics."

"Very good," said Bazarov. "You can say that I cursed all Anglomaniacs."

"All right. What do you suppose that man thinks about us now?" continued Pavel Petrovich, pointing at the same peasant who had driven the hobbled horses past Bazarov a few minutes before the duel, and who was now going back again along the same road and took off his cap at the sight of the "masters."

"Who knows him!" answered Bazarov. "Most likely of all he thinks about nothing. The Russian peasant is that mysterious unknown person about whom Mrs. Radcliffe used to say so much. Who can understand him? He doesn't understand himself."

"Ah, so that's what you think," Pavel Petrovich began, then suddenly exclaimed, "Look what your fool of a Pyotr has done! Here's my brother galloping towards us."

Bazarov turned round and saw Nikolai Petrovich sitting in a droshky, his face pale. He jumped out before it had stopped and ran up to his brother.

"What does this mean?" he called out in an agitated voice. "Evgeny Vassilich, what is this?"

"Nothing," answered Pavel Petrovich, "they have alarmed you quite unnecessarily. We had a little dispute, Mr. Bazarov and I – and I have had to pay for it a little."

"But for heaven's sake, what was it all about?"

"How shall I explain? Mr. Bazarov alluded disrespectfully to Sir Robert Peel. I hasten to add that I am the only person to blame in all this, and Mr. Bazarov has behaved honorably. I challenged him."

"But you're covered with blood!"

"Well, did you suppose I had water in my veins? But this bloodletting positively does me good. Isn't that so, doctor? Help me to get into the droshky and don't give way to gloomy thoughts. I shall be quite well tomorrow. That's it; excellent. Drive off, coachman."

Nikolai Petrovich followed the droshky on foot. Bazarov lagged behind ...

"I must ask you to look after my brother," Nikolai Petrovich said to him, "until we get another doctor from the town."

Bazarov nodded his head without speaking. An hour later Pavel Petrovich was already lying in bed with a skillfully bandaged leg. The whole house was upset; Fenichka felt ill; Nikolai Petrovich was silently wringing his hands, while Pavel Petrovich laughed and joked, especially with Bazarov; he had put on a fine cambric nightshirt, an elegant morning jacket, and a fez; he did not allow the blinds to be drawn down, and humorously complained about the necessity of not being allowed to eat.

Towards night, however, he grew feverish; his head ached. The doctor arrived from the town. (Nikolai Petrovich would not listen to his brother, nor did Bazarov want him to; he sat the whole day in his room, looking yellow and angry, and only went in to the invalid for as brief a visit as possible; twice he happened to meet Fenichka, but she shrank away from him in horror.) The new doctor advised a cooling diet; he confirmed, however, Bazarov's assurance that there was no danger. Nikolai Petrovich told him that his brother had hurt himself accidentally, to which the doctor replied "Hm!" but on having twenty-five silver rubles slipped into his hand on the spot, he remarked, "You don't say so! Well, such things often happen, of course."

No one in the house went to bed or undressed. Nikolai Petrovich from time to time went in on tiptoe to his brother's room and tiptoed out again; Pavel Petrovich dozed, sighed a little, told his brother in French *"Couchez-vous,"* and asked for something to drink. Nikolai Petrovich sent Fenichka in to him once with a glass of lemonade; Pavel Petrovich looked at her intently and drank off the glass to the last drop. Towards morning the fever had increased a little; a slight delirium started. At first Pavel Petrovich uttered incoherent words; then suddenly he opened his eyes, and seeing his brother beside his bed, anxiously leaning over him, he murmured, "Don't you think, Nikolai, Fenichka has something in common with Nellie?"

"What Nellie, Pavel dear?"

"How can you ask that? With Princess R . Especially in the upper part of the face. *C'est de la même famille.*"

Nikolai Petrovich made no answer, but inwardly he marveled at the persistent vitality of old passions in a man. "This is what happens when it comes to the surface," he thought.

"Ah, how I love that empty creature!" groaned Pavel Petrovich, mournfully clasping his hands behind his head. "I can't bear that any insolent upstart should dare to touch..." he muttered a few minutes later.

Nikolai Petrovich only sighed; he never even suspected to whom these words referred.

Bazarov came to see him on the following day at eight o'clock. He had already managed to pack and had set free all his frogs, insects and birds.

"You have come to say good-by to me?" said Nikolai Petrovich, getting up to meet him.

"Exactly."

"I understand and fully approve of you. My poor brother is of course to blame; but he has been punished for it. He told me that he made it impossible for you to act otherwise. I believe that you could not avoid this duel, which ... which to some extent is explained by the almost constant antagonism of your different points of view." (Nikolai Petrovich began to get rather mixed up in his words.) "My brother is a man of the old school, hot-tempered and obstinate ... thank God that it has only ended in this way. I have taken all possible precautions to avoid publicity."

"I'll leave you my address, in case there's any fuss," said Bazarov casually.

"I hope there will be no fuss, Evgeny Vassilich ... I am very sorry that your stay in my house should have come to ... such an end. It distresses me all the more on account of Arkady's..."

"I expect I shall see him," replied Bazarov, in whom every kind of "explanation" and "pronouncement" always aroused a feeling of impatience. "In case I don't, may I ask you to say good-by to him for me and to accept the expression of my regret."

"And I, too, ask..." began Nikolai Petrovich with a bow. But Bazarov did not wait for him to finish his sentence and went out of the room.

On hearing that Bazarov was going, Pavel Petrovich expressed a desire to see him and shook him by the hand. But even then Bazarov remained as cold as ice; he realized that Pavel Petrovich wanted to display magnanimity. He found no opportunity of saying goodby to Fenichka; he only exchanged glances with her from the window. Her face struck him by its sad look. "She'll come to grief, probably," he said to himself, "though she may pull through somehow!"

Pyotr, however, was so overcome that he wept on his shoulder, until Bazarov cooled him down by asking if he had a constant water supply in his eyes; and Dunyasha felt obliged to run away into the plantation to hide her emotion. The originator of all this distress climbed into a country cart, lit a cigar, and when, three miles further on at a bend in the road, he saw for the last time the Kirsanovs' farmstead and its new manor house standing together on the sky line, he merely spat and muttering, "Damned noblemen," wrapped himself more tightly in his cloak.

Pavel Petrovich was soon better; but he had to lie in bed for about a week. He bore his captivity, as he called it, fairly patiently, though he took great trouble over his toilet and had everything scented with eau de Cologne. Nikolai Petrovich read papers to him; Fenichka waited on him as before, brought him soup, lemonade, boiled eggs and tea; but a secret dread seized her every time she came into his room. Pavel Petrovich's unexpected action had alarmed everyone in the house, and her most of all; Prokovich was the only person not troubled by it, and he discoursed on how gentlemen used to fight in his day only with real gentlemen, but such low scoundrels they would have ordered to be horsewhipped in the stables for their insolence.

Fenichka's conscience scarcely reproached her, but she was tormented at times by the thought of the real cause of the quarrel; and Pavel Petrovich, too, looked at her so strangely ... so that even when her back was turned she felt his eyes fixed on her. She grew thinner from constant inward agitation and, as it happened, became still more charming.

One day – the incident took place in the early morning – Pavel Petrovich felt better and moved from his bed to the sofa, while Nikolai Petrovich, having previously made inquiries about his brother's health, went off to the threshing floor. Fenichka brought him a cup of tea, and setting it down on a little table, was about to withdraw, Pavel Petrovich detained her.

"Where are you going in such a hurry, Fedosya Nikolayevna," he began, "are you so busy?"

"No ... yes, I have to pour out tea."

"Dunyasha will do that without you; sit down for a little while with an invalid. By the way, I must have a talk with you."

Fenichka sat down on the edge of an arm-chair without speaking.

"Listen," said Pavel Petrovich, pulling at his mustache, "I have wanted to ask you for a long time; you seem somehow afraid of me."

"I...?"

"Yes, you. You never look me in the face, as if your conscience were not clear."

Fenichka blushed but looked up at Pavel Petrovich. He seemed so strange to her and her heart began quietly throbbing. "Surely you have a clear conscience?" he asked her.

"Why should it not be clear?" she whispered.

"Why indeed. Besides, whom could you have wronged? Me? That is unlikely. Any other people living in the house? That is also a fantastic idea. Could it be my brother? But surely you love him?"

"I love him."

"With your whole soul, with your whole heart?"

"I love Nikolai Petrovich with my whole heart."

"Truly? Look at me, Fenichka." (He called her by that name for the first time.) ... "You know, it is a great sin to tell lies!"

"I am not lying, Pavel Petrovich. If I did not love Nikolai Petrovich, there would be no point in my living any longer."

"And you will never give him up for anyone else?"

"For whom else could I give him up?"

"For whom indeed! Well, what about that gentleman who has just gone away from here?"

Fenichka got up.

"My God, Pavel Petrovich, why are you torturing me? What have I done to you? How can you say such things?"

"Fenichka," said Pavel Petrovich in a sad voice, "you know I saw..."

"What did you see?"

"Well, there ... in the summerhouse."

Fenichka blushed to the roots of her hair and to her ears. "How can I be blamed for that?" she pronounced with an effort.

Pavel Petrovich raised himself up. "You were not to blame? No? Not at all?"

"I love Nikolai Petrovich and no one else in the world and I shall always love him!" cried Fenichka with sudden force, while sobs rose in her throat. "As for what you saw, I will say on the dreadful day of last judgment that I am innocent of any blame for it and always was, and I would rather die at once if people can suspect me of any such thing against my benefactor, Nikolai Petrovich..."

But here her voice failed, and at the same moment she felt that Pavel Petrovich was seizing and pressing her hand ... She looked at him and was almost petrified. He had turned even paler than before; his eyes were shining, and most surprising of all – one large solitary tear was rolling down his cheek. "Fenichka!" he said in a strange whisper. "Love him, love my brother! He is such a good kind man. Don't give him up for anyone, don't listen to anyone else's talk. Only think, what can be more terrible than to love and not to be loved in return. Never leave my poor Nikolai!" Fenichka's eyes were dry and her fright had vanished – so great was her amazement. But what were her feelings when Pavel Petrovich, Pavel Petrovich of all people, pressed her hand to his lips and seemed to pierce into it without kissing it, only breathing convulsively from time to time...

"Good heavens!" she thought, "is he suffering from some attack?"

At that moment his whole ruined life stirred within him.

The staircase creaked under rapidly approaching footsteps.... He pushed her away from him and let his head drop back on the pillow. The door opened, and Nikolai Petrovich came in, looking cheerful, fresh and ruddy. Mitya, just as fresh and rosy as his father, with nothing but his little shirt on, was frisking about in his arms, snatching with bare little toes at the buttons of his rough country coat.

Fenichka simply flung herself upon him and clasping him and her son together in her arms, dropped her head on his shoulder. Nikolai Petrovich was astonished; Fenichka, so shy and modest, never demonstrated her feelings for him in front of a third person.

"What's the matter?" he said, and glancing at his brother he handed Mitya to her. "You don't feel worse?" he asked, going up to Pavel Petrovich, who buried his face in a cambric handkerchief.

"No ... not at all ... on the contrary, I am much better."

"You shouldn't have been in such a hurry to move to the sofa. Where are you going?" added Nikolai Petrovich, turning towards Fenichka, but she had already closed the door behind her. "I was bringing my young hero in to show you; he has been crying for his uncle. Why did she carry him off? What's wrong with you, though? Has anything happened between you?"

"Brother!" said Pavel Petrovich gravely. "Give me your word to carry out my one request."

"What request, tell me."

"It is very important; it seems to me the whole happiness of your life depends on it. I have been thinking a lot all this time about what I want to say to you now ... Brother, do your duty, the duty of an honest and generous man, put an end to the scandal and the bad example you are setting – you, the best of men!"

"What do you mean, Pavel?"

"Marry Fenichka ... she loves you; she is – the mother of your son."

Nikolai Petrovich moved a step backwards and threw up his hands. "You say that, Pavel? You, whom I always took for the most relentless opponent of such marriages! You say that! But don't you know that it was only out of respect for you that I have not done what you rightly called my duty!"

"Your respect for me was quite mistaken in this case," said Pavel Petrovich with a weary smile. "I begin to think that Bazarov was right when he accused me of being an aristocratic snob. No, dear brother, let us stop worrying ourselves about the opinion of the outside world; we are elderly humble people by now; it's high time we laid aside all these empty vanities. We must do our duty, just as you say, and maybe we shall find happiness that way in addition."

Nikolai Petrovich rushed over to embrace his brother. "You have really opened my eyes," he exclaimed. "I was right in always maintaining that you are the kindest and wisest man in the world, and now I see you are just as reasonable as you are generous-minded."

"Softly, softly," Pavel Petrovich interrupted him. "Don't knock the leg of your reasonable brother who at close on fifty has been fighting a duel like a young lieutenant. So, then, the matter is settled; Fenichka is to be my ... *belle-soeur*."

"My darling Pavel! But what will Arkady say?"

"Arkady? He'll be enthusiastic, of course! Marriage is not a principle for him, but on the other hand his sentiment of equality will be gratified. Yes, and after all what is the good of caste divisions *au dix-neuvième siècle?*"

"Ah, Pavel, Pavel! let me kiss you once more! Don't be afraid, I'll be careful."

The brothers embraced each other.

"What do you think, shouldn't you tell her straight away what you intend to do?"

"Why should we hurry?" answered Nikolai Petrovich. "Did you have a conversation with her?"

"A conversation, between us? *Quelle idée!*"

"Well, that's all right. First of all, you must get well; it won't run away from us, and meanwhile we must think it over and consider..."

"But surely you have made up your mind?"

"Of course I have, and I thank you from the bottom of my heart. I will leave you now; you must rest; any excitement is bad for you ... But we will talk it over another time. Go to sleep, my dear, and God grant you good health!"

"Why does he thank me like that?" thought Pavel Petrovich, when he was left alone. "As if it did not depend on himself! Then as soon as he marries I will go away somewhere, far from here, to Dresden or Florence, and I will live there till I expire." Pavel Petrovich moistened his forehead with eau de Cologne and closed his eyes. Lit up by the brilliant daylight, his beautiful emaciated head lay on the white pillow like the head of a dead man ... And indeed he was a dead man.

Chapter 25

At Nikolskoe Katya and Arkady were sitting in the garden on a turf seat in the shade of a tall ash tree; Fifi had placed herself on the ground near them, giving her long body that graceful curve which is known among sportsmen as the "hare's bend." Both Arkady and Katya were silent; he held in his hands a half-open book, while she was picking out of a basket some remaining crumbs of white bread and throwing them to the small family of sparrows which with their peculiar cowardly impudence were chirping and hopping around right up to her feet. A faint breeze, stirring the ash leaves, kept gently moving pale gold patches of sunlight up and down across the shady path and over Fifi's back; an unbroken shadow fell on Arkady and Katya; only from time to time a bright streak gleamed in her hair. Both were silent, but the way in which they were silent and sitting together indicated a certain confidential friendliness; each of them seemed not to be thinking of the other, while secretly rejoicing at each other's presence. Their faces, too, had changed since we saw them last; Arkady seemed more composed and Katya brighter and more self-confident.

"Don't you think," began Arkady, "that the ash has been very well named in Russian *Yasen;* not a single other tree is so light and translucently clear *(yasno)* against the sky."

Katya raised her eyes upwards and murmured, "Yes," and Arkady thought, "Well, she doesn't reproach me for talking poetically."

"I don't care for Heine," said Katya, glancing at the book which Arkady held in his hands, "either when he laughs or when he weeps. I like him when he is thoughtful and sad."

"And I like him when he laughs," remarked Arkady.

"Those are the relics of your old satirical tendency." ("Relics," thought Arkady. "If Bazarov could have heard that!") "Wait a bit; we shall transform you."

"Who will transform me? You?"

"Who? My sister, Porfiry Platonovich, whom you've stopped quarreling with, my aunt, whom you escorted to church the day before yesterday."

"Well, I couldn't refuse. But, as for Anna Sergeyevna, you remember she agreed with Evgeny in a great many things."

"My sister was under his influence then, just as you were."

"As I was! Have you noticed that I've already shaken off his influence?"

Katya remained silent.

"I know," continued Arkady, "you never liked him."

"I'm unable to judge him."

"Do you know, Katerina Sergeyevna, every time I hear that answer, I don't believe it ... there is no one beyond the capacity of judgment of any of us! That is just a pretext for getting out of it."

"Well, I'll tell you then, he is ... not because I don't like him, but I feel he is quite alien to me, and I am alien to him ... and you too are alien to him."

"Why is that?"

"How can I tell you? He's a wild beast, while we are both domestic animals."

"And am I a domestic animal?"

Katya nodded her head.

Arkady scratched his ear. "Listen, Katerina Sergeyevna, surely that is in the nature of an insult."

"Why, would you rather be wild?"

"Not wild, but powerful, energetic."

"It's no good wishing to be that ... your friend, you see, doesn't wish for it, but he has it."

"Hm! So you suppose he had a great influence on Anna Sergeyevna?"

"Yes. But no one can keep the upper hand of her for long," added Katya in a low voice.

"Why do you think that?"

"She's very proud ... I didn't mean to say that ... she values her independence very much."

"Who doesn't value it?" asked Arkady, and the thought flashed through his mind: "What is it for?" The same thought occurred to Katya. Young people who are friendly and often together constantly find themselves thinking the same thoughts.

Arkady smiled and, coming a little closer to Katya, he said in a whisper: "Confess, you are a little afraid of her."

"Of whom?"

"Of her," repeated Arkady significantly.

"And how about you?" asked Katya in her turn.

"I am also. Please note I said, I am *also.*"

Katya wagged her finger at him threateningly.

"I wonder at that," she began; "my sister has never felt so friendly towards you as just now; much more than when you first came here."

"Fancy that!"

"And you haven't noticed it? Aren't you glad about it?"

Arkady became thoughtful.

"How have I succeeded in winning Anna Sergeyevna's favor? Could it be because I brought her your mother's letters?"

"Both for that and for other reasons which I won't tell you."

"Why?"

"I shan't say."

"Oh, I know, you're very obstinate."

"Yes, I am."

"And observant."

Katya cast a sidelong glance at Arkady. "Perhaps so; does that annoy you? What are you thinking about?"

"I'm wondering how you have grown to be so observant as you certainly are. You are so shy and distrustful; you keep everyone at a distance…"

"I live so much alone; that in itself leads to thoughtfulness. But do I keep everyone at a distance?"

Arkady flung a grateful glance at Katya.

"That's all very well," he went on; "but people in your position – I mean with your fortune, seldom possess that gift; it is hard for them, as it is for emperors, to get at the truth."

"But, you see, I am not rich."

Arkady was surprised and did not at once understand Katya. "Why, as a matter of fact, the property is all her sister's!" struck him suddenly; the thought was not disagreeable to him.

"How nicely you said that," he remarked.

"What?"

"You said it nicely, simply, without either being ashamed or making much of it. By the way, I imagine there must always be something special, a kind of pride in the feeling of a person who knows and says that he is poor."

"I have never experienced anything of that sort, thanks to my sister. I referred to my position just now only because it happened to come up in our conversation."

"Well, but you must admit that even you have something of that pride I spoke of just now."

"For instance?"

"For instance, surely you – excuse my question – you wouldn't be willing to marry a rich man?"

"If I loved him very much ... no, probably even then I wouldn't marry him."

"There, you see!" cried Arkady, and after a moment's pause he added, "And why wouldn't you marry him?"

"Because even in the ballads unequal matches are always unlucky."

"Perhaps you want to dominate, or..."

"Oh, no! What's the good of that? On the contrary, I'm ready to obey; only inequality is difficult. But to keep one's self-respect and to obey – that I can understand; that is happiness; but a subordinate existence ... no, I've had enough of that as it is."

"Had enough of that," repeated Arkady after Katya. "You're not Anna Sergeyevna's sister for nothing; you're just as independent as she is; but you're more reserved. I'm sure you would never be the first to express your feelings, however strong or sacred..."

"Well, what would you expect?" asked Katya.

"You are equally intelligent; you have as much character, if not more, than she..."

"Don't compare me with my sister, please," interrupted Katya hurriedly; "it puts me too much at a disadvantage. You seem to forget that my sister is beautiful and clever and ... you in particular, Arkady Nikolaich, ought not to say such things and with such a serious face too."

"What does that mean? 'You in particular.' And what makes you conclude that I'm joking?"

"Of course you're joking."

"Do you think so? But what if I'm convinced of what I say? If I find that I've not even put it strongly enough?"

"I don't understand you."

"Really? Well, now I see that I certainly overestimated your powers of observation."

"How is that?"

Arkady made no answer and turned away, but Katya searched for a few more crumbs in the basket and began throwing them to the sparrows; but she moved her arm too vigorously and the birds flew away without stopping to pick them up.

"Katerina Sergeyevna," began Arkady suddenly, "it is probably a matter of indifference to you; but you should know, I would not exchange you, neither for your sister, nor for anyone else in the world."

He got up and walked quickly away, as if he were frightened by the words which had burst from his lips.

Katya let her two hands drop together with the basket, on to her knees, and with bowed head she gazed for some time after Arkady. Gradually a crimson flush spread a little to her cheeks, but her lips did not smile, and her dark eyes had a look of perplexity and of some other still undefined feeling.

"Are you alone?" sounded the voice of Anna Sergeyevna, quite close to her. "I thought you came into the garden with Arkady."

Katya slowly raised her eyes to her sister (elegantly, almost elaborately dressed, she was standing on the path and tickling Fifi's ears with the tip of her parasol) and slowly answered, "I'm alone."

"So I see," answered the other sister with a laugh. "I suppose he has gone back to his room."

"Yes."

"Were you reading together?"

"Yes."

Anna Sergeyevna took Katya under the chin and raised her face.

"You didn't quarrel, I hope."

"No," said Katya, quietly moving away her sister's hand.

"How solemnly you answer. I thought I should find him here and was going to suggest a walk with him. He keeps on asking me about it. They have brought your new shoes from the town; go and try them on; I noticed yesterday that your old ones are quite worn out. Really you don't pay enough attention to these things; but all the same you've got such lovely little feet! And your hands are good ... only rather large; so you must make the most of your feet. But you're not a flirt."

Anna Sergeyevna went farther down the path, her beautiful dress rustling slightly as she walked.

Katya rose from the bench, and taking Heine with her, also went off – only not to try on the new shoes.

"Lovely little feet," she thought, as she slowly and lightly mounted the stone steps of the terrace which were burning from the heat of the sun. "Lovely little feet, you call them ... Well, he shall be at my feet."

But a feeling of shame came over her at once, and she ran swiftly upstairs.

Arkady was going along the passage to his room when he was overtaken by the butler, who announced that Mr. Bazarov was sitting in his room.

"Evgeny!" muttered Arkady in a startled tone. "Has he been here long?"

"He has arrived only this minute, and gave orders not to be announced to Anna Sergeyevna but to be shown straight up to you."

"Can any misfortune have happened at home?" thought Arkady, and running hurriedly up the stairs he opened the door at once. The sight of Bazarov immediately reassured him, though a more experienced eye would probably have discerned signs of inward excitement in the sunken but still energetic face of the unexpected visitor. With a dusty cloak over his shoulders, and a cap on his head, he was sitting by the window; he did not even get up when Arkady flung himself on his neck with loud exclamations.

"Well, how unexpected! What good luck has brought you?" he kept on repeating, bustling about the room like someone who both imagines and wants to show that he is pleased. "I suppose everything is all right at home; they're all well, aren't they?"

"Everything is all right there, but not everyone is well," said Bazarov. "But don't go on chattering, get them to bring me some kvass, sit down and listen to what I'm going to tell you, in a few, but, I hope, fairly vigorous sentences."

Arkady kept quiet while Bazarov told him about his duel with Pavel Petrovich. Arkady was greatly surprised and even upset, but he did not think it necessary to show this; he asked only whether his uncle's wound was really not serious, and on receiving the reply that it was – most interesting, though not from a medical point of view – he gave a forced smile, but he felt sick at heart and somehow ashamed. Bazarov seemed to understand him.

"Yes, brother," he said, "you see what comes of living with feudal people. One becomes feudal oneself and takes part in knightly tournaments. Well, so I set off for my father's place," Bazarov concluded, "and on the way I turned in here ... to tell you all this, I should say, if I didn't think it a useless and stupid lie. No, I turned in here – the devil knows why. You see it's sometimes a good thing for a man to take himself by the scruff of the neck and pull himself away, like a radish out of its bed; that's what I've just done ... But I wanted to take one more look at what I've parted company with, at the bed where I've been sitting."

"I hope that those words don't apply to me," retorted Arkady excitedly. "I hope you don't think of parting from me."

Bazarov looked at him intently; his eyes were almost piercing.

"Would that upset you so much? It strikes me that you have parted from me already; you look so fresh and smart ... your affairs with Anna Sergeyevna must be proceeding very well."

"What do you mean by my affairs with Anna Sergeyevna?"

"Why, didn't you come here from the town on her account, my little bird? By the way, how are those Sunday schools getting on? Do you mean to tell me you're not in love with her? Or have you already reached the stage of being bashful about it?"

"Evgeny, you know I've always been frank with you; I can assure you, I swear to you, you're making a mistake."

"Hm! A new story," remarked Bazarov under his breath, "but you needn't get agitated about it, for it's a matter of complete indifference to me. A romantic would say: I feel that our roads are beginning to branch out in different directions, but I will simply say that we're tired of each other."

"Evgeny..."

"There's no harm in that, my good soul; one gets tired of plenty of other things in the world! And now I think we had better say good-by. Ever since I've been here I've felt so disgusting, just as if I'd been reading Gogol's letters to the wife of the Governor of Kaluga. By the way, I didn't tell them to unharness the horses."

"Good heavens, that's impossible!"

"And why?"

"I say nothing of myself, but it would be the height of discourtesy to Anna Sergeyevna, who will certainly want to see you."

"Well, you're mistaken there."

"On the contrary, I'm convinced that I'm right," retorted Arkady. "And what are you pretending for? For that matter, haven't you come here because of her?"

"That might even be true, but you're mistaken all the same." But Arkady was right. Anna Sergeyevna wanted to see Bazarov and sent a message to him to that effect through the butler. Bazarov changed his clothes before he went to her; it turned out that he had packed his new suit in such a way as to be able to take it out easily.

Madame Odintsov received him, not in the room where he had so unexpectedly declared his love to her, but in the drawing room. She held her finger tips out to him amiably, but her face showed signs of involuntary tension.

"Anna Sergeyevna," Bazarov hastened to say, "first of all I must set your mind at rest. Before you stands a simple mortal, who came to his senses long ago, and hopes that other people too have forgotten his follies. I am going away for a long time, and though I'm by no means a soft creature, I should be sorry to carry away with me the thought that you remember me with abhorrence."

Anna Sergeyevna gave a deep sigh like one who has just climbed to the top of a high mountain, and her face lit up with a smile. She held out her hand to Bazarov a second time and responded to his pressure.

"Let bygones be bygones," she said, "all the more so, since, to say what is on my conscience, I was also to blame then, either for flirting or for something else. In a word, let us be friends as we were before. The other was a dream, wasn't it? And who remembers dreams?"

"Who remembers them? And besides, love ... surely it's an imaginary feeling."

"Indeed? I am very pleased to hear that." Anna Sergeyevna expressed herself thus and so did Bazarov; they both thought they were speaking the truth. Was the truth, the whole truth, to be found in their words? They themselves did not know, much less could the author. But a conversation ensued between them, just as if they believed one another completely.

Anna Sergeyevna asked Bazarov, among other things, what he had been doing at the Kirsanovs'. He was on the point of telling her about his duel with Pavel Petrovich, but he checked himself with the thought that she might suppose he was trying to make himself interesting, and answered that he had been working the whole time.

"And I," observed Anna Sergeyevna, "had a fit of depression to start with, goodness knows why; I even planned to go abroad, just fancy! But that passed off; your friend Arkady Nikolaich arrived, and I settled down to my routine again, to my proper function."

"And what is that function, may I ask?"

"To be an aunt, guardian, mother – call it what you like. Incidentally, do you know I used not to understand before your close friendship with Arkady Nikolaich; I found him rather insignificant. But now I have got to know him better, and I recognize his intelligence ... but he is young, so young, it's a great thing ... not like you and me, Evgeny Vassilich."

"Is he still shy in your presence?" asked Bazarov.

"But was he..." began Anna Sergeyevna, and after a short pause she went on. "He has grown more trustful now; he talks to me; formerly he used to avoid me; though, as a matter of fact, I didn't seek his society either. He is more Katya's friend."

Bazarov felt vexed. "A woman can't help being a hypocrite," he thought.

"You say he used to avoid you," he said aloud with a cold smile; "but probably it's no secret to you that he was in love with you?"

"What? He too?" ejaculated Anna Sergeyevna.

"He too," repeated Bazarov, with a submissive bow. "Can it be that you didn't know it and that I've told you something new?"

Anna Sergeyevna lowered her eyes. "You are mistaken, Evgeny Vassilich."

"I don't think so. But perhaps I ought not to have mentioned it."

"And don't you try to fool me any more," he added to himself.

"Why not mention it? But I imagine that here as well you attach too much importance to a transitory impression. I begin to suspect that you are inclined to exaggerate."

"We had better not talk about that, Anna Sergeyevna."

"And why?" she replied, but herself diverted the conversation into another channel. She still felt ill at ease with Bazarov, though she had both told and assured herself that everything was forgotten. While exchanging the simplest remarks with him, even when she joked with him, she was conscious of an embarrassed fear. Thus do people on a steamer at sea talk and laugh carelessly, for all the world as if they were on dry land; but the moment there is some hitch, if the smallest sign appears of something unusual, there emerges at once on every face an expression of peculiar alarm, revealing the constant awareness of constant danger.

Anna Sergeyevna's conversation with Bazarov did not last long. She began to be absorbed in her own thoughts, to answer absentmindedly and ended by suggesting that they should go into the hall, where they found the princess and Katya.

"But where is Arkady Nikolaich?" asked the hostess, and on hearing that he had not been seen for more than an hour, she sent someone to look for him. He was not found at once; he had hidden himself away in the wildest part of the garden, and with his chin propped on his folded hands, he was sitting wrapped in thought. His thoughts were deep and serious, but not mournful. He knew that Anna Sergeyevna was sitting alone with Bazarov, and he felt no jealousy as he had before; on the contrary, his face slowly brightened; it seemed as if he was at once wondering and rejoicing and deciding to do something.

Chapter 26

The late Odintsov had disliked innovations, but he admitted "a certain play of ennobled taste" and had consequently erected in his garden, between the hothouse and the lake, a building in the style of a Creek temple, made of Russian brick. Along the windowless back wall of this temple or gallery were placed six niches for statues, which Odintsov proceeded to order from abroad. These statues were intended to represent Solitude, Silence, Meditation, Melancholy, Modesty and Sensibility. One of them, the Goddess of Silence, with her finger on her lips, had been delivered and placed in position; but on the very same day some of the farm boys knocked off her nose, and although the neighboring plasterer undertook to make her a new nose, "twice as good as the previous one," Odintsov ordered her to be removed, and she could still be seen in the corner of the threshing barn, where she had stood for many years, a source of superstitious terror to the peasant women. The front part of the temple had long ago been overgrown with thick bushes; only the capitals of the columns could be seen above the thick green. Inside the temple itself it was cool even at midday. Anna Sergeyevna did not like visiting this place ever since she had seen a snake there; but Katya often came and sat on a wide stone seat constructed under one of the niches. Here, surrounded by shade and coolness, she used to read and work, or give herself up to that sensation of perfect peace, known probably to everyone, the charm of which consists in the half-conscious mute listening to that vast current of life which uninterruptedly flows both around us and within us.

On the day after Bazarov's arrival, Katya was sitting on her favorite stone seat, and Arkady was sitting beside her again. He had begged her to come with him to the temple.

It was about an hour before lunchtime; the dewy morning had given place to a hot day. Arkady's face retained the expression of the preceding day; Katya looked preoccupied. Her sister, immediately after their morning tea, had called her into her study, and after some preliminary caresses – which always rather alarmed Katya – advised her to be more guarded in her behavior with Arkady, and to avoid solitary talks with him, which had attracted the attention of her aunt and the household. Apart from that, Anna Sergeyevna was still in a bad mood from the evening before, and Katya herself felt embarrassed, as if she had done something wrong. When she yielded to Arkady's entreaties, she said to herself that it was for the last time.

"Katerina Sergeyevna," he began with a sort of bashful carelessness, "ever since I have had the happiness of living under the same roof with you, I have discussed many things with you, but meanwhile there is one very important question – for me – which

I have not yet touched on. You remarked yesterday that I have been transformed here," he went on, at once catching and avoiding the inquiring look which Katya fixed on him. "In fact I have changed a lot, and you know that better than anyone else – you to whom above all I owe this change."

"I...? Me...?" said Katya.

"I am no longer now the conceited boy I was when I arrived here," went on Arkady. "I've not reached the age of twenty-three for nothing; as before I want to be useful, I want to devote all my powers to the truth; but I don't look for my ideals where I used to look before; they have shown themselves to me ... so much nearer. Up till now I failed to understand myself, I set myself tasks which were beyond my strength ... My eyes have recently been opened, thanks to one feeling ... I'm not expressing myself quite clearly, but I hope you understand me..."

Katya made no reply, but she stopped looking at Arkady.

"I suppose," he began again, this time in a more agitated voice, while above his head a chaffinch sang its song heedlessly among the leaves of a birch tree, "I suppose it is the duty of every honest person to be absolutely frank with those ... with those people, who ... in a word, with those who are near to him, and so I ... I intend..."

But at this point Arkady's eloquence abandoned him; he fumbled for words, stammered and was obliged to pause for a while. Katya still did not raise her eyes. It seemed as though she did not even understand what he was leading up to with all this, as though she were awaiting something.

"I foresee that I shall surprise you," began Arkady, pulling himself together again with an effort; "all the more since this feeling is connected in a certain way – in a certain way, remember – with you. You reproached me yesterday, you remember, for a lack of seriousness," Arkady went on with the air of a person who has walked into a swamp, feels that he is sinking in deeper and deeper at every step, and yet hurries forward in the hope of crossing it quicker; "that reproach is often aimed ... often falls ... on young men even when they no longer deserve it; and if I had more self-confidence..." ("Come, help me, do help me," Arkady was thinking in desperation, but Katya kept her head averted as before.) "If I could hope..."

"If I could feel convinced of what you said," sounded at that moment the clear voice of Anna Sergeyevna.

Arkady fell silent at once and Katya turned pale. Alongside the very bushes which screened the temple ran a little path. Anna Sergeyevna was walking along it accompanied by Bazarov. Katya and Arkady could not see them, but they heard every word, the rustle of their clothes, their very breathing. They walked on a few steps and then, as if on purpose, stopped right opposite the temple.

"You see," continued Anna Sergeyevna, "you and I made a mistake; we have both passed our first youthful stage, I particularly; we have seen life, we are tired; we are both intelligent – why pretend otherwise? – at first we were interested in each other, our curiosity was aroused ... and afterwards..."

"And afterwards my interest fell flat," interposed Bazarov.

"You know that was not the cause of our misunderstanding. But however that may be, we did not need each other, that's the main thing; there was in us ... how shall I put it? ... too much of the same thing. We did not realize that straight away. Now Arkady, on the contrary..."

"Do you need him?" asked Bazarov.

"Stop, Evgeny Vassilich. You say he is not indifferent to me, and it always seemed to me that he liked me. I know that I could well be his aunt, but I don't want to conceal from you that I have begun to think about him more often. In that fresh youthful feeling there is a special charm..."

"The word *fascination* is more often used in such cases," interrupted Bazarov; a violent suppressed bitterness could be detected in the steady but hollow tone of his voice. "Arkady was secretive with me about something yesterday, and wouldn't talk about either you or your sister ... that's a serious symptom."

"He's just like a brother with Katya," remarked Anna Sergeyevna, "and I like that in him, though perhaps I ought not to have let them become so intimate."

"Is that idea prompted by your feelings ... as a sister?" said Bazarov, dragging out his words.

"Of course ... but why are we standing here? Let us go on. What a strange talk we're having, aren't we? I could never have believed I should talk to you like this. You know, I'm afraid of you ... and at the same time I trust you, because at bottom you are very good."

"In the first place, I'm far from good; and in the second place I no longer mean anything to you, and you tell me that I am good ... It's just like placing a wreath of flowers round the head of a corpse."

"Evgeny Vassilich, we are not masters..." began Anna Sergeyevna; but a gust of wind blew across, started the leaves rustling and carried away her words.

"Of course, you are free," said Bazarov after a pause. Nothing more could be distinguished; the steps went farther away ... all became quiet again.

Arkady turned to Katya. She was sitting in the same position, but her head bent still lower.

"Katerina Sergeyevna," he said; his voice shook and he clenched his hands; "I love you – forever and irrevocably, and I love no one except you. I wanted to tell you this, to find out what you will say and to ask you to marry me, because, of course, I'm not rich and I feel ready for any kind of sacrifice ... You don't answer? You don't believe me? Do you think I'm talking lightly? But remember these last days! Surely you must be convinced by now that everything else – you understand me – absolutely everything else has vanished long ago and left no trace? Look at me, say one word to me ... I love ... I love you ... believe me."

Katya turned her eyes to Arkady with a grave and radiant look, and after a long reflective pause, she murmured, smiling slightly, "Yes."

Arkady jumped up from the seat.

"Yes! You said 'yes,' Katerina Sergeyevna! What does that word mean? Just that I love you, that you believe me ... or ... I daren't go on..."

"Yes," repeated Katya, and this time he understood her. He seized her large beautiful hands and, breathless with enthusiasm, he pressed them to his heart. He could hardly stand on his feet, and only kept on repeating, "Katya, Katya..." and she began to weep in such an innocent way, smiling gently at her own tears. Whoever has not seen such tears in the eyes of a beloved person has not yet experienced to what an extent, overwhelmed with gratitude and awe, a human being may find happiness on earth.

The next day in the early morning, Anna Sergeyevna sent a message asking Bazarov to come to her study, and with a strained laugh she handed him a folded sheet of notepaper. It was a letter from Arkady, in which he asked for her sister's hand in marriage.

Bazarov quickly read through the letter, and could only with some effort conceal the malicious impulse which at once flared up within him.

"So there it is," he remarked, "and apparently you thought no longer ago than yesterday that his feelings for Katerina Sergeyevna were of the brotherly sort. What do you intend to do now?"

"What would you advise me to do?" asked Anna Sergeyevna, continuing to laugh.

"Well, I suppose," answered Bazarov, also with a laugh, though he felt anything but gay and no more wanted to laugh than she did; "I suppose you ought to give the young people your blessing. It's a good match from every point of view; Kirsanov is tolerably well off, he's the only son, and his father's a good-natured fellow; he won't object."

Madame Odintsov walked up and down the room. Her face flushed and turned pale by turns.

"You think so?" she said. "Well, I see no obstacles ... I'm glad for Katya ... and for Arkady Nikolaich. Of course, I shall wait for his father's answer. I will send him in person to him. So it turns out that I was right yesterday when I told you that we have both become old people.... How was it I noticed nothing? That surprises me."

Anna Sergeyevna laughed again and quickly turned her head away.

"The younger generation of today has grown painfully cunning," remarked Bazarov, and he also gave a short laugh. "Good-by," he began again after a short silence. "I hope you will bring this affair to the most agreeable conclusion; and I will rejoice from a distance."

Madame Odintsov turned to him quickly. "Are you going away? Why shouldn't you stay *now?* Do stay ... it's such fun talking to you ... one seems to be walking on the edge of a precipice. At first one feels timid, but one gets somehow exhilarated as one goes along. Won't you stay?"

"Thank you for the invitation, Anna Sergeyevna, and for your flattering opinion of my conversational talents. But I find I've already been moving around for too long in a sphere which is alien to me. Flying fish can hold out for a time in the air, but soon they have to splash back into the water; you must allow me too to flop down into my natural element."

Madame Odintsov looked at Bazarov. A bitter smile twisted his pale face. "This man loved me," she thought, and she felt sorry for him and held out her hand with sympathy.

But he too understood her. "No," he said, stepping back a pace. "I'm a poor man, but I've never accepted charity so far. Good-by and good luck."

"I am sure that we are not seeing each other for the last time," said Anna Sergeyevna with an unconscious movement.

"Anything can happen in this world," answered Bazarov, and he bowed and went out.

"So you propose to build yourself a nest?" he said the same day to Arkady, crouching on the floor as he packed his trunk. "Well, it's a good thing. Only you needn't have been such a humbug about it. I expected you'd go in quite a different direction. Perhaps, though, it took you unawares?"

"I certainly didn't expect this when I left you," answered Arkady; "but why are you being a humbug yourself and calling it a 'good thing,' as if I didn't know your opinion of marriage?"

"Ah, my dear friend," said Bazarov, "how you express yourself. You see what I'm doing; there happened to be an empty space in my trunk, and I'm putting hay into it; that's how it is with the luggage of our life; we would stuff it up with anything rather than leave a void. Don't be offended, please; you probably remember what I always thought of Katerina Sergeyevna. Many a young lady is called intelligent simply because she can sigh intelligently; but yours can hold her own, and indeed she'll hold it so well that she'll have you under her thumb – well, and that's quite as it should be." He slammed the lid and got up from the floor. "And now I say again, farewell ... because it's useless to deceive ourselves; we are parting forever, and you know it yourself ... you acted sensibly; you were not made for our bitter, rough, lonely existence. There's no daring in you, no hatred, though you've got youthful dash and youthful fervor; that's not enough for our business. Your sort, the nobility, can never go farther than noble resignation or noble indignation, but those things are trifles. For instance, you won't fight – and yet you fancy yourselves as brave fellows – but we want to fight. So there! Our dust would get into your eyes, our mud would soil you, but you're not up to our standard, you unconsciously admire yourselves and you enjoy finding fault with yourselves; but we're fed up with all that – we want something else! We want to smash people! You're a fine fellow, but all the same you're a mild little liberal gentleman – *ay volatoo,* as my parent would say."

"You are bidding good-by to me for ever, Evgeny," said Arkady sadly, "and you have nothing else to say to me."

Bazarov scratched the back of his head.

"Yes, Arkady, I have other things to say to you, but I won't say them, because that's romanticism – that means sentimental trash. But you hurry up and marry, settle down in your nest and have as many children as you like. They'll have the gumption to be born in a better time than you and me. Aha! I see the horses are ready. It's time to go. I've said good-by to everyone ... well, what's this? Embracing, eh?"

Arkady threw himself on the neck of his former teacher and friend, and tears fairly streamed from his eyes.

"That's what comes of being young!" remarked Bazarov calmly. "But I rely on Katerina Sergeyevna. You'll see how quickly she can console you."

"Farewell, brother," he called out to Arkady, as he was already climbing into the cart, and pointing to a pair of jackdaws, sitting side by side on the roof of the stables, he added, "There you are! Learn from the example."

"What does that mean?" asked Arkady.

"What? Are you so weak in natural history or have you forgotten that the jackdaw is a most respectable family bird! An example to you...! Good-by."

The cart creaked and rolled away.

Bazarov spoke the truth. Talking that evening with Katya, Arkady had completely forgotten about his former teacher. He had already begun to follow her lead, and Katya felt this and was not surprised. He was to set off the next day to Maryino to see Nikolai Petrovich. Anna Sergeyevna had no wish to hamper the freedom of the young people, but on account of decorum she did not leave them alone for too long. She generously kept the princess out of their way; the old lady had been reduced to a state of tearful frenzy by the news of the approaching marriage. At first Anna Sergeyevna was afraid that the sight of their happiness would prove rather upsetting to herself, but it turned out to the contrary; it not only did not upset her to see their happiness, it occupied her mind, and in the end it even soothed her heart. This outcome both gladdened and grieved Anna Sergeyevna. "Evidently Bazarov was right," she thought, "I have curiosity, nothing but curiosity, and love of a quiet life, and egoism..."

"Children," she said aloud, "do you think love is an imaginary feeling?"

But neither Katya nor Arkady even understood her. They were shy with her; the fragment of conversation which they had accidentally overheard haunted their minds. But Anna Sergeyevna soon relieved their anxieties, and that was not difficult for her; she had set her own mind at rest.

Chapter 27

Bazarov's old parents were all the more overjoyed by their son's sudden arrival on account of its complete unexpectedness. Arina Vlasyevna was so agitated, continually bustling about all over the house, that Vassily Ivanovich said she was like a partridge; the short flat tail of her little jacket certainly gave her a birdlike look. He himself made noises and bit the amber mouthpiece of his pipe, or, clutching his neck with his fingers, turned his head round, as though he were trying to find out if it was properly screwed on, then suddenly opened his wide mouth and laughed noiselessly.

"I've come to stay with you for six whole weeks, old man," Bazarov said to him. "I want to work, so please don't interrupt me."

"You will forget what my face looks like, that's how I will interrupt you!" answered Vassily Ivanovich.

He kept his promise. After installing his son in his study as before, he almost hid himself away from him and he restrained his wife from any kind of superfluous demonstration of affection. "Last time Enyushka visited us, little mother, we bored him a little; we must be wiser this time." Arina Vlasyevna agreed with her husband, but she gained nothing thereby, since she saw her son only at meals and was in the end afraid to say a word to him.

"Enyushenka," she would sometimes start to say – but before he had time to look round she would nervously finger the tassels of her handbag and murmur, "Never mind, I only...." and afterwards she would go to Vassily Ivanovich and ask him, her cheek leaning on her hand, "If only you could find out, darling, what Enyusha would like best for dinner today, beet-root soup or cabbage broth?" "But why didn't you ask him yourself?" "Oh, he'll get tired of me!" Bazarov, however, soon ceased to shut himself up; his fever for work abated and was replaced by painful boredom and a vague restlessness. A strange weariness began to show itself in all his movements; even his walk, once so firm, bold and impetuous, was changed. He gave up his solitary rambles and began to seek company; he drank tea in the drawing room, strolled about the kitchen garden with Vassily Ivanovich, smoked a pipe with him in silence and once even inquired after Father Alexei. At first Vassily Ivanovich rejoiced at this change, but his joy was short-lived.

"Enyusha is breaking my heart," he plaintively confided to his wife. "It's not that he's dissatisfied or angry – that would be almost nothing; but he's distressed, he's downcast – and that is terrible. He's always silent; if only he would start to scold us; he's growing thin, and he's lost all the color in his face."

"Lord have mercy on us!" whispered the old woman. "I would hang a charm round his neck, but of course he won't allow it."

Vassily Ivanovich tried several times in a very tactful manner to question Bazarov about his work, his health, and about Arkady ... But Bazarov's replies were reluctant and casual, and once, noticing that his father was trying gradually to lead up to something in the conversation, he remarked in a vexed tone, "Why do you always seem to be following me about on tiptoe? That way is even worse than the old one."

"Well, well, I didn't mean anything!" hurriedly answered poor Vassily Ivanovich. So his diplomatic hints remained fruitless.

One day, talking about the approaching liberation of the serfs, he hoped to arouse his son's sympathy by making some remarks about progress; but Bazarov only answered indifferently, "Yesterday I was walking along the fence and heard our peasant boys, instead of singing an old folk song, bawling some street ditty about 'the time has come for love' ... that's what your progress amounts to."

Sometimes Bazarov went into the village and in his usual bantering tone got into conversation with some peasant. "Well," he would say to him, "expound your views on life to me, brother; after all, they say the whole strength and future of Russia lies in your hands, that a new era in history will be started by you – that you will give us our real language and our laws." The peasant either answered nothing, or pronounced a few words like these, "Oh, we'll try ... also, because, you see, in our position..."

"You explain to me what your world is," Bazarov interrupted, "and is it the same world which is said to rest on three fishes?"

"No, *batyushka,* it's the land that rests on three fishes," the peasant explained soothingly in a good-natured patriarchal sing-song voice; "and over against our 'world' we know there's the master's will, because you are our fathers. And the stricter the master's rule, the better it is for the peasant."

After hearing such a reply one day, Bazarov shrugged his shoulders contemptuously and turned away, while the peasant walked homewards.

"What was he talking about?" inquired another peasant, a surly middle-aged man who from the door of his hut had witnessed at a distance the conversation with Bazarov. "Was it about arrears of taxes?"

"Arrears? No fear of that, brother," answered the first peasant, and his voice had lost every trace of the patriarchal sing-song; on the contrary, a note of scornful severity could be detected in it. "He was just chattering about something, felt like exercising his tongue. Of course, he's a gentleman. What can he understand?"

"How could he understand!" answered the other peasant, and pushing back their caps and loosening their belts they both started discussing their affairs and their needs. Alas! Bazarov, shrugging his shoulders contemptuously, he who knew how to talk to the peasants (as he had boasted in his dispute with Pavel Petrovich), the self-confident Bazarov did not for a moment suspect that in their eyes he was all the same a kind of buffoon....

However, he found an occupation for himself at last. One day Vassily Ivanovich was bandaging a peasant's injured leg in his presence, but the old man's hands trembled and he could not manage the bandages; his son helped him and from that time regularly took part in his father's practice, though without ceasing to joke both about the remedies he himself advised and about his father, who immediately applied them. But Bazarov's gibes did not upset Vassily Ivanovich in the least; they even comforted him. Holding his greasy dressing gown with two fingers over his stomach and smoking his pipe, he listened to Bazarov with enjoyment, and the more malicious his sallies, the more good-humoredly did his delighted father chuckle, showing all his discolored black teeth. He even used to repeat these often blunt or pointless witticisms, and for instance, with no reason at all, went on saying for several days, "Well, that's a far away business," simply because his son, on hearing that he was going to the early church service, had used that expression. "Thank God, he has got over his melancholy," he whispered to his wife. "How he went for me today, it was marvelous!" Besides, the idea of having such an assistant filled him with enthusiasm and pride. "Yes, yes," he said to a peasant woman wearing a man's cloak and a horn-shaped hood, as he handed her a bottle of Goulard's extract or a pot of white ointment, "you, my dear, ought to be thanking God every minute that my son is staying with me; you will be treated now by the most up-to-date scientific methods; do you know what that means? The Emperor of the French, Napoleon, even he has no better doctor." But the peasant woman, who had come to complain that she felt queer all over (though she was unable to explain what she meant by these words), only bowed low and fumbled in her bosom where she had four eggs tied up in the corner of a towel.

Once Bazarov pulled out a tooth for a traveling pedlar of cloth, and although this tooth was quite an ordinary specimen, Vassily Ivanovich preserved it like some rare object and incessantly repeated, as he showed it to Father Alexei, "Only look, what roots! The strength Evgeny has! That pedlar was just lifted up in the air ... even if it had been an oak, he would have rooted it up!"

"Admirable!" Father Alexei would comment at last, not knowing what to answer or how to get rid of the ecstatic old man.

One day a peasant from a neighboring village brought over to Vassily Ivanovich his brother, who was stricken with typhus. The unhappy man, lying flat on a truss of straw, was dying; his body was covered with dark patches, he had long ago lost consciousness. Vassily Ivanovich expressed his regret that no one had taken any steps to secure medical aid earlier and said it was impossible to save the man. In fact the peasant never got his brother home again; he died as he was, lying in the cart.

Three days later Bazarov came into his father's room and asked him if he had any silver nitrate.

"Yes; what do you want it for?"

"I want it ... to burn out a cut."

"For whom?"

"For myself."

"How for yourself? What is that? What sort of a cut? Where is it?"

"Here, on my finger. I went today to the village where they brought that peasant with typhus, you know. They wanted to open the body for some reason, and I've had no practice at that sort of thing for a long time."

"Well?"

"Well, so I asked the district doctor to help; and so I cut myself."

Vassily Ivanovich suddenly turned completely white, and without saying a word rushed into his study and returned at once with a piece of silver nitrate in his hand. Bazarov was about to take it and go away.

"For God's sake," muttered Vassily Ivanovich, "let me do it myself."

Bazarov smiled.

"What a devoted practitioner you are!"

"Don't laugh, please. Show me your finger. It's a small cut. Am I hurting you?"

"Press harder; don't be afraid."

Vassily Ivanovich stopped.

"What do you think, Evgeny; wouldn't it be better to burn it with a hot iron?"

"That ought to have been done sooner, now really even the silver nitrate is useless. If I've caught the infection, it's too late now."

"How ... too late...?" murmured Vassily Ivanovich almost inaudibly.

"I should think so! It's over four hours ago."

Vassily Ivanovich burned the cut a little more.

"But hadn't the district doctor got any caustic?"

"No."

"How can that be, good heavens! A doctor who is without such an indispensable thing!"

"You should have seen his lancets," remarked Bazarov, and went out.

Till late that evening and all the following day Vassily Ivanovich kept seizing on every possible pretext to go into his son's room, and though, far from mentioning the cut, he even tried to talk about the most irrelevant subjects, he looked so persistently into his son's face and watched him with so much anxiety that Bazarov lost patience and threatened to leave the house. Vassily Ivanovich then promised not to bother him, and he did this the more readily since Arina Vlasyevna, from whom, of course, he had kept it all secret, was beginning to worry him about why he did not sleep and what trouble had come over him. For two whole days he held firm, though he did not at all like the look of his son, whom he kept watching on the sly ... but on the third day at dinner he could bear it no longer. Bazarov was sitting with downcast eyes and had not touched a single dish.

"Why don't you eat, Evgeny?" he inquired, putting on a perfectly carefree expression. "The food, I think, is very well prepared."

"I don't want anything, so I don't eat."

"You have no appetite? And your head," he added timidly, "does it ache?"

"Yes, of course it aches."

Arina Vlasyevna sat bolt upright and became very alert.

"Please don't be angry, Evgeny," went on Vassily Ivanovich, "but won't you let me feel your pulse?"

Bazarov got up.

"I can tell you without feeling my pulse, I'm feverish."

"And have you been shivering?"

"Yes, I've been shivering. I'll go and lie down; and you can send me in some lime-flower tea. I must have caught cold."

"Of course, I heard you coughing last night," murmured Arina Vlasyevna.

"I've caught cold," repeated Bazarov, and left the room.

Arina Vlasyevna busied herself with the preparation of the lime-flower tea, while Vassily Ivanovich went into the next room and desperately clutched at his hair in silence.

Bazarov did not get up again that day and passed the whole night in heavy half-conscious slumber. At one o'clock in the morning, opening his eyes with an effort, he saw by the light of a lamp his father's pale face bending over him, and told him to go away; the old man obeyed, but immediately returned on tiptoe, and half-hidden behind the cupboard door he gazed persistently at his son. Arina Vlasyevna did not go to bed either, and leaving the study door a little open, she kept coming up to it to listen "how Enyusha was breathing," and to look at Vassily Ivanovich. She could see only his motionless bent back, but even that have her some kind of consolation. In the morning Bazarov tried to get up; he was seized with giddiness, and his nose began to bleed; he lay down again. Vassily Ivanovich waited on him in silence; Arina Vlasyevna went up to him and asked him how he felt. He answered, "Better," and turned his face to the wall. Vassily Ivanovich made a gesture to his wife with both hands; she bit her lip to stop herself from crying and left the room. The whole house seemed to have suddenly darkened; every person had a drawn face and a strange stillness reigned; the servants carried off from the courtyard into the village a loudly crowing cock, who for a long time was unable to grasp what they were doing with him. Bazarov continued to lie with his face to the wall. Vassily Ivanovich tried to ask him various questions, but they wearied Bazarov, and the old man sank back in his chair, only occasionally cracking the joints of his fingers. He went into the garden for a few minutes, stood there like a stone idol, as though overwhelmed with unutterable amazement (a bewildered expression never left his face), then went back again to his son, trying to avoid his wife's questions. At last she caught him by the arm, and convulsively, almost threateningly, asked, "What is wrong with him?" Then he collected his thoughts and forced himself to smile at her in reply, but to his own horror, instead of smiling, he suddenly started to laugh. He had sent for a doctor at daybreak. He thought it necessary to warn his son about this, in case he might be angry.

Bazarov abruptly turned round on the sofa, looked fixedly with dim eyes at his father and asked for something to drink.

Vassily Ivanovich gave him some water and in so doing felt his forehead; it was burning.

"Listen, old man," began Bazarov in a slow husky voice, "I'm in a bad way. I've caught the infection and in a few days you'll have to bury me."

Vassily Ivanovich staggered as though someone had knocked his legs from under him.

"Evgeny," he muttered, "what are you saying? God have mercy on you! You've caught cold..."

"Stop that," interrupted Bazarov in the same slow, deliberate voice; "a doctor has no right to talk like that. I've all the symptoms of infection, you can see for yourself."

"What symptoms ... of infection, Evgeny? ... Good heavens!"

"Well, what's this?" said Bazarov, and pulling up his shirt sleeve he showed his father the ominous red patches coming out on his arm.

Vassily Ivanovich trembled and turned cold from fear.

"Supposing," he said at last, "supposing ... even supposing ... there is something like an infection..."

"Blood poisoning," repeated Bazarov severely and distinctly; "have you forgotten your textbooks?"

"Well, yes, yes, as you like ... all the same we shall cure you!"

"Oh, that's rubbish. And it's not the point. I never expected to die so soon; it's a chance, a very unpleasant one, to tell the truth. You and mother must now take advantage of your strong religious faith; here's an opportunity of putting it to the test." He drank a little more water. "But I want to ask you one thing – while my brain is still under control. Tomorrow or, the day after, you know, my brain will cease to function. I'm not quite certain even now, if I'm expressing myself clearly. While I was lying here I kept on imagining that red dogs were running round me, and you made them point at me, as if I were a blackcock. I thought I was drunk. Do you understand me all right?"

"Of course, Evgeny, you talk perfectly clearly."

"So much the better. You told me you'd sent for the doctor ... you did that to console yourself ... now console me too; send a messenger..."

"To Arkady Nikolaich?" interposed the old man.

"Who's Arkady Nikolaich?" said Bazarov with some hesitation ... "Oh, yes, that little fledgeling! No, leave him alone, he's turned into a jackdaw now. Don't look surprised, I'm not raving yet. But you send a messenger to Madame Odintsov, Anna Sergeyevna, she's a landowner near by – do you know?" (Vassily Ivanovich nodded his head.) "Say 'Evgeny Bazarov sends his greetings, and sent to say he is dying.' Will you do that?"

"I will ... But is it a possible thing, that you should die, you, Evgeny ... judge for yourself. Where would divine justice be after that?"

"I don't know; only you send the messenger."

"I'll send him this minute, and I'll write a letter myself."

"No, why? Say, I send my greetings, and nothing more is necessary. And now I'll go back to my dogs. How strange! I want to fix my thoughts on death, and nothing comes of it. I see a kind of patch ... and nothing more."

He turned over heavily towards the wall; and Vassily Ivanovich went out of the study and, struggling as far as his wife's bedroom, collapsed on his knees in front of the sacred images.

"Pray, Arina, pray to God!" he groaned. "Our son is dying."

The doctor, that same district doctor who had been without any caustic, arrived, and after examining the patient, advised them to persevere with a cooling treatment and threw in a few words about the possibility of recovery.

"Have you ever seen people in my state not setting off for the Elysian fields?" asked Bazarov, and suddenly snatching the leg of a heavy table standing near his sofa, he swung it round and pushed it away.

"There's strength enough," he murmured. "It's all there still, and I must die ... An old man has time at least to outgrow the habit of living, but I ... well, let me try to deny death. It will deny me, and that's the end of it! Who's crying there?" he added after a pause. "Mother? Poor mother! Whom will she feed now with her wonderful cabbage soup? And I believe you're whimpering too, Vassily Ivanovich! Why, if Christianity doesn't help you, be a philosopher, a Stoic, and that sort of thing! Surely you prided yourself on being a philosopher?"

"What kind of philosopher am I!" sobbed Vassily Ivanovich, and the tears streamed down his cheeks.

Bazarov got worse with every hour; the disease progressed rapidly, as usually happens in cases of surgical poisoning. He had not yet lost consciousness and understood what was said to him; he still struggled. "I don't want to start raving," he muttered, clenching his fists; "what rubbish it all is!" And then he said abruptly, "Come, take ten from eight, what remains?" Vassily Ivanovich wandered about like one possessed, proposing first one remedy, then another, and ended by doing nothing except cover up his son's feet. "Try wrapping up in cold sheets ... emetic ... mustard plasters on the stomach ... bleeding," he said with an effort. The doctor, whom he had begged to stay, agreed with everything he said, gave the patient lemonade to drink, and for himself asked for a pipe and for something "warming and strengthening" – meaning vodka. Arina Vlasyevna sat on a low stool near the door and only went out from time to time to pray. A few days previously, a little mirror had slipped out of her hands and broken, and she had always considered this as a bad omen; even Anfisushka was unable to say anything to her. Timofeich had gone off to Madame Odintsov's place.

The night passed badly for Bazarov ... High fever tortured him. Towards the morning he felt a little easier. He asked Arina Vlasyevna to comb his hair, kissed her hand and swallowed a few sips of tea. Vassily Ivanovich revived a little.

"Thank God!" he repeated, "the crisis is near ... the crisis is coming."

"There, think of that!" muttered Bazarov. "What a lot a word can do! He's found one; he said 'crisis' and is comforted. It's an astounding thing how human beings have faith in words. You tell a man, for instance, that he's a fool, and even if you don't thrash him he'll be miserable; call him a clever fellow, and he'll be delighted even if you go off without paying him."

This little speech of Bazarov's, recalling his old sallies, greatly moved Vassily Ivanovich.

"Bravo! splendidly said, splendid!" he exclaimed, making as though to clap his hands.

Bazarov smiled ruefully.

"Well, so do you think the crisis is over or approaching?"

"You're better, that's what I see, that's what rejoices me."

"Very well; there's never any harm in rejoicing. And, do you remember, did you send the message to her?"

"Of course I did."

The change for the better did not last long. The disease resumed its onslaughts. Vassily Ivanovich was sitting close to Bazarov. The old man seemed to be tormented by some particular anguish. He tried several times to speak – but could not.

"Evgeny!" he ejaculated at last, "My son, my dear, beloved son!"

This unexpected outburst produced an effect on Bazarov ... He turned his head a little, evidently trying to fight against the load of oblivion weighing down on him, and said, "What is it, father?"

"Evgeny," went on Vassily Ivanovich, and fell on his knees in front of his son, who had not opened his eyes and could not see him. "You're better now; please God, you will recover; but make good use of this interval, comfort your mother and me, fulfill your duty as a Christian! How hard it is for me to say this to you – how terrible; but still more terrible would be ... forever and ever, Evgeny ... just think what..."

The old man's voice broke and a strange look passed over his son's face, though he still lay with his eyes closed.

"I won't refuse, if it's going to bring any comfort to you," he muttered at last; "but it seems to me there's no need to hurry about it. You say yourself, I'm better."

"Yes, Evgeny, you're better, certainly, but who knows, all that is in God's hands, and in fulfilling your duty..."

"No, I'll wait a bit," interrupted Bazarov. "I agree with you that the crisis has come. But if we're mistaken, what then? Surely they give the sacrament to people who are already unconscious."

"For heaven's sake, Evgeny,..."

"I'll wait, I want to sleep now. Don't disturb me."

And he laid his head back on the pillow. The old man rose from his knees, sat down on a chair and clutching at his chin began to bite his fingers....

The sound of a carriage on springs, a sound so remarkably distinguishable in the depths of the country, suddenly struck upon his hearing. The light wheels rolled nearer and nearer; the snorting of the horses was already audible.... Vassily Ivanovich jumped up and ran to the window. A two-seated carriage harnessed with four horses was driving into the courtyard of his little house. Without stopping to consider what this could mean, feeling a kind of senseless outburst of joy, he ran out into the porch ... A livened groom was opening the carriage door; a lady in a black shawl, her face covered with a black veil, stepped out of it...

"I am Madame Odintsov," she murmured. "Is Evgeny Vassilich still alive? Are you his father? I have brought a doctor with me."

"Benefactress!" exclaimed Vassily Ivanovich, and seizing her hand, he pressed it convulsively to his lips, while the doctor brought by Anna Sergeyevna, a little man in spectacles, with a German face, climbed very deliberately out of the carriage. "He's still alive, my Evgeny is alive and now he will be saved! Wife! Wife! An angel from heaven has come to us..."

"What is this, my God!" stammered the old woman, running out of the drawing room, and understanding nothing, she fell on the spot in the hall at Anna Sergeyevna's feet and began kissing her skirt like a mad woman.

"What are you doing?" protested Anna Sergeyevna; but Arina Vlasyevna did not heed her and Vassily Ivanovich could only repeat, "An angel! An angel!"

"*Wo ist der Kranke?* Where is the patient?" said the doctor at last in some indignation.

Vassily Ivanovich came to his senses.

"Here, this way, please follow me, *werthester Herr Kollege*," he added, remembering his old habits.

"Ah!" said the German with a sour grin.

Vassily Ivanovich led him into the study.

"A doctor from Anna Sergeyevna Odintsov," he said, bending right down to his son's ear, "and she herself is here."

Bazarov suddenly opened his eyes.

"What did you say?"

"I tell you that Anna Sergeyevna is here and has brought this gentleman, a doctor, with her."

Bazarov's eyes looked round the room.

"She is here ... I want to see her."

"You will see her, Evgeny; but first we must have a talk with the doctor. I will tell him the whole history of your illness, as Sidor Sidorich (this was the district doctor's name) has gone, and we will have a little consultation."

Bazarov glanced at the German.

"Well, talk away quickly, only not in Latin; you see I know the meaning of *'jam moritur.'*"

"*Der Herr scheint des Deutschen mächtig zu sein,*" began the new disciple of Aesculapius, turning to Vassily Ivanovich.

"*Ich ... gabe ...* We had better speak Russian," said the old man.

"Ah! so that's how it is ... by all means..." And the consultation began.

Half an hour later Anna Sergeyevna, accompanied by Vassily Ivanovich, entered the study. The doctor managed to whisper to her that it was hopeless even to think that the patient might recover.

She looked at Bazarov, and stopped short in the doorway – so abruptly was she struck by his inflamed and at the same time deathlike face and by his dim eyes fixed on her. She felt a pang of sheer terror, a cold and exhausting terror; the thought that she would not have felt like this if she had really loved him – flashed for a moment through her mind.

"Thank you," he said in a strained voice; "I never expected this. It is a good deed. So we see each other once more, as you promised."

"Anna Sergeyevna was so good..." began Vassily Ivanovich.

"Father, leave us alone ... Anna Sergeyevna, you will allow it, I think, now..." With a motion of his head he indicated his prostrate helpless body.

Vassily Ivanovich went out.

"Well, thank you," repeated Bazarov. "This is royally done. They say that emperors also visit the dying."

"Evgeny Vassilich, I hope..."

"Ah, Anna Sergeyevna, let's speak the truth. It's all over with me. I've fallen under the wheel. So it turns out that there was no point in thinking about the future. Death is an old joke, but it comes like new to everyone. So far I'm not afraid ... but soon I'll lose consciousness and that's the end!" (He waved his hand feebly.) "Well, what have I to say to you ... I loved you? That had no sense even before, and less than ever now. Love is a form, but my own form is already dissolving. Better for me to say – how wonderful you are! And now you stand there, so beautiful..."

Anna Sergeyevna involuntarily shuddered.

"Never mind, don't be agitated ... Sit down over there ... Don't come close to me; you know my disease is infectious."

Anna Sergeyevna walked quickly across the room and sat down in the arm-chair near the sofa on which Bazarov was lying.

"Noble-hearted," he whispered. "Oh, how near, and how young, fresh and pure ... in this disgusting room! Well, good-by! Live long, that's best of all, and made the most of it while there is time. You see, what a hideous spectacle, a worm, half-crushed, but writhing still. Of course I also thought, I'll break down so many things, I won't die, why should I? There are problems for me to solve, and I'm a giant! And now the only problem of this giant is how to die decently, though that too makes no difference to anyone ... Never mind; I'm not going to wag my tail."

Barazov fell silent and began feeling with his hand for the glass. Anna Sergeyevna gave him some water to drink, without taking off her glove and breathing apprehensively.

"You will forget me," he began again. "The dead is no companion for the living. My father will tell you what a man Russia has lost in me ... That's nonsense, but don't disillusion the old man. Whatever toy comforts the child ... you know. And be kind to my mother. People like them can't be found in your great world even if you search for them by day with a torch ... Russia needed me ... no, clearly I wasn't needed.

And who is needed? The shoemaker's needed, the tailor's needed, the butcher ... sells meat ... the butcher – wait a bit, I'm getting mixed up ... there's a forest here..."

Bazarov put his hand on his forehead.

Anna Sergeyevna bent over him. "Evgeny Vassilich, I am here..."

He at once took his hand away and raised himself.

"Good-by," he said with sudden force, and his eyes flashed with a parting gleam. "Good-by ... Listen ... you know I never kissed you then ... Breathe on the dying lamp and let it go out."

Anna Sergeyevna touched his forehead with her lips.

"Enough," he murmured, and fell back on the pillow. "And now ... darkness..."

Anna Sergeyevna slipped softly out.

"Well?" Vassily Ivanovich asked her in a whisper.

"He has fallen asleep," she answered, almost inaudibly.

Bazarov was not destined to awaken again. Towards evening he sank into a complete coma, and the following day he died. Father Alexei performed the last rites of religion over him. When they anointed him, and the holy oil touched his breast, one of his eyes opened, and it seemed as though, at the sight of the priest in his vestments, of the smoking censer, of the candle burning in front of the image, something like a shudder of horror passed through his death-stricken face. When at last he had stopped breathing and a general lamentation arose in the house, Vassily Ivanovich was seized by a sudden fit of frenzy.

"I said I should rebel!" he shouted hoarsely, his face red and distorted, and shaking his fist in the air as if he were threatening someone. "And I rebel, I rebel!"

But Arina Vlasyevna, all in tears, flung her arms round his neck and both fell on their knees together. "So side by side," related Anfisushka afterwards in the servants' room, "they bowed their poor heads like lambs in the heat of noon-day..."

But the heat of noonday passes and is followed by evening and night, and there comes the return to a quiet refuge where sleep is sweet for the tormented and weary...

Chapter 28

Six months passed. White winter had set in with the cruel stillness of cloudless frosts, with its thick crunching snow, rosy hoarfrost on the trees, pale emerald sky, wreaths of smoke curling above the chimneys, steam emerging from momentarily opened doors, with those fresh faces which look bitten by cold, and the hurried trot of shivering horses. A January day was drawing to its close; the evening cold pierced keenly through the motionless air, and a brilliant sunset was rapidly dying away. Lights were burning in the windows of the house at Maryino; Prokovich in a black tail coat and white gloves, with an air of unusual solemnity, was laying the table for seven. A week earlier in the small parish church, two weddings had taken place quietly, almost without witnesses – Arkady's marriage to Katya and that of Nikolai Petrovich to Fenichka; and on this day Nikolai Petrovich was giving a farewell dinner for his brother, who was going away to Moscow on some business. Anna Sergeyevna had also gone there directly the wedding was over, after making generous presents to the young couple.

Punctually at three o'clock the whole company assembled at the table. Mitya was brought along too and with him appeared a nurse in an embroidered peasant headdress. Pavel Petrovich sat between Katya and Fenichka; the husbands sat next to their wives.

Our friends had somewhat changed lately; they all seemed to have grown better looking and stronger; only Pavel Petrovich had become thinner, which, incidentally, still further enhanced the elegant and *"grand seigneur"* quality of his expressive features ... Fenichka, too, was different. In a fresh-colored silk dress with a wide velvet headdress on her hair, and a gold chain round her neck, she sat respectfully motionless, respectful towards herself and everyone around her, and smiled, as if she wanted to say: "Excuse me, I'm not to blame." And not only she – the others also all smiled and seemed to excuse themselves; they all felt a little awkward, a little sad, but fundamentally happy. They all helped each other with an amusing attentiveness, as if they had agreed in advance to act some good-natured comedy. Katya was quieter than any of the others; she looked confidently around her, and it was already noticeable that Nikolai Petrovich had managed to become quite devoted to her. Just before the dinner was over he stood up and, holding his glass in his hand, turned to Pavel Petrovich.

"You are leaving us ... you are leaving us, dear brother," he began, "not for long, of course; but still I can't help telling you what I ... what we ... how much I ... how much we ... That's the worst of it, we don't know how to make speeches. Arkady, you speak."

"No, daddy, I'm not prepared for it."

"And I'm so well prepared! Well, brother, I simply say, allow us to embrace you, to wish you all the best, and come back to us soon!"

Pavel Petrovich exchanged kisses with everyone, not excluding Mitya, of course; moreover, he kissed Fenichka's hand, which she had not yet learned to offer properly, and drinking off his refilled glass, he said with a deep sigh: "Be happy, my friends! Farewell!" This English ending passed unnoticed; but everyone was deeply touched.

"To Bazarov's memory," whispered Katya in her husband's ear as she clinked glasses with him. Arkady pressed her hand warmly in response, but he did not venture to propose that toast aloud.

This would seem to be the end; but perhaps some of our readers would care to know what each of the characters we have introduced is doing now, at the present moment. We are ready to satisfy that interest.

Anna Sergeyevna has recently married again, not for love but out of reasonable conviction, a man who may be one of the future leaders of Russia, a very clever lawyer with vigorous practical sense, a strong will and a remarkable gift of eloquence – still young, good-natured, and cold as ice. They live very harmoniously together and may live to the point of attaining happiness ... perhaps even love. Princess X. is dead, forgotten on the day of her death. The Kirsanovs, father and son, live at Maryino. Their fortunes are beginning to mend. Arkady has become assiduous in the management of the estate, and the "farm" now yields a fairly substantial income. Nikolai Petrovich has become one of the arbitrators in the land reforms and works with all his energy; he is constantly driving about the district, delivers long speeches (he belongs to those who believe that the peasants must be "made to understand," meaning that by frequent repetition of the same words they should be brought into a state of quiescence); and yet, to tell the truth, he does not fully satisfy either the cultured landowners, talking with a hiss or with a sigh about the emancipation (pronouncing it like a French word) or the uncultured ones who without ceremony curse the "damned emancipation." He is too softhearted for either set. Katerina Sergeyevna has a son, Kolya, and Mitya already runs about fearlessly, and talks a lot. Fenichka, Fedosya Nikolaevna, after her husband and Mitya, adores no one so much as her daughter-in-law, and when Katerina plays the piano, she would gladly spend the whole day at her side. A passing word about Pyotr. He has grown quite rigid with stupidity and self-importance, and pronounces all his *o's* like *u's,* but he too is married, and received a respectable dowry with his wife, the daughter of a market gardener in the town, who had refused two excellent suitors, only because they had no watches; while Pyotr not only had a watch – he even had a pair of patent leather shoes.

In Dresden on the Brühl terrace, between two and four o'clock – the most fashionable time for walking

– you may meet a man of about fifty, already quite grey and looking as though he suffered from gout, but still handsome, elegantly dressed and with that special style which comes only to those who have long been accustomed to move in the higher ranks of society. This man is Pavel Petrovich. From Moscow he went abroad for his health, and has settled down in Dresden, where he associates chiefly with English people and with Russian visitors. With the English he behaves simply, almost modestly, but with dignity; they find him a trifle boring but respect him for being, as they say, "a perfect gentleman." With Russians he is more free and easy, gives vent to his spleen, makes fun of them and of himself, but he does all this very agreeably, with an air of ease and civility. He holds Slavophil views; this is known to be regarded in the best society as *très distingué.* He reads nothing in Russian, but on his writing-desk there stands a silver ash tray in the shape of a peasant's plaited shoe. He is much sought after by our Russian tourists. Matvei Ilyich Kolyazin, happening to be "in temporary opposition," paid him a ceremonious visit on his way to a Bohemian watering place; and the local population, with whom, incidentally, he has little to do, treat him with an almost awestruck veneration. No one can so readily and quickly secure tickets for the court choir and the theater as the *Herr Baron von Kirsanov.* He does as much good as he can; he still causes some stir in the world, not for nothing was he once such a great social lion; but his life is a burden to him ... a heavier burden than he himself suspects. One should look at him in the Russian church: when leaning against the wall on one side, he stands absorbed in thought without stirring for a long time, bitterly compressing his lips, then suddenly recollects himself and begins almost imperceptibly to cross himself...

Madame Kukshina also settled abroad. She is now in Heidelberg, and is no longer studying natural history but has turned to architecture, in which, according to her own account, she has discovered new laws. As before, she associates with students, especially with young Russians studying physics and chemistry with whom Heidelberg is crowded, and who at first astonish the naïve German professors by their sober outlook on things, but later on astound the same professors by their complete incapability and absolute laziness. In company with two or three such young chemistry students, who cannot distinguish oxygen from nitrogen, but are brimming over with destructive criticism and conceit, Sitnikov, together with the great Elisyevich, also prepares to become a great man; he roams about in Petersburg, convinced that he is carrying on the "task" of Bazarov. There is a story that someone recently gave him a beating, but that he secured his revenge: in an obscure little article, hidden away in some obscure little periodical, he hinted that the man who had beaten him was – a coward. He calls this irony. His father bullies him as before, while his wife regards him as a fool ... and a literary man.

There is a small village graveyard in one of the remote corners of Russia. Like almost all our graveyards, it has a melancholy look; the ditches surrounding it have long been overgrown; grey wooden crosses have fallen askew and rotted under their once painted gables; the gravestones are all out of position, just as if someone had pushed them from below; two or three bare trees hardly provide some meager shade; the sheep wander unchecked among the tombs ... But among them is one grave untouched by human beings and not trampled on by any animal; only the birds perch on it and sing at daybreak. An iron railing surrounds it and two young fir trees have been planted there, one at each end; Evgeny Bazarov is buried in this tomb. Often from the near-by village two frail old people come to visit it – a husband and wife. Supporting one another, they walk with heavy steps; they go up to the iron railing, fall on their knees and weep long and bitterly, and gaze intently at the silent stone under which their son lies buried; they exchange a few words, wipe away the dust from the stone or tidy up some branches of a fir tree, then start to pray again and cannot tear themselves away from that place where they seem to be nearer to their son, to their memories of him ... Can it be that their prayers and their tears are fruitless? Can it be that love, sacred devoted love, is not all powerful? Oh, no! However passionate, sinful or rebellious the heart hidden in the tomb, the flowers growing over it peep at us serenely with their innocent eyes; they tell us not only of eternal peace, of that great peace of "indifferent" nature; they tell us also of eternal reconciliation and of life without end.

Books For ALL Kinds of Readers

At ReadHowYouWant we understand that one size does not fit all types of readers. Our innovative, patent pending technology allows us to design new formats to make reading easier and more enjoyable for you. This helps improve your speed of reading and your comprehension. Our EasyRead printed books have been optimized to improve word recognition, ease eye tracking by adjusting word and line spacing as well as minimizing hyphenation. Our EasyRead SuperLarge editions have been developed to make reading easier and more accessible for vision-impaired readers. We offer Braille and DAISY formats of our books and all popular E-Book formats.

We are continually introducing new formats based upon research and reader preferences. Visit our web-site to see all of our formats and learn how you can Personalize our books for yourself or as gifts. Sign up to Become A RHYW Registered Reader.

www.readhowyouwant.com

Made in the USA
Middletown, DE
04 January 2017